Accla

'An accomplished, entertaining blend of historical fiction and dark fantasy.'

THE TIMES

'Rich historical insight and compelling storytelling.'

WATERSTONE'S BOOK QUARTERLY

'A bloody good tale.'

PUBLISHERS WEEKLY

'Leaks Russia from its very pages.'

SAN FRANCISCO BOOK REVIEW

'You will love Jasper Kent for all eternity. I sure do.'

ELITIST BOOK REVIEWS

'A brilliant book.'

HISTORICAL NOVEL SOCIETY

Also by Jasper Kent

The Danilov Quintet

An epic saga of vampires and tsars, spanning a century of Russian history.

Twelve
Thirteen Years Later
The Third Section
The People's Will
The Last Rite

All published in the UK by Bantam Press.

Short Stories

The Sergeant and the General
from the collection *A Fantasy Medley 2*

Ben
from the collection *Full Fathom Forty*

The Tangled Web
from the collection *Thou Shalt Not*

Plays

Beside the Kitchen Table
Comin' Thro' the Rye

LATE WHITSUN

Jasper Kent

www.jasperkent.com

Copyright © Jasper Kent 2016

Jasper Kent has asserted his right under the Copyright, Designs and Patents Act 1988 to be identified as the author of this work.

All rights reserved.

This book is sold subject to the condition that it shall not, by way of trade or otherwise, be lent, resold, hired out, or otherwise circulated without the author's prior consent in any form of binding or cover other than that in which it is published and without a similar condition including this condition being imposed on the subsequent publisher.

This book is a work of fiction. Any resemblance to actual persons, living or dead, is purely coincidental.

ISBN-13: 978-1537739571
ISBN-10: 1537739573

Cover design by Jasper Kent. Images by Shutterstock.

Typeset in 11/14pt Garamond.

Brighton, 1938 …

CHAPTER 1

There are ways to make a girl look prettier; changes that no one can quite put their finger on, but are what the man – or occasionally the girl herself – is paying for. Some of it's just tidying up, things she should have done for herself before she stepped outside, like neatening the line of the eyebrow or defining the lip more clearly. Some of it's more major: a little off the nose – or, once in a while, on. The same for the chin. The easiest thing to improve is the complexion; you're starting with a blank sheet there. Sometimes it's just a case of giving her a better hat.

But you can't go too far. It has to be the same face you started with – recognizable. You don't want the prospective mother-in-law coming round and asking 'Who's that?' only to be told, with shuffling feet, that it's her own daughter. And you don't want to end up with something so beautiful that it eclipses the original, a Galatea for the man to gawp at and wonder what might have been, or for the girl herself to turn away from whenever she sees it, knowing that reality is its poor reflection.

This girl wouldn't take much work. She was a real looker. She knew it, and he knew it. They were engaged, so the ring on her finger declared, and recently too, judging by the way she rested her hands in her lap to ensure that everyone could see it. They were down from London, as were more than half the people who paraded along the Palace Pier that day, the last Saturday in May. So far, 1938 hadn't been a great season. Easter had been late this year, and so Whitsun would not be with us until the beginning of June, the following weekend. But then the bank holiday would bring them to Brighton in droves. If the weather was good then even more would come, but today the sun was coy, just visible as a glowing disk through the light cloud, not strong enough to cast much of a shadow.

I was nearly done. I'd got the chin wrong, but only slightly, and it didn't do to rub anything out – not when the punter could see you. The hardest bit had been getting a smile out of her. That wasn't something you could guess the look of. It wasn't that she was unhappy, but neither of them seemed the sort to show their emotions in public; they were above that. They'd probably only come down this particular weekend to avoid the riff-raff that Whitsun would bring to the town. Eventually her fiancé said something that coaxed a grin out of her, though she immediately tried to conceal it. After that, she'd given me a quiet, apologetic smile, and that's what I used – not quite the Mona Lisa, but something close.

I changed her hat. The one she was wearing was a couple of years out of fashion. I was good with hats. I spent a lot of time looking at them in the window of Hanningtons, especially when the new season began. I gave her what they called a 'sport' hat – a kind of fedora for ladies. It suited her. I'd seen a photograph of Rita Hayworth in one, but they had them in the shops in Brighton too. Maybe, if she liked the drawing, she'd get her fiancé to buy her one. I often wondered if I shouldn't be charging the milliners some sort of commission.

I signed the sketch at the bottom, 'C. K. Woolf'. It would probably be hidden by the frame – if they bothered to frame it. I handed it to the girl and she smiled again. It was a shame she didn't do it more often. Her chap gave me a curt nod and handed over a crown. It was what I'd put on the sign: 'Portraits 5/-. Graduate of the Royal College of Art.' It was true, but for the word 'graduate'. Sometimes they felt inspired to offer me a little more, but this one didn't. He barely even glanced at what he was paying for.

The couple continued on their way up the pier. They passed two or three other artists who tried to catch their interest, but then noticed what she was holding. Business wasn't good, not at this time of year, nor this time of day. Whitsun would be different. But, for now, I took whatever trade I could drum up. I had the best pitch, close to the turnstiles.

A short girl of about twenty was hovering nearby, considering the sign. I smiled at her, but she didn't seem bothered enough to look at the artist himself. She tugged the sleeve of the man beside her, who turned to look.

'Makes a lovely memento of your day together,' I said. 'Only five shillings.'

'We could get a photo for less,' he replied, not taking the cigarette from his mouth to speak.

'A photograph won't bring out the young lady's true beauty.'

The girl grinned broadly, demonstrating that she didn't understand the full implication of what I was saying. She was no looker, but I could improve on reality. Her fellow, on the other hand, seemed to get the idea.

'Will it take long?' he asked.

'Ten minutes,' I said.

He nodded and the girl sat down on the little wooden chair opposite me. I began to work my magic. To be honest, he'd have done better to spend his five bob in Boots, getting her some make-up and the free advice that comes with it. Her face was sweet enough, but there was more she could have done with it, if only she had the nous. No sisters, I guessed, and a mother who didn't approve of such things.

I didn't make small talk – I'd learned not to over the years. It looked like flirting and, however much the subject might like it, it wasn't she who was paying. Sometimes you'd get a couple of girls come down to Brighton together, and each take a turn in the chair. Then it was a different matter.

'Very good!' The words, laden with sincerity, came from behind me.

I didn't need to look – and I didn't want to. I

recognized the voice.

'Thanks,' I said curtly.

'It's amazing what he can do, you know,' O'Connor continued, still out of sight. He was addressing the girl now, or perhaps the man. Both looked up in his direction.

I raised my hand slightly. 'Could you just keep still there?' I said. It didn't matter for the drawing, but there was a chance it would curtail the conversation. However flattering O'Connor's words might have been to begin with, it wasn't going to last.

'You wouldn't believe some of the material he has to work with.' He sucked air through his teeth to emphasize the point. 'But they all end up looking lovely on the page.'

The girl was still smiling, responding to O'Connor's tone, rather than his words. The man had cottoned on quicker. His face had become still – not angry yet, but ready to have his suspicions of what O'Connor meant confirmed.

'Real sow's ears, some of them,' the voice continued behind me with a slight laugh. There couldn't be much doubt left for either of them now.

I swivelled round on my stool and looked up at him. 'Take a hike, why don't you, old man? I'm sure we can manage without hearing your opinions.'

He raised his hands apologetically. 'All right, I'll go!' He tried to make himself sound hard-done-by. I turned back to my efforts and sensed him beginning to move away, but still he wouldn't shut up. 'Some people just can't take a compliment, can they? She looks beautiful in that picture.' He paused – his timing exquisite – then concluded, 'You wouldn't recognize her.'

The girl's face fell into an expression that was every bit the classic mask of tragedy. She looked up at her suitor, who was already on the move, pulling up his sleeves as he strode towards O'Connor. I stood and got myself between the two of them, though why I cared I wasn't sure. He pushed against me, though if he'd really been trying, he could easily have knocked me down.

'What are you saying?' he growled at O'Connor over my shoulder. O'Connor made no attempt at an explanation. I managed to push the younger man away until he was at arm's length.

'I can only apologize,' I said. 'You get a lot of his type on the pier. They've got nowhere to go during the day.' The man calmed a little. 'Look,' I continued, 'let me finish the drawing – no charge.'

I showed him what I'd done already; it was almost complete. He took it from me and stepped back a few paces, staring at it. Then he looked up at the girl and back to the drawing. 'No,' he said thoughtfully. 'No, he's right.' He crumpled the paper and threw it on to the decking, then marched towards the turnstiles. The girl stood there, abandoned and insulted, wondering which of us to be more upset with. She looked at the retreating figure of her beau, then at O'Connor and then at me, her eyes blazing. I felt the sting of her hand slapping my cheek before I spotted any movement. She'd had to stretch up to reach my face, but still managed quite a blow. A few stars twinkled in the left of my field of vision, but it didn't seem they would amount to anything serious. She turned and walked briskly after her man, but he was already off the pier. She broke into a run. I heard laughter behind me. O'Connor was leaning against the railing, grinning triumphantly, his belly stretching the buttons of his shirt. He offered me his hand to shake, but I didn't take it.

'How's business, Big-Bad?' he asked.

Walt Disney had a lot to answer for. O'Connor had starting calling me 'Big-Bad' five years before, when we were still working together. He would sing the song day in day out, cutting out the 'the' so it would make sense: '*Who's afraid of Big Bad Woolf?*' He hoped the name would catch on, but few others took it up. Still he persisted.

'It was all right until you turned up.'

'Five bob a pop? And how many of those do you get a

day? I meant your other business.'

'Not bad. How about you?'

'Since we parted company, I've gone from strength to strength. More work than I can handle. Which is what I wanted to talk to you about.'

'Not interested, thanks all the same.' I sat back down and picked up my pad and pencil, looking around for likely clients.

'Well, let me buy you a drink, then. For old times' sake.'

'Later maybe.'

'They'll be closed soon.'

I glanced up at the clock tower. He was right. It was well after two. There'd be a rush of trade on the pier when the pubs turned out, so now would be a good time for me to get a drink – especially a free one.

We headed across to the Royal Albion. There was an empty table in the corner of the bar, close to the window where we could look back out at the Palace Pier and the sea. A waiter came over quickly.

'Tamplin's, isn't it?' O'Connor asked. 'A pint?'

'Scotch,' I said, 'since you're buying.'

'Two Scotches,' he instructed the waiter.

We sat in silence until the drinks arrived. O'Connor poured a dribble of water into his from the jug that came with them. He looked at me but I shook my head.

'So how you been, Big-Bad?'

'As well as ever.'

'Still getting the headaches?'

'Now and then.' I glanced around the room as I spoke, not to take in the surroundings, but to see if anything else was there, creeping in from the side. The slap I'd received on the pier probably wasn't enough to start anything – but I was due.

'Never stopped you working, though, did they?'

I was bored already, and the whisky wasn't going to last me long. 'What's this about, O'Connor?'

'Why do you never call me "Al"?'

I couldn't picture him as an American gangster, and besides, his name was Alan, not Alphonse. Though I could hardly throw stones on that score myself. 'What's it about?' I repeated.

'I was wondering if you needed a little work.'

'Not your kind of work.'

'I'm a detective, just like you ... when you're not drawing pictures on the pier.'

'We investigate different things.'

He shrugged, tricky though that was with his corpulent body wedged into a hotel armchair. 'All I'm looking for is a courier.' He reached into his case and brought out a large brown envelope. 'I need this taken up to a man in London.'

'Try the Royal Mail.'

He shook his head. 'They might take a peek.'

'And I wouldn't?'

'Maybe, but you'd deliver it anyway.'

I tried to judge what might be in there. I could make a good guess, but that wouldn't quite explain why he refused to trust it to the post. 'Why not go yourself?' I asked. 'It's only London.'

He paused, choosing his words. 'I don't want him to know who it's from.'

'So he'd recognize you?'

O'Connor nodded. 'But not you.'

'What's it worth?' I asked, taking another sip.

'In return, he'll give you the sum of fifty pounds, in cash.'

I scarcely needed to pretend to choke. 'Fifty quid? For a delivery?'

'For content *and* delivery. You can keep ten.'

It was still a good fee. 'How do you know I won't keep it all?'

'You're an honest man. That's why we don't work together anymore.'

'But you're happy to work with me now?'

'That depends. Are *you* happy to work for *me*?'

'I'll think about it,' I said. 'When do you need to know?'

'It has to be delivered tonight.'

I looked at the envelope. He was holding it by opposite corners, twirling it between his fingers. I could see no name or address on it. I reached out my hand and the rotation stopped.

'You agree, then?' he asked.

'I said I'll think about it.'

'Then I'd best keep this for now.' He slid the envelope back into his case and brought out a notebook. He scribbled something on a page, which he then tore out and handed to me. 'Call me on this number,' he said. 'Make it before seven or I'll find someone else.'

'Why not just find someone else, anyway?'

He smiled. 'Maybe I will. Call me and you'll find out.'

He downed what was left of his drink and stood up. It would have been impressive but for the way the chair rose with him for a few inches. He pushed his hands against the arms and it dropped back on to the carpeted floor with a quiet thud. He straightened his tie and headed across the bar to the door. I finished my Scotch, but remained seated, staring out of the window. Soon O'Connor reappeared outside. He crossed the road as if heading back on to the pier, but then glanced around furtively and squeezed into one of the red telephone boxes just beside the ice-cream kiosk, his backside preventing the door from quite closing behind him.

*

After I left the Royal Albion, I went back to my pitch on the pier. As I'd expected, business picked up during the afternoon, but then it began to rain. I packed up soon after four. I didn't have much to take with me – the chair and my stool folded up nice and small, and the sketch pad was no weight. Even so, the rain persuaded me to take a tram. I popped into the newsagent's and bought a copy of the *Argus*, along with a few other things, then walked the last few yards home. I trotted up the steps to the front door, trying to avoid looking at the chequered pattern of tiles that covered them. As usual for that time of day, the door wasn't locked. Once inside, I shouted.

'Mrs Croft?'

'That you, Mr Woolf?' Her voice came from the kitchen at the end of the hallway. There were few other places she was likely to be.

'Indeed it is.' I put my head around the door. Her hands were plunged in a large mixing bowl, her forearms coated in flour. 'Any telephone calls?'

'Your mother rang. We had a good long chat.'

'That's nice.'

'She wanted to remind you you're going there for lunch on Wednesday. She wants to know if you're bringing anyone.'

'Thanks.'

'Well, are you?'

'Am I what?'

'Bringing anyone.'

It would have been easy just to tell her, but it was none of her business. 'Any other calls?'

'Your friend Mr O'Connor.'

'What did he want?' I hardly needed to ask.

'He didn't say. He didn't even leave his name, but I knew it was him.'

'Thanks, Mrs Croft.' I stepped back into the hallway.

'Will you be in for dinner?'

It was a good question. I still hadn't decided about O'Connor's offer. 'No, thank you. I'll find something for myself,' I shouted back. Perhaps I had decided.

I went upstairs and unlocked the door to my rooms.

My office was at the front of the house, facing south, so even on a cloudy day like today it was still bright. This was where I received my clients, when I had any. Two other doors led off to my private rooms – a bedroom and a living room. I dumped the two seats and the rest of what I'd been carrying in a corner, then sat down at the desk. I opened my diary where the strip of gold braid marked the current week, then turned the page. Only one word was written there, under Wednesday: *Mum*. I could hardly count her as a client. I turned the page again. The Whitsun bank holiday was printed in there on the Monday, but there was nothing that I'd filled in. I didn't bother to look any further. I had no work coming. Not the kind of work I wanted.

I'd been right in what I said to O'Connor: we investigated different things. The things he concerned himself with happened every day; for me it was once in a blue moon. And so he got the cases and I didn't. When we'd worked as partners there had been more of a mixture, but he'd always been keener to deal with the simple, lucrative stuff. And that, in a word, meant divorces. O'Connor was a genius at finding evidence of adultery, but my heart wasn't in it. That was why we'd gone our separate ways – that and a few other things. His business was thriving, from what I'd heard – not least from his own lips. I hadn't been offered a case in weeks.

There wasn't much room for a private detective in Brighton, not between the police and the gangs. The police dealt with the normal crime, the offences you'd find in any town: burglary, assault, the occasional murder. But Brighton also had the fun crimes, the crimes that ensnared willing victims: gambling, drinking, prostitution. That was what the tourists came down from London for – some of them, at least. And those things didn't just happen; they needed organization. If people got out of line, they had to be dealt with. Brighton Borough Police didn't want to get involved and so the gangs policed themselves. Sometimes there was an overlap of jurisdiction, and that would lead to trouble, but it meant that there wasn't much room in the middle for a privateer like me.

So in my case it was mostly persons gone missing, or the occasional blackmail. And there'd been none of either for a while. I reached into my pocket and pulled out the phone number that O'Connor had given me. Ten pounds was good money. I'd sold three drawings on the pier that day – fifteen shillings' worth. It wasn't that I was desperate for income. Mum was always willing to give me some, but that would mean she'd have won. And there was more to it than that. Ten pounds wasn't just good money – it was ridiculous. There was more to this than being a simple delivery boy; more to it than an envelope full of photographs of some rich husband caught *in flagrante delicto* to be delivered into the hands of the aggrieved wife's solicitor. O'Connor could have done that for himself. So perhaps it would lead on to something more interesting: a real case.

I went back down to the hallway. From the kitchen I could hear Mrs Croft singing to herself, picking a new key for almost every phrase. *'Isn't it romantic? Music in the night; a dream that can be heard. Isn't it romantic?'* The telephone was on a stand at the bottom of the stairs. I picked up the receiver and dialled the number. It rang three times and then a woman answered.

'Hullo?'

'Mrs O'Connor?' I began. I'd never used her first name. I wasn't even sure I could remember it.

'Who's that?' She sounded annoyed.

'It's Woolf. Charlie Woolf.'

'Who?' It must have been a bad line – she couldn't have forgotten me.

'Is Alan there?' I remembered that she, like me, was loathe to abbreviate his name.

'Al!' she shouted, turning away from the receiver. It seemed I'd remembered wrongly, or times had changed.

Moments later another voice spoke. 'Hullo?'
'O'Connor?' I said. 'It's me. Is that job still going?'

CHAPTER 2

O'Connor was waiting by the departures board when I arrived at the station. It was just after eight – still light, though the sun would have set by the time I got to London.

'Thanks for this, Big-Bad,' he said as he shook my hand. 'It gets me out of a real fix.'

I nodded, but didn't say anything. He presented me with the same envelope that he'd shown me before.

'I got you a ticket, too,' he continued, offering it to me. I took it.

'When do you want the money delivered?'

He seemed nervous. 'I'll call you,' he said. 'It may be a few days.'

The horrible feeling that I was being set up began to develop in me, though I could fathom neither how nor why. Besides, I was too curious to back out.

'You know what to do when you get to Victoria?' he asked.

'You told me. Trust me.'

'I do, Big-Bad.' He forced a laugh. 'You know I do. But get a move on; the train's off in a few minutes.'

I showed my ticket at the gate and walked down the long platform as it curved gently to the left. I remembered the thrill of coming here as a kid, the excitement not just of wherever we were going to, but of the journey itself, carried along by those great, noisy, smelly machines. It was different now, especially the smell. There were still a few steam engines that came into the station, but most of it was electric – certainly on the route I was taking up to London. They had a smell to them, too, but it wasn't a real smell: the odour of exertion, of blazing coal releasing its energy to make the train move. This was the quiet, meek scent of electricity doing its work in a modern, efficient, passionless way. It didn't even need a locomotive;

everything required was hidden beneath the carriages. The driver got a tiny cabin to operate in, not even as big as a third-class compartment.

I got on close to the front, where the platform jutted out from under the iron-vaulted roof and into the open air. It had begun to rain again, which put people off from coming this far, despite the fact that up here we'd be closest to the barriers at Victoria. As a result the carriages were almost empty. There were only two other people in my compartment – a couple who'd been down for the day. Likely as not they'd passed me on the pier, though they hadn't stopped for a portrait. As I opened the door I got the impression of them moving apart a little. It seemed my presence was going to spoil their journey somewhat, but I didn't care. I sat in the opposite corner to them and looked out of the window, up at the man-made cliffs that had been cut and blasted when the railway was built, a hundred years before, and at the houses perched on top of them.

The train began to move. That was all that could be said of the process: it merely *began*. There was no whoosh of steam, no sense of a gargantuan strength pulling its load. Electric current was applied and the wheels began smoothly to turn. As we picked up speed, another train came in, passing just feet away and making the windows rattle. Then it was quiet again but for the gentle hum of the motors and the click of the wheels as they passed from one section of track to the next.

At first we called at all stations but nobody else got on, and after Haywards Heath I knew we wouldn't be stopping for a while. The couple opposite had begun reading a newspaper, shared between them. Occasionally she would point at an article or picture and make some comment. I felt safe to begin my investigations.

The envelope O'Connor had given me was just as I'd first seen it in the bar of the Royal Albion: unmarked, sealed with gum. I took out my pocket knife and slit it open at the top, then reached inside. As I'd suspected, they were photographs. I could feel the glossy side facing away from me. I flipped the envelope round; I didn't want to shock that couple by showing them these pictures, not if they were what I assumed they were.

There were sixteen of them; large prints – almost foolscap size – typical of O'Connor's work. He had no eye for composition, but the circumstances couldn't have been ideal. It was a nice big room, obviously in a hotel – the Metropole to judge by the décor. The bedclothes were in a heap on the floor. That always helped in getting a clear view. Sometimes O'Connor would turn up the heating just to discourage the happy couple from snuggling modestly beneath the sheets. In a divorce case that wouldn't matter – just getting into bed together was sufficient grounds, regardless of what they did there. But I was beginning to suspect that this was about something other than divorce.

The girl was in her twenties, with a little of Claudette Colbert about her – perhaps even more petite, if that were possible. She wore her dark hair long and waved, though in the earlier shots she had it tied up in a bun. The more I looked at her, the prettier she seemed. If I'd been drawing her, there would have been nothing to fix, but I'd still have taken my time over it. The man was around ten years older with short, neat dark hair. He was about six feet tall and had a physique that wasn't disproportionate. His face was marred by a slightly undersized chin.

But none of that really held my attention.

I'd seen nudes before, of course, of both sexes, at the Royal College. I'd sketched them there. But there were rules – rules that hadn't changed much over the centuries – as to how they should be posed. It was quite unrealistic, as these pictures demonstrated, but that was art. O'Connor had taken this sort of photo before, and I'd seen some of the results, but he'd never gone this far. Or if he had, he'd destroyed the more extreme photographs. It seemed unnecessary, even for blackmail.

In only one of the pictures were they not touching –

simply gazing at one another across the fresh, white sheets. In another they were kissing, her naked breasts pressed against his chest, their loins together and therefore hidden from view. The remaining images were truly shocking – not so much in what they depicted but in that they depicted it at all. What a man and a woman did together was no one's concern but their own, but for it to be recorded like this, available for display, was something different; something appalling, and yet also thrilling.

I was no stranger to it – to the act, that is. The art world in London in the late Twenties had been what they called Bohemian. Girls were liberated and men – myself included – took advantage. I'd had no father to explain it to me, but my headmaster had assumed the role. His description was mechanical, directed towards the single-minded goal of procreation. There was one way it could be done, and one reason it should be done. I soon learned differently. There were so many things that a man and a woman could do together – things that did not even involve sex, at least not in the narrow way my headmaster defined it.

These two in the photos clearly knew them all, and O'Connor's camera had captured those activities in lurid, stark detail, turning love into shame. And, by looking, I was contributing to that shame. Not simply by looking – by enjoying; I couldn't deny it, nor did I resist it.

I glanced up across the compartment. At the same moment the girl sitting opposite happened to look in my direction. For an instant our eyes met and I was certain that she knew what was in the photographs and suspected that, when I looked at her, it was in the same way I looked at those pictures. I dropped my eyes and felt blood rushing to my face. I was mad to have taken on this job. If I was caught with those pictures, I'd end up in front of a magistrate. I'd probably escape prison, but the humiliation would be worse. No wonder O'Connor didn't want to run this errand himself.

I raised my eyes again. The girl was still looking in my direction with half a smile on her face. A sudden anxiety hit me: I was next to the window and it was getting dark outside. I looked over my shoulder to judge whether she might be able to see anything in the reflection. It seemed unlikely, but still I angled the photographs a little further away from the glass.

I forced myself to calm down and think. I was in no danger. I understood perfectly well what was going on here. This was not a divorce case. It was blackmail. I could guess who I'd be meeting in London. I'd recognize him from the photographs. I wouldn't even need to see his face – any part of his body would do.

Or was I being old-fashioned? Why should I assume that it was the man who had the most to lose? What reasons might the girl have for keeping these pictures to herself? She could be married. She might come from a good family. Would it be she who handed over an envelope full of money in exchange for them? Or perhaps her father, terrified of the dishonour that might befall his name?

But, looking at them again, I began to doubt it. In too many of the images the girl's eyes betrayed her. She was not staring at her lover's face, nor at any other part of him. Her gaze was instead turned outwards, like Manet's Olympia, at the viewer – at me – or, in truth, at the camera concealed somewhere in the room. She *knew*. I could almost see the curl of a smile on her lips, the pride that an actress takes in her performance. But the man never looked at the camera. His eyes were always … where any man's would be. In fact, in none of the pictures could more than just the profile of his face be seen – sometimes less. For a photographer as experienced as O'Connor, it was a mistake: it made the man harder to recognize, to identify. But I supposed that didn't matter much. Anyone who knew him would be certain of his identity, even from these pictures. It was obvious that *he* was the victim of the blackmail.

Even then I began to harbour doubts. Just fifty pounds for *those* pictures. It was very little. And, besides that, there was something missing. I reached down into the envelope again, but there was nothing else there. No negatives. That was usually part of the deal, otherwise the blackmailer – O'Connor – could just manufacture more prints. Perhaps fifty pounds was a mere down payment.

The train began to slow; we were coming into East Croydon. We'd fill up there, and that would mean people sitting next to me. I reached into my bag and took out the envelope I'd bought earlier in the day, just in case. It was the same size as the one O'Connor had given me; perhaps a slightly lighter shade of buff. I slid the sixteen photographs inside and then licked the flap and sealed it shut. I was lucky that O'Connor hadn't written anything on the outside, but even if he had, it was unlikely I'd have been caught out. Blackmailer and victim would hardly compare notes on such matters.

The train came to a halt and the door opened. Seconds later the compartment was full. I kept the envelope flat on my lap, with my hands resting on it. I glanced again at the girl sitting opposite, but she was now looking out of the far window.

Twenty minutes later we were at Victoria Station. I cut across the concourse and out through the side exit on to Wilton Road, opposite the cinema. The sun had set by now and the twilight was fading. I turned right, back along the side of the station, and then left. Soon I was in Eccleston Square, where O'Connor had told me my rendezvous was to be. The place was surrounded by trees thick with leaves. If it wasn't for a few lampposts scattered around, the darkness would have been impenetrable. O'Connor had explained that there was a bench on the south-western side. I was to be there at 10 o'clock. It was now a quarter to. I sat down to wait.

A few people crossed the square – some in couples,

others alone. I kept my eyes open for anyone looking like the man in the pictures, or even the girl. There was one that might have been him when I saw him from the front, but then he turned and his profile was all wrong. By ten-fifteen no one had come. I stood and took a walk around the square in case there'd been a mix up as to which bench, but there was no one to be seen. It took me only two or three minutes to do a complete circuit but, as I came back towards the bench where I'd been sitting, I saw that the other participant in our meeting had arrived.

As expected, it was a man – I could tell that much from his build. He was standing with his back to me, staring down on the bench as if wondering why I wasn't there. Both his hands were stuffed into the pockets of a fawn raincoat. On his head sat a brown trilby. I skirted around to the side of him, keeping my distance, hoping to see his profile and confirm that it was who I expected. As I approached, the face began to take shape, but what I saw made no sense to me.

His nose was enormous – the only significant feature of his face. It was as if the tip of a normal nose had been grabbed and pulled, stretching the flesh of the entire face out into a cone, and then allowed to droop over the mouth and chin. I began to move closer towards him, so that I could get a clearer view. He heard me and turned, and now I could see him full on.

His eyes were huge, flat and round, glinting in the lamplight but with no structure of iris or pupil to be seen. Mouth and nose had merged into one feature, a round, flat, protruding snout. As a human face it made no more sense now than it had when viewed from the side. The only conclusion I could draw was that I was not looking at a human.

I was staring into the face of some giant, upright, clothed pig.

CHAPTER 3

It could not be so. My next thought was that some new, hideous form of migraine aura had forced itself upon me. At its worst it could make a normal, human face splinter into facets as though rendered in a cubist painting, but I had never been the victim of anything like this before, and I felt none of the other usual symptoms. I flicked my eyes from side to side, observing this bizarre apparition at different points in my field of vision, but it remained steady – a physical reality, not an artefact of my mind.

The figure raised a hand to me in a friendly greeting; and it *was* a hand – not a cloven trotter – wearing a black leather glove. We approached one another, and what I was seeing became clear. It was merely a man, a man wearing a coat, a trilby and a gas mask. It was an unfamiliar sight, but not a complete novelty. I'd seen them in the newsreels, as everyone had. If it came to war, we'd all be issued with them. I remembered my dad's wheezing lungs and blistered skin after the Germans had used mustard gas. I can't have been much older than eight or nine at the time. He'd had a gas mask, little help though it had been. But there was no poison gas here in Pimlico. I could only deduce that this fellow was afraid I might recognize him – or that O'Connor might have.

The figure spoke, but I could make no sense of it. His voice was muffled by the mask.

'What?' I demanded, not trying to hide my irritation at the farcical nature of it all.

He spoke louder and I could just about make out what he said. 'You got them?'

'You got the money?' I countered.

He reached inside his coat and pulled out a wad of notes, rolled up and fastened with a rubber band. He held it up between his thumb and forefinger, so that I could see it clearly, then tossed it on to the bench alongside him. I offered him the envelope. He took a step towards me and grabbed it. Immediately his fingers were at the flap, scrabbling to tear it open. He raised his hand to his face, then let out a gasp of annoyance. He tucked the envelope under his arm and pulled the glove from his right hand by using his left. I realized that his instinct had been to use his teeth, but the mask prevented him.

With his fingers freed he was finally able to open the envelope. He stepped into the lamplight to see better and tipped the photographs out into his other hand. As he did so I noticed a tattoo on his forearm, stretching down to the back of his hand itself. It looked like an anchor. That told me something: this was not the man in the photographs. I'd seen pretty much every inch of his body, and there were no tattoos – not anywhere. Whatever the reason he was hiding his face, it wasn't that.

He held the photographs at arm's length, as though he needed reading glasses, and turned his head to one side. The gas mask evidently didn't make things easy. I wondered how he might be reacting to the sight of them. Disgust? Shock? Arousal? Whatever his expression beneath it, the mask remained impassive. He didn't bother to go through all of the prints – the first few were enough to verify their nature. He slipped them back into the envelope.

'Take it and go,' he said, gesturing towards the roll of money lying on the bench.

I walked over and picked it up, pulling the rubber band off and on to my wrist. They were all one-pound notes. I half expected the masked man to say something along the lines of 'It's all there,' but perhaps I'd seen too many talkies. It didn't take long to count the notes. There was exactly fifty quid. I put the rubber band back around them and slid the roll into an inside pocket.

The man jerked his head in the direction of the gate. There was nothing else for me to do here, so I turned and walked away. At the gate I paused and looked back, but he had already gone.

I walked briskly back to Victoria Station, my hands buried in my pockets, feeling the lump of banknotes pressing against my chest. It was a lot of cash to be carrying around. Only two other people knew about it: one of them had just given it to me and the other would soon be receiving it, minus my cut. Even so, I felt nervous. I'd learned to my cost more than once what a blabbermouth O'Connor could be, and I knew nothing of the other bloke. It still felt like a set-up and I wasn't going to play it all O'Connor's way. At the station I sat down. I'd bought two envelopes earlier in the day. The second one was smaller and padded. I scribbled an address on the front, making some slight attempt to disguise my handwriting, then unrolled the notes and slipped them inside. I put a stamp on and then posted it in the pillar box on the station concourse. I'd missed the last collection, but at least I felt safe.

I looked up at the departure board. There was a train in ten minutes. I'd soon be home.

*

It was getting on for midnight when we rolled into Brighton. The station was quiet but not deserted. Almost as soon as I was off the concourse, I doubled back on myself and went down Trafalgar Street, descending into the tunnel where the station itself had been built over the roadway. It was somewhere around there that I first realized I was being followed. I stopped to light a cigarette and took the opportunity to look back. He stopped a second later, ostensibly to tie his shoelace. It took him a long time. I'd seen him at the ticket barrier – blond crew haircut and pimples – but not thought much of it then.

LATE WHITSUN

He'd been standing with his back to the platforms, not a very helpful position if you've been tipped off about a chap carrying fifty quid on his way back from London. He was scarcely twenty, but I'd known younger kids who could manage a better tail. Employed them, too, on more than one occasion.

I carried on down Trafalgar Street and stopped at the phone box on the corner of Pelham Square. I went inside and pretended to make a call. He fell for it. He knew I'd spot him if he loitered for too long, so he had to give himself a reason to be there. He stood just outside, pretending he was waiting to use the telephone. I finished my 'call' and stepped out, holding the door open for him. He was hoist on his own petard; his only option was to pretend to make a call of his own. He went in and I hovered for a moment, finishing my cigarette, while he affected an earnest conversation into the receiver. In truth I was indulging in what I believe the Japanese call 'origami', busily transforming the now empty envelope that O'Connor had given me, folding it into a wedge.

I threw my cigarette stub to the ground and bent forward, slipping the folded paper under the crack at the bottom of the door. It wouldn't detain him for long, but long enough. I walked swiftly away and soon heard the sound of him banging against the glass. I turned a corner and began to run, quickly losing myself in the grid of tiny streets that make up North Laine. There was no sign of him following, but I went home the long way, just in case, crossing the Victoria Gardens and sticking to the side streets before making my way back home via the Level.

As I turned into my street I saw that it was busy – busier than it ever should be at that time of night, and with a very specific kind of visitor. Three police cars – black Wolseleys – were parked outside my house. On the steps up to the front door two coppers stood chatting. There was no point in avoiding them, so I carried on walking, trying to look calm and wondering why I shouldn't be. In the distance I saw another figure coming along the pavement towards me, from the other end of the street. As we got closer I recognized him: the pimply kid who'd followed me from the station. Giving someone the slip was pretty pointless if they knew where you lived. He offered me an embarrassed smile then held out his hand, gesturing that I should go first into my own home. I mounted the steps.

'You Woolf?' asked one of the policemen.

I nodded. He took a step through the open door and shouted up the stairs. 'Governor? He's here.'

A sudden fear took hold of me. 'Mrs Croft – is she …?' I couldn't finish the sentence.

'The landlady?'

I nodded again.

'She's fine. A bit shaken. It was her that called us.'

I went on in. Along the hall I could see Mrs Croft sitting in the kitchen, drinking from a teacup which I guessed had something stronger in it. The police inspector, dressed in civvies, was looking down from the first floor landing.

'Woolf?' he asked.

I climbed the stairs, always looking up at him. He was a tall man, balding, with a ginger moustache from behind which peeked a thin, white scar. I recognized him immediately.

'Marchant, isn't it?' I said.

'That's right. Been a couple of years. You were working with Alan O'Connor back then, weren't you?'

I was tempted to reveal I still was, but for now the less said the better. 'What's happened?' I asked.

'Come and look.'

It wasn't far from the top of the stairs to my rooms. The door had been forced open, the splintered jamb left leaning against the wall.

'*My* boys, I'm afraid,' said Marchant. 'Your landlady heard a shot, so we had to get in quick.'

He indicated I should go first. My office was still reasonably tidy, but I could tell someone had been there. Each of the three filing cabinets had a drawer left open. There were some papers spread out on my desk that I hadn't put there. God only knew what might have been taken.

'Looks like I've been burgled,' I said.

'Looks like it, yes,' Marchant replied.

'You said there was a shot?'

He pointed to my living room. 'Through there.' I went in.

This was in much more of a mess. The window was broken. The standard lamp that I used to read by was lying on the floor, the green cotton lampshade knocked askew and the bulb shattered. I felt oddly relieved to see that my wireless set appeared undamaged. A uniformed constable stood next to my armchair. I wondered if he might have been sitting in it until he heard us coming.

'Move your arse, Foster,' said Marchant.

The constable stepped aside, revealing what I had evidently been brought in here to see. Between my armchair and the wall, a body lay face down. The upper part of it was still hidden by the chair but, now that the copper had moved, the legs were there for all to see.

'This is how it was when we got here,' continued the inspector.

'You haven't even turned him over?' I asked.

'We have, but we thought you'd like to see exactly how we found things.' He gestured to the constable, who grabbed my chair by the arm and began to pull it across the room. I wanted to complain about how he was rucking the carpet, but thought better of it. The entirety of the body could be seen now. It wasn't a dainty figure. The hair was matted with blood, as though he'd been hit on the back of the head, but I remembered there had been a shot.

'You can see the exit wound clearly,' said Marchant helpfully.

There was something else strange too: what looked like a dark strap of cloth pressing down and flattening his hair. Marchant took a step towards the body, but I remained still. He looked at me, then took my arm and led me forward, somewhere between guiding me and dragging me.

'He must have spun around as he fell.'

We were standing just feet away now. I noticed there was a patch of blood on the wall behind my chair, just above a man's height, splattering outwards. At its centre, the plaster was cracked. Another bloodstain had soaked into the carpet around the body's head, bigger than the first.

'Turn him over,' said Marchant.

Foster grimaced and rubbed his face, then leaned over the corpse. He reached across and under, grabbing it by the trousers and the shirt, then heaved until the body rolled on to its back. I felt a horrible certainty that I would recognize the face once I saw it, but for a moment the constable remained crouched, blocking my view. At last he moved.

I recognized the face all right – if you could call it that – but I couldn't put a name to it. No one could. It was the same face I'd seen in London, in Eccleston Square just hours before. The dangling snout of the nose was the same. The two great wide eyes were the same. It was a gas mask – just like the one I had seen before.

Except that there was one difference. In the right eyehole the flat glass disc remained just as it should do. But the left one was shattered. A few jagged splinters remained in place; the rest had been blasted inwards. Through the gap, even in the dim light of my living room, I could see some of the face beneath, or I should have been able to. But all I could make out was the glistening bloody pulp that remains when a bullet penetrates a human eye.

CHAPTER 4

They put me in a cell in the Police Station in the centre of town, occupying part of the same building as the Town Hall itself. I had to wait for an age or more until they called me up for interview. It was now into the small hours, but I didn't know quite when. They'd taken my watch along with everything else in my pockets.

Marchant was there, accompanied by a detective sergeant called Purvis, who didn't talk much. It was obvious I was considered a suspect. Marchant's first question was a cliché, but it also came as a relief.

'Where were you between the hours of nine and ten this evening?'

So that told me when the victim had died, and I had an alibi. It wouldn't have been too hard for them to work out the time of death; Mrs Croft had heard the shot. And they'd have taken the body temperature and done the calculations, just in case she was mistaken, or lying.

'London,' I said.

'Any witnesses?'

'Possibly.'

'What do you mean, "possibly"?'

I told him the whole story, or most of it: how O'Connor had first approached me on the pier and asked me to act as courier for him; how I'd rung him later and agreed; our meeting at Brighton Station; the rendezvous in Eccleston Square; the journey home; the man who'd followed me from the station.

'But, then, you know about that part,' I concluded.

Marchant nodded. 'After we found the body, DC Langley was sent to the station to look out for you. Once he'd extricated himself from that telephone box, he made his way back to your flat.'

'So you knew I was in London anyway?' I said.

'No.' Marchant spoke deliberately, as if explaining things to a child. 'When we found a body in your flat, we thought you might attempt to leave the town. That's what Langley was looking out for. We had someone at Hove Station as well ... and at Pool Valley in case you decided to catch a bus.'

It was laughable. Even in the grim interview room, I couldn't help but smile.

'What's so funny?'

'This isn't the sort of town you can put a cordon around, not if you sent out the entire force. There's half a dozen other stations. And I could have got on a bus anywhere.'

'We found you, didn't we?'

'Only because I wasn't trying to hide. And you caught me coming in, not going out.'

He looked at me sourly and changed the subject. 'So who can verify your story?'

'Anybody. The passengers on the train. The ticket collectors at either end. The man in Eccleston Square.'

'Anyone you could actually name?'

'O'Connor, obviously, though he can't prove I really went up to London.'

Marchant and Purvis exchanged an uncomfortable glance. Purvis took up the questioning. 'So what about this bloke you met? You can at least tell us what he looked like.'

On that part of the story I'd overlooked some details, but I had to tell them sometime.

'He looked,' I said, 'rather like the deceased.'

'What?'

'He was wearing a gas mask, just like the body in my flat.'

'*Just* like?' asked Marchant.

'Apart from the shattered eyepiece, they looked pretty much the same. The same type.'

Marchant again spoke slowly, precisely. 'So you're

saying that the dead man in your room is the same man you met in London?'

'I'm not saying anything,' I snapped, 'other than that they were both wearing gas masks.' My immediate instinct, on seeing the body lying in my room, had been that it was the same man, but that was difficult to make any sense of. 'I don't see how it can be, though. We were in London. He couldn't have been in my flat at 9.30 to be shot, any more than I could have been there to shoot him.'

'You seem to know very precisely when he was killed.'

'You said between nine and ten. I split the difference. So when *was* he killed?'

Marchant paused, but decided there was nothing to be gained by not telling me. 'Your landlady called us at twenty to ten. She said it couldn't have been more than two minutes since she heard the shot. You left Brighton at…?'

'I caught the 8:18.'

'And you got back…?

'Ask Langley.'

'I'm asking you.'

It wasn't worth a fight. 'Around midnight,' I conceded.

'And the murder took place slap-bang in the middle of your little *sojourn*.' He pronounced the last word as though it was new to his vocabulary. 'Quite convenient.'

'You're saying my alibi's just too good?'

'Your alibi's a pile of shit. You've got no one to confirm it.'

'You could at least ask O'Connor!' I hadn't meant to raise my voice.

He directed the same look towards Purvis that he had before, and shook his head resignedly. 'Let's get back to your trip to London. What was in the envelope?'

'I didn't look,' I lied. I'd exchanged obscene material for money; they could get me on that as a purveyor.

'And how much did he give you for conveying it?'

'Fifty pounds.'

'So where is it? We didn't find more than a few quid on

you.'

'I posted it. To a friend.'

'Who?'

'I'd rather not say.'

'It could save your neck.'

The words hung in the air. He might have been right. The postmark might give them some idea of when I was at Victoria – show that I'd been there late enough to miss the last collection. It could help prove my story.

'If it comes to that, I'll tell you,' I said.

'You'd do better to just tell me now.'

'Cobblers,' I muttered.

'What about this bloke in the gas mask, then. You really think he could make it back to Brighton quicker than you? *And* get himself killed?'

'I can't see how. I saw him in London after you say he was already dead – unless one of us has got the timings wrong. And, anyway, the mask is the only similarity. The coats they were wearing are different – and the gloves.'

'Odd thing that, for a bloke to notice another bloke's clothes.'

'I have a trained eye.'

'I've not heard it called that before.' Purvis gave a chuckle to please his boss. 'What about the build?' Marchant continued.

I shrugged. 'I'd say the corpse was fatter, but it's hard to compare. One standing up, alive; the other … a body expands when the muscles stop holding it in shape.'

'You've seen a lot of bodies, then?'

'One or two.'

'And you've no idea who the man in London was?'

'Not a clue.'

'And the man who died in your flat?'

'How could I? I couldn't see either of their faces.'

'You have an eye for "couture". An eye for a man's body.'

'I don't know him,' I insisted. Even then I wondered if

I might be mistaken.

He paused and took a deep breath, blowing it out through his teeth. 'Let's take another look, shall we?'

Purvis stood up and banged on the door, which was opened from the other side. Marchant beckoned me with a single finger and I followed him out. Purvis took up the rear. The corridor turned twice before descending a half flight of steps. It felt suddenly cold. The inspector turned sharply left. In the room beyond lay the cadaver, stretched out on a marble slab. It was still fully dressed, still wearing the gas mask. A man in a white coat stood nearby, surprised at our entrance.

'Why have you left the mask on?' I asked. I felt an intense anger at this indignity, which must have come across as an air of authority. The doctor glanced from Marchant to me and then back again.

'But ... you told me to put it back,' he said.

Marchant shook his head and exhaled, but said nothing.

'Have you confirmed the time of death?' Purvis asked.

'Any time between eight-thirty and when you found him,' the doctor replied.

I took a step forward to get a closer look at the corpse.

'Sure you don't recognize him?' said Purvis.

'Just take the fucking mask off,' I growled. I was bored with the play-acting.

Purvis looked to Marchant for confirmation and did as I had asked. He reached his hands under the body's head to loosen the straps. The blood was drying now, but even so some of it came away on his hands as a sticky burgundy paste. He peeled the gas mask off and looked around for somewhere to put it. The doctor took it from him. Purvis cradled the corpse's chin in his hand and turned the face in my direction.

I shouldn't have been surprised. Despite the mess that remained of his left eye, the chubby face was still recognizable. The clothes were not the ones he'd been wearing earlier in the day, but they were still undoubtedly his style. His portly physique had been disguised as death had moulded it into the corner of my living room, but it was still the same body that had squeezed itself into a chair in the bar of the Royal Albion only that afternoon. Here was the man who was my best chance of an alibi – an alibi in his own murder.

It was Alan O'Connor.

*

They took me back to the cells. I lay on the bunk and gazed up at the ceiling, tracing the cracks in the plasterwork with my eyes, thinking over what had happened. I couldn't make much sense of it all. Eventually I fell asleep. I don't recall dreaming but, when I awoke, I seemed to have formulated some kind of arrangement of the pieces that made sense. A constable delivered a simple breakfast and I kicked my heels for a couple of hours before they took me up for more questioning. This time it was just Marchant.

'Care to change your story?' he asked.

'Nope.'

'All right, then. Why don't you tell me what *you* think happened? You call yourself a detective – of sorts.'

I considered. It wouldn't hurt to tell him – I doubted he was part of it. 'I've been set up,' I told him.

'Really?'

'Sent to London on a fool's errand to get me out of the way.'

'A fool's errand? For fifty pounds? That's presuming the money really exists.'

'Obviously, whatever he was looking for was worth it.'

'Looking for?' Marchant was genuinely puzzled.

'In my rooms. My files had been searched.'

'O'Connor you mean?' Marchant laughed loudly and genuinely. 'So he framed you for his own murder?'

'I don't suppose getting murdered was part of his plan,' I said weakly.

There was a pause. He sat down, his whole attitude suddenly more conciliatory, but I could tell it was just an act. 'Look at it from my point of view, Charlie. I find a dead man in your living room. I don't know what he was doing there. Maybe he *was* raking through your files. Maybe you caught him at it. Maybe that's why you did it. The whole town remembers how badly you two fell out, that time.'

'I was in London.'

'And that's just the thing. There's not much in your story that can be verified – and even the bits that can don't hold water.'

'What?' Evidently he had something new. The whole conversation had been leading up to this.

'You said you got home yesterday around five, yeah?'

'That's right.'

'And soon after that you telephoned O'Connor.'

'Yes.' I exaggerated the tone of boredom in my voice.

'And his wife answered.'

'Like I told you.'

He stood up again and paced around the room. 'Now why, I ask myself, would you lie about a thing like that?'

'What?'

'We've spoken to her – had to break the bad news. But we questioned her too. You didn't ring. No one did. O'Connor wasn't even home.'

'Then she's lying,' I said, before I'd even considered the implication of his words.

'And why would she do that?'

'Her husband's dead, for one thing.'

'*Cherchez la femme*, you mean?'

'She lied, didn't she?'

'One of you did.'

There was a knock at the door. Marchant went to it and spoke briefly, then left the room. It might have been deliberate – an opportunity for me to sweat. I found it hard to believe that O'Connor's wife had anything to do with what had happened, but she must have had a reason to lie – if Marchant wasn't just making that up to unnerve me. It looked more and more like the envelope with the money – the postmark on it – was my best hope. But even that wasn't conclusive: I could have got someone to post it for me. Maybe if I dug deep enough, I'd be able to unearth the name of the man in the gas mask. But even if I found him, what use would it be? Who was going to admit to handing over a wad of cash in exchange for an envelope full of smut in a London park?

It was about twenty minutes later when Marchant came back in. His hands were clasped behind his back, his eyes fixed on the floor in thought. I watched him as he slowly walked across the room and came to a halt on the opposite side of the wooden table.

'You say you never looked at what was in the envelope?'

I nodded.

He brought his hands from behind his back. He was now wearing gloves and in his right hand he held a large manila envelope. I had no doubt as to what was in it. He tipped the contents on to the table. The images were entirely familiar. Still obscene. Still fascinating. The one thing of note was that only about half of the original set were there.

'So, if I had these examined, I wouldn't find your dabs on them?'

There was no point trying to pretend anymore. I leaned back in my chair with a sigh. 'All right, I did look.'

'Like what you saw?'

'Do you?'

He picked one up and examined it. It wasn't a good shot to identify either of the participants, but he let his eyes linger. 'You think this is the man you met?' he asked.

'It could be, I don't know.' I didn't mention the tattoo and its absence in the photographs. If I could just get the police looking further into things, they might eventually find something to clear me. 'Where the hell did you get those, anyway?' I'd let more emotion than intended creep into my voice. It showed I was nervous, and Marchant would read that as guilt.

He didn't answer my question. Instead he tidied up the pictures and returned them to the envelope, then went to the door and opened it. Another man entered the room, and I felt a distant stab of recognition. He was around ten years older than me, perhaps not quite in his forties. Nothing about him suggested he was a policeman. His suit was perfectly tailored – Savile Row, I guessed. His dark hair had a slight wave in it. As he approached, I caught a hint of cologne. He put down his hat and the suitcase he was carrying and offered me his hand.

'Tremaine,' he announced with a disarming smile. 'Ralph Tremaine.' His accent was pure Oxford.

'Charlie Woolf,' I replied, shaking his hand.

'Sorry to leave you stewing here, but I've only just made it down from London.'

I tried to make sense of what he was saying. He'd spoken as if I should have been expecting him, and he seemed to be on my side, though that could be a trick. There was only one explanation I could come up with but, even then, it didn't make much sense. 'So what are you?' I asked. 'A solicitor?'

He laughed in a way that was unconvincing without being rude. 'Let's just say I'm a different kind of policeman.' It sounded patronizing, but I suspected the tone was directed more towards Marchant than me. I noticed that the inspector had suddenly made himself appear insignificant. Tremaine continued, 'Now why don't you take me through what happened to you yesterday?'

I told my story again and this time I didn't hold much

back. I admitted to looking at the photographs, and explained how I'd swapped the envelopes to cover up my prying. I still didn't tell them where I'd sent the money, nor did I mention the tattoo – God knows why not. It seemed much easier recounting it all to him than it had been to Marchant, but that demonstrated the skill of a good interrogator.

'So you didn't recognize the man you met?'

'He was wearing a gas mask.' I wondered how many times I'd explained it already.

'What about his voice?'

It was a smarter question than anything I'd been asked so far, but it still wouldn't be much help. 'It was muffled by the mask. I could barely make out what he was saying.'

Tremaine nodded thoughtfully. 'I suppose so.' His mood suddenly lightened. 'Do you recognize *me*, by the by?'

I smiled. 'Actually, I do. But I can't place you.'

'We met briefly,' he explained. 'It was back in '33. You'd been working on a case with O'Connor, God rest his soul. You had to give evidence at the Old Bailey – as did I. We exchanged a few words in the waiting room.'

As soon as he mentioned it, I could picture every detail. Tremaine had looked younger, of course, and had been wearing a uniform. Royal Navy, a lieutenant-commander. It had been more O'Connor's case than mine – and a real investigation for once. 'Leopold Gilbert,' I said, remembering the name. 'He was sent down for —'

'I don't think we need worry about that now,' interrupted Tremaine, tapping the side of his nose and giving Marchant a furtive glance. 'Small world, though.'

'Not really enough of an acquaintanceship that you could act as a character witness for me,' I said.

'No.' He spoke with a firmness that suggested he might never be prepared to attest to my good character, even if he'd known me all my life. 'But I may be able to do rather better.'

He grinned and turned away, then laid his suitcase on the floor. I heard the clasps flick open. He rummaged inside but, with his back to me, I couldn't see what he was doing. I glanced over at Marchant, who had a better view. His face carried a look of sturdy confusion – the expression of a man accustomed to not understanding what he was seeing and able to cope with the fact.

Tremaine turned and stood up in a single rapid motion. He leaned forwards with his hands on the table, so that our faces were just inches apart.

'Recognize me now?' His voice was loud, but muffled in a way that was now familiar. The whole thing was becoming ridiculous. The dangling snout and porthole eyes became less shocking on each encounter. Once again I found myself face to face with the cold, blank countenance of a gas mask.

CHAPTER 5

'Sorry to be so theatrical,' Tremaine chuckled, as he removed the mask. He stared down at it, as though he were Hamlet contemplating Yorick.

'So it was you!' I couldn't disguise my surprise.

'Guilty as charged.'

'What was *you*?' asked Marchant, stepping back towards the table.

Tremaine turned and held the respirator up to his face again. 'The man in the mask.' His voice was less muffled now that the rubber was not sealed tight against his skin.

'*You* met him in London?' said Marchant. 'In Eccleston Square?'

'I'd presumed you cottoned on to that when I gave you the photographs,' Tremaine replied.

I sat back in my chair. It took a moment for the sense of relief to wash over me. I had my alibi, and from a source I'd least expected. Whatever subterfuge Tremaine had gone through in acquiring those photographs, he now had no shame in announcing his possession of them. It left many questions unanswered, but none seemed of any immediate significance. The only thought running through my mind was that I was free.

'So who is it in the photographs?' asked Marchant, evidently less distracted than I had been by this new development. The two men sat down.

'As I explained to you when I arrived,' – Tremaine directed his words towards the inspector – 'I work in a government department that has a special interest in the activities of certain foreign nationals resident in this country. The gentleman in the photographs is one such, and I doubt very much whether he'd like his paymasters back home to find out what he's been up to over here – or, indeed, his wife.'

'So it *is* blackmail,' I said.

Tremaine twisted his mouth as if chewing something sour. 'Blackmail of the noblest kind: not for money but for the safety of England.'

'And you've shown him the pictures? He's agreed to help you?'

'Not yet, but we're pretty sure he will.'

'We?' I asked.

'My department.'

'I don't think that's any concern of ours, Woolf,' interjected Marchant. He oozed deference.

'No, but I've put you both to considerable inconvenience. I'm happy to tell you what I can.'

'Who's the girl?' I asked.

'I've no idea. Some tart O'Connor got hold of.'

'So O'Connor did take the pictures?' I said. 'Down here in Brighton?'

'I presume so.'

I already knew so. I'd recognized the room as being in the Metropole. I looked towards Marchant. He must have known that as well as I did – he'd been a Brighton copper for twenty years. Like me, he kept the knowledge to himself.

'Do you recognize her?' I asked the inspector.

He shook his head. 'She may not have been here long. Some of them come down just for the summer, when the trade's good. She'll be hoping for a rainy Whitsun.'

'You could find out,' I suggested. 'Show the pictures around the station.'

'There'd be a riot.' He seemed genuinely concerned.

'I'd rather you didn't,' said Tremaine. We both looked at him. 'The poor girl's done great service to her country. I'm sure she'd rather be left in peace.'

'She knew what she was doing, then?' I asked.

Tremaine cracked a smile that turned into a leer. 'I think the photographs make that quite evident. Don't you?'

'I mean,' I said patiently, 'she knew *why*.'

'I doubt she bothered to ask, once she saw the money. Even if she had, O'Connor didn't know very much.'

'But why didn't O'Connor just give you the pictures himself?' asked Marchant. 'Why send Woolf?'

'I should have thought that was fucking obvious.' Tremaine pronounced the word to rhyme with 'barking'. It sounded almost pleasant on his lips.

'Not to me,' said Marchant.

'And to you, Mr Woolf?'

'Yeah, it's plain enough,' I said.

Tremaine smiled at me, acknowledging that I'd joined in his game of trying to irritate the policeman. 'Inspector,' he said, 'what was the first thing O'Connor did after he'd seen our friend here off on the train to Victoria?'

'How should I know?'

'What's the first thing you *do* know he did?'

'He went to Woolf's flat.'

'And, once there, what did he proceed to do?'

'He proceeded to get himself shot.' Marchant allowed his anger at being patronized to show through.

'He didn't go there to get shot, though, did he?'

'You still think he sent you up to London deliberately? Got you out the way so he could search your office?'

'Seems likely,' I said.

'And while he was there,' said Tremaine, 'somebody killed him.'

'I don't suppose you have any idea who?' asked Marchant.

'Who'd have a reason to? Who had something against him?'

Marchant looked blank. I felt equally bewildered, but tried not to show it. Tremaine picked up the brown envelope and poured its contents on to the table, forming a jumble of eyes, ears, skin and hair. Again my thoughts turned to the fractured structure of a cubist painting. Tremaine's gloved finger pointed to the top picture: at the man's face squashed against the back of the girl's neck.

'Who'd he been taking dirty pictures of?'

*

Despite Tremaine's personal evidence that I'd been fifty miles away at the time of O'Connor's death, I was sent back down to my cell. It was understandable, I suppose. Marchant needed to verify what Tremaine had told him, and that was better done in my absence. It was only for another half hour. Then they took my fingerprints, gave me back my personal effects, and told me I was free to go. I looked at my watch: it was five to eleven on Sunday morning.

I headed down Market Street to the seafront, looking for somewhere to get a drink. It was too early for the pubs to be open, but a cup of tea would be enough. The first place I came to was the Hollywood Hotel. I went in and sat by a window overlooking the sea, like I had done with O'Connor just the day before, in the Royal Albion. A waitress came up and I ordered, scarcely even looking at her, which wasn't like me. I was free but I wasn't happy. There was just too much tommyrot in this whole thing. In broad terms it made sense, but a hundred little details still needed explanation.

A leather-gloved hand tapped at the window. A face loomed close – for once simply human, not hidden behind a mask. It was Tremaine. He pointed to himself and then to the door to indicate that he was coming in.

'I thought I'd better catch up with you,' he said, as he sat down. 'I imagine you might have one or two questions.'

'One or two.'

'Not unlike our friend the inspector, but he's rather easier to deal with than I imagine you will be.'

Before I could ask what he meant, the waitress arrived with my pot of tea. Tremaine beamed up at her. 'How lovely. Do you think I might have the same? And perhaps some cake?' He turned to me. 'You like cake, do you?' I nodded. 'Cake, then,' he continued. 'What cakes do you have?' She listed them with a degree of enthusiasm I suspected was reserved for customers such as him. 'Ginger, did you say? That sounds delightful. Ginger cake for us both, please.'

I was beginning to like him. He was of my class, or at least of the class I'd been born into. However much I hid myself away here in Brighton, I couldn't escape it. He pulled off his gloves and put them on the table, far more smoothly this time than he had managed it the previous night in Eccleston Square. As then I caught a glimpse of the ship's anchor tattoo on his forearm. It fitted with his having been in the navy.

'Why is Marchant so easy to deal with?' I asked.

'He's a public servant and has therefore a duty to obey orders. With you I can only appeal to your sense of patriotism. I take it you have one?'

It would sting any Englishman even to be asked. 'My father died in the war,' I replied coldly.

'I'm sorry. I didn't mean to …' He petered out. 'I lost my elder brother.'

'Just be straight with me,' I said. 'I'm not going to blab about it to anyone.'

The waitress returned with the tea and cake. Once she'd gone Tremaine leaned forward and spoke softly. 'As you'll have guessed, I'm with the Security Service. I also don't suppose I need to tell you that within a few years this country is likely once more to be at war with Germany.'

'You think so? That they'd be so stupid again?'

He seemed to take my comment almost personally. 'Mr Woolf, please don't presume to tell me my business. I'm privy to far more information on this than you get from the newspapers.'

'But I thought it had all calmed down. Hitler said he wasn't interested in the Sudetenland, not with France and

Russia prepared to stand up to him.'

'What Herr Hitler says to the world is very different from what he says in private. Do you really think he'll stop at Austria?'

I opened my mouth, but had nothing to say. I must have looked like a fish.

'Anyway,' Tremaine continued, 'what you or I think hardly matters. It's my job to gather all the information I can on the Nazis.' He pronounced the 'z' as a Germanic 'ts'.

'So the chap in the photographs – he's a German?'

Tremaine nodded. 'Works at the embassy in London. We've been watching him for months. We noticed how he liked to pop down to Brighton every now and again. It was easy enough to guess why.'

'It could be for any number of reasons.'

Tremaine slipped a hand into his jacket and brought out a silver cigarette case. He offered me one. It had been hours since I'd had a drag of anything and I hadn't realized how much I needed it. He lit both mine and his and then stared out of the window as he drew in the smoke.

'You ever read Wells?' he asked, apropos of nothing.

'I have done.'

'*The Time Machine*?'

I nodded.

'The fellow's a socialist, of course, but that doesn't stop him from being spot on. You see all these trippers?' he waved his hand towards the window. Outside, Kings Road was beginning to fill with tourists, either down for the day or emerging from their hotels into the sunlight. It was brighter than yesterday. 'They're like the Eloi in the novel: seemingly contented, leisurely, their every need catered for. And they're fed by the Morlocks – that's you, the people of Brighton. You feed them when they come down, entertain then, draw sketches of them. You take their money at the races. Girls like whoever-she-may-be will even fuck them. But who's really the superior partner?

Who's really being fucked? This town doesn't have any other substantive trade; even the fishermen are going out of business. In the end the Morlocks ate the Eloi, but here you don't need to go that far. That would be killing the goose that lays the golden eggs. You just let them keep coming back every weekend, every bank holiday, and you keep chiselling.'

'Charming,' I said.

He turned to me and smiled, acknowledging that he might have gone too far. 'Perhaps I should leave the social commentary to gentlemen such as Mr Wells. My point is that when we come across a German diplomat popping down to Brighton every other week, we suspect he's here for more than just a paddle in the sea. He's coming for one of the many pleasures a town like this can offer. In his case it turns out to be the ladies.'

'Couldn't he find anyone willing in London?' I asked.

'You'd think so, wouldn't you? But there's something about this place that adds a certain … *frisson*. Perhaps it's the sea air, or the fact that one has to make a journey – that sense of anticipation as one travels down by train. And, of course, one doesn't like to shit on one's own doorstep.'

'So you set him up and got O'Connor to take the photos?'

'I left it all to O'Connor. He knows the territory.'

'Why O'Connor?'

'I remembered him from that same court case where we two met. I looked him up.'

I thought back to what O'Connor had said about his reasons for employing me as a courier. 'So he wasn't worried you'd recognize him if he showed up with the photos himself.'

Tremaine shook his head. 'It would seem to be just as you suspected: his sending you was merely a ruse so that he could break into your flat.'

The obvious implication didn't appear to strike him,

though I doubted he was that stupid, and I was happy to demonstrate that I wasn't either. 'But if you already knew one another,' I asked, 'and if you were expecting O'Connor to meet you in London, why did *you* need to be wearing a mask?'

He raised his hands in mock surrender. 'I'm afraid I must confess to some involvement in this little deception. O'Connor telephoned yesterday to tell me that you would be bringing the photographs in his place. I assure you, I had no idea what he had planned while you were safely out of the way. Even so, I was severely peeved by the arrangement, I can tell you, but I couldn't force him to come, and he swore that you were a man to be trusted. It did present me with the additional problem that you and I had met before, however briefly. There was always the chance you'd recognize me, or identify me later. I decided it was better to keep things simple.'

To me things seemed anything but simple. 'But you're not worried about me recognizing you now?'

'It's got more serious. I wasn't going to leave you to rot in gaol.'

'And what about O'Connor? He just happened to be wearing a gas mask as well. Coincidence?'

'That hardly seems likely, does it? It was he who suggested the idea to me. I complained that you'd recognize who I was and he said that he found a gas mask the ideal way to conceal one's identity. I was hardly to know he was going to pull the selfsame trick while burgling you.'

'Why a gas mask? Why not simply … tie a handkerchief across your face?' When I'd begun the sentence, I'd imagined I could come up with a dozen ideas – but it wasn't so easy.

'A little bit too Wild West, don't you think? The gas mask seemed to fit the bill – and it appealed to my sense of the absurd.'

'And you just happened to have one to hand?' I asked

sceptically.

He leaned forward, glancing around to verify he wasn't overheard, but making more of it than he needed to. 'My dear boy, I've seen plans detailing how every citizen of this nation – man, woman and child – will be issued with a respirator within a year or so. Fortunately, there are certain government departments whose staff are regarded as a little more indispensable than the hoi polloi. That's why we've already received ours.'

'And where did O'Connor get his?'

Tremaine shrugged, leaning back. 'How should I know? They're easy enough to acquire, for those who are thinking ahead.'

'Wouldn't he have been worried it would connect the two of you?'

'You knew the man. Don't give him more credit than he deserves. But, anyway, why should he worry? He wouldn't have expected anyone to see us both. I doubt he was planning on getting killed.'

I paused. 'Theatrical' was the word he'd used earlier, at the police station. It was certainly that. But there was some kind of sense to it. 'Any idea what O'Connor was after?' I asked. 'In my flat, I mean?'

Tremaine drew on his cigarette. 'He confided nothing to me. I can only suppose it was something in your files. It would hardly be your common-or-garden burglary.'

'And then he was killed by this German, you reckon … what was his name?'

'I'm afraid I can't tell you that, but it does seem the most likely possibility. Of course, O'Connor could have unearthed something even more squalid about him. Do you have any idea what else he was investigating?'

'Until yesterday I hadn't seen him for over a year.'

'It could be related to whatever he was after in your office,' Tremaine suggested. 'And let's not forget the effort that was made to put *you* in the frame. If I'd not been able to confirm your alibi, you'd still be banged up.'

Another thought occurred to me. 'You were pretty quick off the mark with that. How did you know to come down?'

'We get reports of serious crime from all the major constabularies. When I got back to Thames House, after meeting you, the Brighton police had already called it in. We only got O'Connor's name later, and I toddled down here right away.'

I nodded thoughtfully. For a spy he seemed surprisingly open. He stood up and offered me his hand. 'I hope I've been of some help,' he said. 'As I explained, I can tell the police what to do – and what not to do. With civilians it's more tricky.'

'But you *are* telling me?'

He grinned and nodded. 'That's the ticket. I'm sure you're angry about the death of your colleague but, believe me, we'll look into it. If our Kraut friend did it, we'll find out.'

He put his gloves back on and tipped his hat briefly. Then he was gone. I looked down at the table and saw that he hadn't touched his cake. I hadn't eaten since the meagre breakfast I'd been given in my cell, so I finished it for him.

I thought about what Tremaine had said, but I couldn't foresee O'Connor's murderer ever being brought to justice. I didn't doubt that the Security Service had the skill to find out if their German diplomat had done it, but what then? There was nothing to be gained by sending him to gaol. It's one thing to have some dirty pictures you can use to persuade a man to betray his country. How much better a nice juicy murder?

CHAPTER 6

Those two small slices of ginger cake wouldn't be enough to keep me going for long, so I found myself some lunch in town before heading back home. I walked rather than taking the tram. It was a sunny day but, more than that, I wanted to delay the moment. I could face going back into the room where O'Connor's body had been found, but it was Mrs Croft's home that had been violated as much as mine; I didn't relish the prospect of looking her in the eye.

I turned into Rose Hill Terrace. It was quiet; there were no police cars here today. I went up the steps and opened the front door. Usually I would have called out her name, but today the words caught in my throat. I looked along the hall. For once the kitchen door was closed. I walked down and was about to knock, when I heard her softly singing beyond the door next to it – the door to her sitting room. It was the same song as yesterday: *Isn't It Romantic?*

I tapped softly and then a little louder, but the singing continued. I felt relieved. I had done my best to speak to her – done my duty. Now I could leave her alone. But I knew that was cowardice talking – the same cowardice that had prevented me from rapping clearly and firmly on the door in the first place. I did so now. The singing stopped. Moments later the door opened and she stood there, a feather duster in her hand.

'Mr Woolf! Oh, thank heavens!'

She took a step forward, as if about to embrace me but then thinking better of it. I wouldn't have objected, but it had never happened before in the eight years I'd lived there. It would be too much of an innovation now.

'Come in,' she said. 'Sit down.'

I walked through the doorway. I'd rarely been in this room before – it was her private retreat. Another door led on to the kitchen, while on the other side of the room a third stood closed. I'd always presumed that this one led to her bedroom.

'I'd just put the tea on,' she continued. After that first moment of our encounter, she had avoided eye contact. She disappeared into the kitchen.

Despite her offer, I didn't sit down immediately. Instead I walked over to inspect the photographs on the mantelpiece. One was of a man in the uniform of a sergeant, dating back to the war. I knew she was a widow but I'd never asked about her husband. Perhaps this was he. Perhaps he'd died in the war, like my father. Dad had been a colonel, not a sergeant, but death was the same for all of them. I thought back to what Tremaine had said about a new war coming; I'd always been optimistic. It wasn't that I trusted the politicians, but I couldn't see how any of them could be insane enough to let it all happen again. But Tremaine must know things that would never be revealed to the rest of us – to the hoi polloi.

The next photo was of three children: two boys and a girl. These I did know about – she talked of them a lot. I'd met two of them on their occasional visits – none of them lived in Brighton any more. The final picture was not a photograph at all, but a pastel I myself had drawn, of Mrs Croft's daughter, Esme, when she had visited a couple of years before. The jagged, abstract patterns I'd used for a background reminded me how I'd had a migraine approaching at the time. I think Mrs Croft had been trying to engineer something between us, but Esme wasn't my type. She wasn't my class. That was my mother talking.

I finally went and sat down. The tea was taking a while. She'd been lying when she said she'd already put the kettle on, but she evidently didn't want to give me any excuse for not staying. Eventually she came back with a pot and two cups on a tray, along with a little plate of rich tea biscuits. She began to pour.

'They let you go, then?' she said.

'They knew it was nothing to do with me. I was up in

London.'

'*I* could have told them that. They have any idea who the poor blighter was?'

They evidently hadn't told her. She knew O'Connor slightly – well enough to recognize his voice on the telephone. I wished it wasn't me who now had to break the news.

'You remember Alan O'Connor – the chap I used to work with? The one who phoned yesterday?'

'Yes.' She said the word cautiously, as if guessing but not wanting to jump to any conclusion.

'It was him, I'm afraid.'

'Good heavens! Really?' I could imagine her sitting there gossiping with her friends. She might have reacted just the same to the news that one of the neighbours had run off with the coalman. She knew how to hide her emotions.

'I don't suppose you saw anything?' I said. I tried to drink my tea quickly, despite its still being painfully hot. I didn't want to be forced to stay here for too long.

'All I heard was the shot. I ran upstairs but your door was locked. They must have come in through the back – I saw the broken window later – but I didn't think to look at the time.'

'I suppose they must have.'

'Then I called the police. They got here very quickly.'

'I'm sure you told them everything you knew.'

'Nothing more than I've just told you. And Mr Crosby's away till Tuesday, so he can't help.'

Crosby rented the rooms on the top floor, above mine. My tea was a little cooler now. I gulped it down and then stood up.

'I'd better go and see what state the place is in,' I explained.

'I had a word with Jack; he says he'll be over to fix your door this afternoon. The window will take longer.'

I was never quite sure of what Jack was to Mrs Croft,

or really of anything about him, but he did all the work around the house that required a man's skills.

'Thanks,' I said, heading for the door. As I reached it, I turned. 'You will be all right, won't you, Mrs Croft?'

She gave me one of her rare smiles. It didn't suit her. 'I'm sure I'll be fine.'

I went upstairs. The door was pulled shut, but the frame was still broken. I pushed it open and went straight to my living room to look around. The place had been straightened up. The standard lamp was upright again, with its shade back in place. Newspaper had been taped over the broken window. The bloodstain on the wall was gone, but the hole in the plaster was bigger now where they'd dug out the bullet. The chair had been put back in place by someone who didn't quite know where it was supposed be. I went and looked down the side of it. The stain in the carpet remained, though it looked as though someone – Mrs Croft presumably – had tried to scrub it out. It was a hopeless task.

I went back out to my office. This was where the real clues would be, or at least the ones I could make sense of. It didn't look like anything had been moved since I'd last seen it the night before. The filing cabinets still had their drawers pulled wide open. Papers remained scattered on the desk.

O'Connor had taught me a lot in the years we worked together. His own path into the world of the private detective had been different from mine. He'd originally worked on the railways as an engineer. I remember when he'd first told me about it. He'd been at pains to point out that he didn't mean 'engineer' in the American sense. He didn't *drive* the locomotives; he maintained them – repaired them. It was – at least in his mind – a far more illustrious job. He'd left the Southern Railway under something of a cloud, but always approached his work with a scientific, mathematical attitude. I still used the filing system he'd devised.

One of its key benefits was in just such a situation as this – it could tell you what was missing. I looked first at the open files on the desk. It seemed self-evident that O'Connor had been studying them. They all began with 'G': 'George Street (Brighton)', 'Geoffreys' and 'Goldstone'. Each file had a number on the back – acting as a unique identifier. I went through them all – not just the three that had been left out, but everything in the cabinets – ticking each one off against the entry in the master list kept separately in a drawer in my desk. It took me about half an hour but by the end it was easy to see that there was just a single file missing: 'Grove Street'. Evidently O'Connor had grabbed all the 'G's and then taken the one he wanted.

And yet he couldn't have. He couldn't have taken anything, because he had never left. It would have been difficult to conceal a file on his body. On the other hand, the police might have taken it before I arrived, but I could see no reason why Marchant wouldn't have then asked me about it. And there was more than that: it was O'Connor's own system that had told me what was missing. He knew that I used it. If he'd wanted to steal something – and hide the fact that it was gone – he'd have altered or destroyed the master list, or at least extracted individual items, not the entire file. It was obvious who *had* taken it: whoever had killed him.

I tried to recall what the Grove Street case had been about. It was from a couple of years before – a Peeping Tom. Someone had been prowling through the back gardens on one side of the street, but there'd been no attempt at burglary, so the police weren't interested. I'd kept an eye on the place for a few nights, and the problem had stopped – and, as far as I knew, never recurred. I got paid for my time. That was about as exciting as most cases got for me. I couldn't see how anything about O'Connor's death could be related to Grove Street. Might it have been him, prowling around behind the houses with his camera, collecting evidence of some sort? But again that assumed *he* had taken the file. It may well have been him that was looking for it – and him that found it. But he certainly didn't *take* it. He took nothing because he never had the chance to leave. It was now in the hands of whoever had killed him. There had to be a reason why that second man hadn't just run for it after pulling the trigger – why he'd made sure to grab the file.

But, try as I might, I couldn't see what a German diplomat, an envoy of Herr Hitler to His Majesty King George VI, would be doing hanging around in the back gardens of a nondescript terrace in Brighton, getting his thrills by peering through the windows at middle-aged women preparing for bed.

*

I decided that I liked Tremaine. I didn't trust him but I liked him – he made good conversation and that was more than many could achieve. And it was only natural for me to distrust him; he was a spy. Deceit was his profession. He'd have been offended if I thought otherwise.

The particular matter over which I didn't trust him was his assertion that he'd had no idea O'Connor planned to break into my rooms. That seemed just a little too generous of him; too much of a distraction from the real task for which he'd hired O'Connor: getting hold of something he could use against the unnamed German. 'Peeved' was the word he'd used to describe his reaction to the news that O'Connor wouldn't be coming to London in person. He'd said he couldn't force O'Connor to run the errand himself, but it didn't sound like he'd even tried. I knew O'Connor and, in circumstances like that, he'd have caved at the slightest pressure. Tremaine would only have allowed it if what O'Connor was doing was likely to be of benefit to *him* – and that meant it must be something to do with the blackmail. It hardly mattered whether O'Connor had actually explained to Tremaine where he was going to look for dirt on the German, but that must have been why he was in my rooms. Somewhere in the Grove Street file there was information relating to the German. After that, the rest seemed obvious. Somehow the German had got wind of things, killed O'Connor and taken the file himself. And then destroyed it, most likely.

There was always another possibility. When you shoot a man in the face, you can usually be pretty certain of exactly who he is. But not in this case; O'Connor had been wearing a mask. Whatever my speculations about why anyone should want to kill O'Connor, they rested on the foundation that someone *did* want to kill him. If his death was merely the result of mistaken identity, then all bets were off.

But I wasn't going to mention any of that at my next port of call. I was in Hove now, walking along Eaton Villas. O'Connor had moved house since I'd been working with him, so the place was new to me, but I had the address. It struck me that I should feel bad at never having visited someone who used to be so close to me, but I felt nothing. It was a nice area; O'Connor had obviously done well for himself with his divorce cases. I went up to the front door and pulled the bell. A face appeared from behind the net curtains at the bay window. The expression was sour; the hair was pinned up and close to the skull, dark but not naturally so. I remembered her name now: Vera. I still knew better than to use it. I could tell by her scowl that she'd recognized me too. A moment later she opened the door.

'Mrs O'Connor ...' I had no chance to say more, but I noticed briefly the tears in her eyes as she turned away and headed along the hall. I could only presume she meant me to follow. I closed the door behind me. She went back into the living room and sat down on the settee. A ginger cat jumped up on to her lap and she began to stroke it. She didn't offer me a chair, so I remained standing close to the door.

'They told me they'd let you go,' she said reproachfully.

'I was miles away.'

'He was in your flat.'

'He broke in.' I knew I'd get more out of her if I appeared contrite, but I had to defend myself.

'I'm sure he had his reasons.'

'That's what I'm trying to find out.'

'Leave it to the police. No sense both of you getting killed.' It was the first hint that she had any sympathy for me at all.

'I'm not sure the police are going to make much effort.'

'Don't be stupid.'

'They've been told to lay off – by someone high up in government.'

She said nothing. This was evidently not news to her.

'He told you, didn't he?' I said.

'He mentioned something. He couldn't tell me very much, of course, and I didn't want to know. But he said it might mean a whole new line of work for him – might earn him enough money to mean we could move out of this place and find somewhere better.'

I looked around the room and found it hard to conceive what was so bad about 'this place'. It was almost as big as Mrs Croft's whole house, and there were only the two of them living here. Only one now.

'Did he mention a man named Tremaine to you?' I asked.

'We agreed from the start: work and home stay separate.' The cat was trying to get away now, but she held it firmly by the back of its neck as she continued to stroke it. 'I didn't ask, and he didn't tell. Even when he had to go away, I didn't ask.'

'Away?'

'He stayed at a lot of hotels; that's all I know.'

'He took his camera?'

She nodded. She must have guessed something; that was why she was so loath to talk. But she probably thought that, for a divorce, it was enough just to get a shot of the unfaithful couple having dinner together. Sometimes it was, but Mrs O'Connor would never guess just how intimate her husband's pictures could be. I wasn't going to disabuse her.

'Did he ever mention anyone German?'

'He was always going on about the Germans. Said what we needed here was our own version of Hitler. Said —'

'Someone he knew personally, I mean.'

She shook her head.

I wasn't getting anywhere. 'And after I telephoned yesterday, where did —?'

'Now, that's what the police said.' Her voice wavered between confusion and anger. 'But you didn't call. No one called. He wasn't even here. He went out at midday and …' She sniffed back tears. '… and I never saw him again.'

It seemed so unnecessary a lie. I'd spoken to her, and then she'd put O'Connor on. That was to say, I'd spoken to someone — I couldn't swear it was her voice, but who else could it be? I could see little benefit in pressing the point, or in asking her anything more.

'Does he still have the office on Blatchington Road?' I asked. That was where we'd worked together as partners. It showed how well he was doing if he could afford to keep the place up as well as this house. For me office and home were separated by only a wooden door.

'You mean "did he".'

I took it as a yes. 'I don't suppose I could borrow a key, just to look around.'

The cat finally escaped her grasp and leapt across the furniture before scuttling quickly past me and out through the door. It was the final straw for her. She threw one hand outwards across the table beside her, knocking over a thin glass vase that contained a single peony. It fell to the floor and didn't break, but spilled water on the carpet. I took a step forward so as to help clear up the mess, but she'd have none of it.

'Haven't you done enough?' She was angry rather than tearful. 'Just go. Get out of my house.'

I didn't argue. Instead I turned and left, walking quickly back along the hall to the front door. But there was one more thing for me to discover here, almost by chance. Between the foot of the stairs and the front door stood a table with a telephone on it – in just the same position as where I lived. I glanced down at it. In the centre of the dial a see-through plastic disk covered a circle of card. On that was written the telephone number in neat pencil. I still had the page of notepaper that O'Connor had given me when he asked me to call. I took it out of my pocket and compared the two numbers. They were not the same.

CHAPTER 7

Blatchington Road was just a block closer to the seafront than Eaton Villas, so I didn't have far to walk. I had no idea what I intended to do when I got there. I had no key and I'd be a fool to break in. Even with my alibi, I was still a suspect in O'Connor's murder. How would it look if I was arrested for burgling his offices? And though Tremaine had been polite enough in warning me off, I was sure he had colleagues who could be very much more persuasive if the need arose.

About halfway along the road, on the other side, I spotted a phone box. I crossed quickly, dodging between the few motor cars that were out for a jaunt on a Sunday afternoon. I put in two pennies and dialled the number on the sheet of paper that O'Connor had given me. It rang three times, then a woman answered.

'Al?' she said. 'Al? Is that you?'

Now that I heard it again, this clearly wasn't Mrs O'Connor's voice. That was no surprise; as good as I was at remembering a face, I was lousy with voices. It was only when I saw the telephone number that I understood Vera O'Connor was not the woman I'd spoken to on Saturday evening. Even now I couldn't be sure that this *was* the woman – but it was certainly the same number. I pressed button A and the coin dropped through.

'Hullo?' I said. Her question had taken me by surprise. I couldn't think what to say. 'To whom am I speaking?'

'Oh, I'm sorry. I was expecting someone else.'

'Alan, you mean?' I said. 'Alan O'Connor?'

'Yes!' There was a slight thrill in her voice, certainly in comparison with her tone moments before. 'You know where he is?'

'Can you tell me who *you* are?' I persisted.

'Please. I've been worried sick. He never came home last night.'

I didn't have the heart to string her along. 'I'm afraid I have some bad news: Alan's dead.'

It was hardly the best way for her to have found out, but what else could I do? Silence followed for a few seconds, then the click of her putting down the receiver. I put in more money and dialled again, but this time there was no answer, not even after twenty rings. I left the phone box and carried on down the road. A kid of about eight emerged from nowhere and ran into the box. I turned to see him rattling button B in the hope that I'd left some change in the machine, but I'd already got my pennies back. I squeezed the coins between my fingers, feeling a pathetic sense of victory, and crossed back over the road.

O'Connor rented a part of a three-storey terraced building on the north side of the street. Steps led up to the front door, but that was a little too grandiose even for him. His office – our office, as it had once been – was situated in the basement. The steps went down from the pavement just beside where others ascended to the front door. They led to a tiny courtyard, only half a storey below street level, and so still high enough to look out and see the feet of passers-by, if there'd been any around on that quiet Sunday. I recalled how bad the drainage was here, and how the yard could flood with water up to your ankles on a rainy day.

The door was right underneath the steps. The place had been built as a house rather than for offices, and this would have been the servants' entrance. I tried the door, but it was locked. I went over to the window overlooking the yard and cupped my hands against it, to peer through. There was movement inside. I heard the sound of the door opening and turned to see who was there. It was Marchant.

'Returning to the scene of the crime?' he said.

'The crime took place at my house, remember. I don't have any choice but to go back *there*.'

'So you've never been here before?'

'You know I have. I used to work here. But not recently. Why, what's happened?'

He beckoned me with his finger and stepped inside again. It was the same gesture he'd used back at the nick. I followed, just as I had then.

It was a familiar scene – familiar in two ways. The first was simply that the office hadn't changed very much since I'd worked there with O'Connor. The layout remained the same: O'Connor's desk by the window, mine in the corner. He'd never found himself a new partner, as far as I was aware. I wondered why he hadn't got rid of my desk. I felt no nostalgia for the old days here, and again surprised myself with my lack of sentiment over his death.

The second cause of familiarity was the state in which the office had been left – much the same as mine had been. Filing cabinets stood with their drawers open. Papers were strewn across both desks. The place had obviously been searched, and by the same person as had searched my own office; the person who killed O'Connor.

'He must have come here straight after the murder,' I said.

'You'd think so, wouldn't you? But it was called in last night at just after nine. That's *before* O'Connor was killed.'

'Took you a while to get here.'

He bridled but kept his composure. 'We're in Hove now, laddie. Not our patch.'

'So what *are* you doing here?'

I wasn't sure why I was trying so hard to irritate him, nor why he bothered to restrain himself, but he didn't rise to the bait. Instead he nodded towards another man who was bending over O'Connor's desk, going through some papers. 'Thankfully, my colleague, DI Chambers, has squared things so that I can take a look.'

The last sentence jarred with me, and I immediately understood why. The word 'squared' was used to make a point. At least half the officers in both the Brighton and

Hove police forces were Freemasons. Over the years I'd got used to picking out the words and phrases they employed to demonstrate the fact. Of course, it could have been an entirely innocent turn of phrase – but it hadn't been so long since I'd bumped into Marchant coming out of the Lodge on Queen's Road.

'I'm surprised you're here at all,' I said. 'Didn't Tremaine warn you off?'

'I could say the same for you.'

'I'm not a servant of the Crown. I don't have to do what I'm told.'

Marchant rubbed his chin. 'Technically,' he explained, 'I'm not investigating the murder. I'm investigating a burglary.' He paused, then looked me straight in the eye. 'I've got to do *something*.'

'So what have you found?'

'He broke in through the rear, just like at your place. A neighbour in a house backing on to this one noticed the smashed window, but he was long gone by then, so it could have been even earlier.'

'What's missing?'

'Hard to tell.'

I smiled. 'I'm not so sure. Did you find his master list?'

'His what?'

'A list of names and numbers – several pages long. He used to keep it in the bottom-left drawer of his desk.'

Chambers shuffled through the documents in front of him and pulled one out. 'This what you mean?' He brought it over and I glanced at it.

'That's right,' I said. 'If you look at each separate file, you'll see a number on the back. That corresponds to the number on the list. If you cross-reference them, you'll find out what's missing.'

'It'll take forever,' said Chambers.

'Better get started, then,' said Marchant. Chambers paused for a moment, then set to work. Whatever the equality of their ranks in the force, Marchant had evidently attained a superior degree at the Lodge. 'How did you know about this?' he asked, turning to me.

'I worked with O'Connor, remember? He taught me all his tricks – some of them, anyway.'

'So you could work out what was taken from your own files in the same way?'

'Could. Did.'

He nodded his head towards the door. 'Come outside.'

'One last thing,' I said. I went over to O'Connor's desk and peered at the telephone. I remembered the original number, but there was a chance he'd changed it. It was written there just like on the phone at his house; the same number that I'd once shared with him. It wasn't the number he'd given me to call him on. That had never seemed likely. 'O'Connor didn't have a secretary, did he?' I asked.

Marchant shrugged. 'Who knows?' He looked around the room. 'But I don't see any feminine touches. Do you?'

With that he headed back out. I followed. In the courtyard he lit a cigarette, then offered me one. We stood in silence for a moment.

'I take it Tremaine explained to you about this German,' Marchant said at last.

'Some of it. Like I said, I'm a civilian, so he had to be careful. He said his department would investigate.'

'You believe him?'

'I'm sure they'll investigate. I'm not so sure what they'll do with anything they find.'

Marchant nodded. 'That was my supposition. All for the good of the country, I suppose.'

'So why are you here?'

He answered me with a question of his own. 'You worked out what was missing from your office, then?'

'Just one file: case of a Peeping Tom on Grove Street.'

'Solved?'

'Resolved … but I can't see a connection. Have you come up with anything?'

'The doctor confirms that the bullet wound was the cause of death. No other signs of injury. Bullet was a .455 – probably from a Webley. There must still be hundreds of them knocking around from the war.'

'Anything else?' I asked, choosing not to mention that I'd inherited just such a revolver from my father. Thankfully I didn't keep it at home.

'We dusted the photographs that Tremaine gave me for prints. Found three sets of them.'

I thought back through the previous evening: my own examination of the pictures on the train; Tremaine peeling off his glove to get them out of the envelope. 'Me, Tremaine and …?'

'And O'Connor himself.'

It made sense, though there was one slight surprise in it. 'Tremaine let you take his prints?' I asked.

'He had a cup of coffee at the station. We got them off that.'

It seemed careless behaviour from a professional like Tremaine. 'I presume you dusted my rooms.'

'Oh, yeah, we found plenty there. It'll take days to go through them, and I doubt we'll find anything. O'Connor was wearing gloves. I imagine this German would have been smart enough to do the same.'

'Any chance I could get a copy of the photos?'

He snorted. 'I never took you for that type. Sends you blind, you know.'

I scowled. 'To help find the girl,' I explained.

'Afraid not. Tremaine's taken them back with him to London – to prevent exactly that, I suspect.'

'O'Connor's darkroom's through there.' I nodded inside. The door at the back of the office led through to where he used to develop his pictures. 'I didn't deliver any negatives. They may still be there.'

'I had a look but there's tons of stuff in there. Another long job, presuming whoever turned this place over was slapdash enough to leave anything like that behind. And even if we find something, I'll have to send it straight to Tremaine.'

'So why look?'

'I'm a copper.' He took a final drag from his cigarette and flicked it to the ground, grinding it to extinction with his heavy boot. 'You'd better get lost. You're still a suspect, officially. If we find what's missing from the files, I'll be in touch.'

He went back inside. I looked at my watch. It was getting on for 7 o'clock. I headed home.

*

Mrs Croft had made meat pie and mash. I was late back for dinner, but she'd kept it warm. I ate it alone in my rooms. Jack had fixed the door, but the window was still covered with paper. The carpet was still stained. After I'd eaten, I listened to the wireless. The BBC got very serious on a Sunday, so I tuned in to Radio Luxembourg instead. I had a half bottle of Scotch tucked away behind a row of books in my living room, which, to my relief, neither the original intruders nor the police had disturbed. I poured myself a glass.

For a good while I sat, listening to the music and contemplating all that had taken place in the past twenty-four hours. The previous day I'd been hoping that a simple courier job would lead to something more interesting. I should have been more careful what I wished for. But at least there was something to investigate – a case, if unpaid. Should I really be sticking my nose in? Tremaine didn't think so, and part of me knew he was right. Churchill and Eden were fearful of Germany, and they seemed to have a better grasp of what was going on than Chamberlain and Halifax. O'Connor's death going unavenged might be a fair enough price to prevent a war. Or help win a war, if it came to that.

But another part of me disagreed. And it wasn't just me. Marchant thought the same – if not he'd have kicked me out of O'Connor's office without a second thought. He couldn't be seen trying to bring this German to book, and so he was giving me the chance to do so – what little chance there was. Tremaine wasn't going to reveal the name of the Jerry in question, and there must have been dozens of them at the embassy in London. Of course, you don't need a name if you have a picture, but then Tremaine had dealt very nicely with that too. Maybe Marchant would find the negatives, but he wouldn't dare let me see them.

But then I didn't actually need to see them.

Bing Crosby had just started crooning *The Moon Got in My Eyes* as I crossed the room to get my sketchpad. I sharpened my pencils and then gazed blankly at the wall, picturing the scenes that had been laid out before me in the photographs. I started by drawing him in simple profile, exactly as in the photos – his short dark hair, his small chin. I did him a few times, each sketch based on what I could remember of a particular photograph, never going beyond what I knew of the right side of his face. I considered my work. He didn't look very Germanic, but I resisted the urge to make alterations on that basis. It was a good representation founded on a good recollection, just like they'd taught me at the RCA. It should have been my career.

I drew the girl, too, wondering whether she was local or had travelled down to Brighton for this special occasion. Could she have been the woman I'd spoken to on the telephone? I wasn't surprised to discover that O'Conner had kept a mistress – he'd never been faithful to his wife while I'd been working with him – but surely even he wouldn't sink so low as to use his own lover in pictures like those. But what did I know? If I could find either woman, I'd discover whether or not they were one and the same. It had been a mistake to think initially how she looked like Claudette Colbert; my first two attempts had more of the movie star in them than of the girl on the bed in the Metropole. I tried again, forcing myself to be strictly accurate. The artistic urge was to create; the technical to reproduce. I'd been trained in both, but also educated to consider when each aspect of my trade was more appropriate. I looked at my finished work and was happy with it. I'd been worried that I was going to make her too good-looking, but it wasn't a mistake. She had been.

I went back to the man and allowed my imagination full rein. I'd only ever seen him from the right-hand side, but I was experienced enough to take a guess at what he might look like full on. I came up with three different possibilities. I couldn't know how close the likeness was – it certainly wouldn't stand up in court – but it might help someone else to recognize him. At the very least it would be interesting to discover how well I'd done, if I ever did find him.

I should have stopped there, but there was more that I remembered – much more. I began a new sheet of paper and started sketching again; not just their faces, but everything I'd seen. Every detail of body touching body, skin rubbing against skin, flesh penetrating flesh. I can't deny that I enjoyed it, much as O'Connor must have enjoyed taking those pictures, perhaps more so. For him the participation was minimal; the simple pressure of a finger on a shutter release. With the drawings, everything came from me, from my hand. It was the closest one could come to touching without actually being there. And I so desired to touch.

Before I looked up at the clock again, I'd recreated all sixteen of the photographs and the Scotch was almost gone. I knew places where I could get good money for my drawings, but I wasn't into that. I cast my eyes over them, admiring my own work in more ways than one. I'd gone beyond my memories in composing these, adding detail no camera could pick up. I had created. But I couldn't be sure I'd got it right. The nudes we'd painted in class never revealed themselves so intimately, and whenever I'd been with women, I'd not been looking at them with the eye of an artist. It didn't matter. The pictures were for no one's benefit but my own. If others saw them, they might not understand. The girl – as I had drawn her, as I had created her, and despite the acts in which I had depicted her – was beautiful. I was happy with what I had done.

Fred Astaire sang *Nice Work If You Can Get It* from the wireless.

*

I must have dozed off. When I awoke, the wireless speaker was hissing nothingness. I looked at the clock. It was almost three in the morning. I stood up to go to the bedroom, pausing to take one last look at my work. It was only then that I remembered the final additions I'd made to one of the drawings.

She was lying on her back, her eyes for once directed at her lover, not at the camera. He was kneeling over her, his hands on her knees, parting them, his eyes looking downwards at where he soon would be. Except that the eyes of neither of them were visible in what I'd drawn, thanks to those late alterations that I'd made through some bizarre inspiration.

Each face was now obscured by the blank, round-eyed anonymity of a gas mask.

CHAPTER 8

The morning took me to Grove Street. It was a steep trek up the hill into Hanover. I couldn't recall the names of anyone I'd spoken to, or the precise addresses, except that all the incidents had occurred on the western side of the street. Once I was there, it all came quickly back to me. I recognized a blue front door, its paint peeling to reveal green underneath. I knocked.

A familiar face greeted me, but I couldn't put a name to it. She was typical of the women who lived around here: in her thirties, but the accumulation of hard work and childbearing pushing her prematurely into her fifties. It was an unambitious man who spied through these windows – but that didn't make it any less unpleasant for the victims.

'It's Mr Woolf, isn't it?' She rubbed her hand on her dirty apron and then across her forehead, leaving a streak of coal dust. 'The fellow that helped us with the lecher.'

'That's right, Mrs …'

'Stephens.' I remembered as soon as she said it. 'That's all sorted now, though, innit?'

'Well, we never caught him.'

'You think he might come back?'

There was no need to alarm her. 'No, that's very unlikely. But I do have a possible suspect.' I showed her one of the drawings I'd done the previous night. Just the man's head in profile. 'Does he look familiar, at all?'

She took it from me, then stepped out into the street to be in the sunlight where she could see it better. She looked for a few seconds, then shook her head. 'Sorry, never saw him before. Mind you, none of us ever got a good look at him.' I handed her another sketch of him, from the front this time, drawn in part from my imagination. She shook her head again.

'What about this one?' It was an off-chance, but I

handed her a picture of the girl – again just the face.

She studied it for longer this time, but with the same conclusion. 'Stranger to me. Pretty, though. Pestering *her* now, is he?'

'I'm afraid I can't say. But many thanks.'

I tried a few more houses, but with no better result. It had been a long shot, but it served a secondary purpose. As I conducted my interviews, memories of the case came back to me: names and faces plus a few details of exactly what they'd seen and heard. But none of it related to a German diplomat, or to O'Connor, or to anything connected with the current case.

I went back down the hill towards the Level, and then climbed the almost as steep Trafalgar Street towards the station. It was just after twelve and so the pubs were open now. It wasn't simply that I needed a drink, though. I went down to the Royal Standard, where I peered through the window and spotted her at the bar. Her red hair – still the precise shade that nature had once, long ago, dictated – curled under just short of her shoulders, as though moulded by an invisible hairnet. She was seated in her usual place. I don't think anyone ever saw her enter or leave; she was simply there.

I took the stool beside her. 'Hey, Lottie,' I said.

She didn't turn her head. Instead she looked at me in the mirror behind the bar, half-camouflaged by the words 'Chivas Regal Blended Scotch Whisky' in red and gold, along with a variety of etched ornaments. Even so, I could see that her face lit up. 'Wotcher, Charlie!' Her voice never ceased to surprise me in its soft-spoken meekness.

'How's business?' I asked.

'You know me, Charlie. I don't need no business. I got a private income.' She tried and failed to roll the 'r' of 'private'.

'You don't have to worry about me,' I said. 'I'm not with the constabulary.'

'You call yourself a detective, don't you?'

'Not much of one,' I muttered.

I felt her hand on my arm. 'I heard about Al,' she said. 'I'm sorry.'

Still she looked at me only via the mirror. I tried to return her gaze, but found it uncomfortable. The patterns on the glass, combined with bottles in the foreground and her reflection behind produced a fractured, overlapping whole which reminded me all too much of the dislocated images my mind would produce before the onset of migraine. I was afraid that it could provide more than a reminder – that it might actually induce an attack. I'd seen mirrors like it before and a headache had never followed, but I'd always looked quickly away. I did so now.

'Can I get you a drink?' I asked.

'That's very kind. A Mackeson's, please.' She addressed the barman as much as she did me, then drained the glass in front of her. I ordered a Tamplin's for myself. The barman brought them both, opening the bottle for her and putting it on the bar, not bothering to pour. She took the empty glass in her left hand and the bottle in her right, staring intently as she tilted both to a precise angle. The milk stout flowed from one to the other, a white head forming above the black liquid. I paid the barman, but kept my eyes on what she was doing. When she had finished, the bottle was completely empty and the foam just peeped over the rim of the glass. She took a sip, then wiped her upper lip.

'Funeral's tomorrow, I hear,' she said.

'Really? When?' I wasn't surprised that Mrs O'Connor hadn't bothered to let me know, but she couldn't keep it off the grapevine.

'Eleven o'clock … at the Borough Crematorium.'

'Thanks.'

'Think they'll catch him?'

'I'm not sure they're trying.'

'What? Why the hell not?' Even in anger, she could barely raise her voice.

I shrugged; it was too complicated to explain.

'It's not right,' she said. '*You* should look into it. Al was your friend.'

I risked a glance at her in the mirror, my eyebrows raised.

'Oh!' she said. 'You already are.'

I reached into my pocket and took out one of the sketches of the girl in the photographs. I showed it to Lottie. 'She one of yours?' I asked.

She glanced at it briefly. 'Pretty. I wish she was but, no, I never seen her.'

'Doesn't work for one of your competitors?'

'Like I say, I never seen her. And I would have unless she's new in town.' She tried to hand the picture back to me.

'Keep it,' I said. 'Ask around.'

'Will it help Al?'

'As much as anything can.'

She reached down for her handbag and slipped the picture inside. We sat in silence for a few minutes, she sipping her stout, I my bitter.

'You should get yourself a nice girl,' she said at length.

I looked directly at her, surprised, but still she didn't turn her head towards me. 'One of yours, you mean?'

'A *nice* girl,' she insisted. 'Someone you could take home to see your mother.' She paused. 'On the other hand, I'm sure I could find someone if you're interested.'

I smiled, pretending to take it as a joke, but I don't know if she noticed. If she could find me just this girl then I would be interested, in more ways than one. I downed my pint quickly, wanting to be out of there, not because her suggestion appalled me; more out of the suspicion that it didn't.

I stood up. 'Thanks, Lottie. Let me know if you hear anything.'

'Will do. And thanks for the drink.'

I strode down Queen's Road, past the clock tower and

on to West Street. The fine weather made it obvious that June would soon be upon us. The streets were busy now; it was lunchtime and office workers were coming out to find something to eat. In an hour or two it would be quiet again. In a week's time things would be different; it would be the bank holiday. Nobody would be at work in the offices, but the population of the town would just about double.

I reached the seafront pretty much halfway between the two piers and turned to the west. Soon I was outside the Grand Hotel. Motor cars pulled in and out of the crescent-shaped driveway that separated its entrance from the main road, doormen in extravagant uniforms helping customers in and out of them. Beyond the Grand stood the Metropole, even grander than the Grand, at least in its physical presence. Management and residents of the two could debate which had the more prestigious reputation. Neither hotel would be proud of the sort of business that I was hoping to discuss, but both gladly took it.

I turned up the side street between the two of them. Out on the Kings Road, the white-painted façade of the Grand made a distinct contrast with the red brick of the Metropole but, as I walked inland, both buildings metamorphosed into unkempt griminess. It wasn't far to one of the Metropole's numerous side entrances. Outside, a couple of bootboys were sharing a fag. I went over.

'Coates working today?' I asked.

One of them nodded. The other drew deeply on the cigarette, using the distraction to get a little more than his fair share.

'There's a tanner in it for you if you'll fetch him.' I held out the coin towards the boy who'd responded. The other one scowled. 'Tell him it's Charlie Woolf.'

The kid ran inside and I waited with his pal, who was still trying to judge whether the sixpence or the smoke was worth more, though it didn't take much calculation for him to know he'd lost out. We stood without exchanging a word, but after a minute or so he broke the silence.

'You want a drag?' he asked, holding out the cigarette. It took me by surprise, but he seemed quite natural in the offer. I looked at the thin tube of paper and tobacco, half burnt down. It was dirty, flattened from the perfect cylinder it should have formed. There was even a small tear in the side. Evidently one of the hotel's clients had dropped it as he took another from the case. This one had been kicked around the lobby, but not for very long. Such a trophy would have been quickly spotted and seized upon.

'I'm all right, thanks,' I said. I lit one of my own Player's, watching his eyes enviously follow the packet as it was returned to my pocket. The cigarette hadn't burnt down very far before the first boy returned along with Coates, who was dressed the only way I'd ever seen him, in his hotel uniform.

'Afternoon, Big-Bad,' he said. 'Terrible news.'

The use of the nickname and his expression of regret were not unrelated. He was more O'Connor's contact than mine.

'You heard, then?' I said.

'It was in the *Argus*. Funeral's tomorrow, they say, but I won't be able to make it. Come on in.'

I gave the half shilling I'd promised to the boy and dropped my fag on the ground. Normally I'd have screwed it flat with the sole of my shoe, but that would just have been mean. As I went inside, I heard them scrabbling for it.

The door took us into a grubby corridor. The sound and the smell of kitchens came from nearby. Coates turned to look at me.

'Was he here much?' I asked.

'Plenty. Business was good for him.'

'When was the last time?'

He looked warily from side to side, though there was no one to overhear us. 'Mr O'Connor prized my discretion very highly,' he said.

'I'm trying to find out who killed him.'

He shrugged. He hadn't been making an ethical point. I took out my wallet and gave him a ten-bob note. It was a lot, but I'd worked with him before often enough to know his price. He'd have landed more for the favours he'd done O'Connor.

'It was last week,' he explained. 'Wednesday. Usual arrangement.'

That fitted with O'Connor giving me the photographs on Saturday. He'd have had plenty of time to develop and print them. I showed Coates one of my drawings. 'This the girl?'

He nodded. 'Pretty thing. You do that yourself?'

I ignored the question and showed him the next picture. 'And this the man?'

'Could be. Looks familiar, so he might have been in the lobby, but I never saw who went up to the room.'

I considered telling him that he was looking at the face of O'Connor's murderer, but it wouldn't help matters. 'Who arrived first?' I asked.

'O'Connor had sorted things out a couple of days before. He'd asked me to look up a reservation for 'Blenkinsop' – phoney name if ever I heard one. There was a booking for Wednesday, just the one night. I made sure that they were allocated a suitable room.'

'Suitable?'

'He had his favourites. A room with a view, he used to say, and he didn't mean of the sea. He showed up about seven o'clock and got a spare key off me.'

'But you didn't see the man – only the girl.'

Coates nodded. 'I wasn't around when they checked in. I did see her waiting in the lounge, though. I always keep my eye open for whoever O'Connor's doing the dirt on. No harm in looking, is there?'

'So it was obvious who she was – why she was here?'

'Not at all. I took her for a lonely heart.'

'A lonely heart?'

'She had a book on the table in front of her, with a red carnation in it – like she wanted someone who didn't know her to recognize her.'

'What was the book?' I asked. I couldn't see that it mattered, but it was the sort of question that suggested an air of professionalism.

'God knows.' He shrugged. 'I didn't realize she was anything to do with it until you showed me that picture just now.'

I felt a pang of regret whose cause I couldn't quite place. Then I understood: it was jealousy. I'd shared her, the girl in my drawings. I'd shared her with another man when I could have kept her to myself.

'Did you see them leave?' I asked.

'O'Connor came back down at around 11.30. Handed me the key.'

'Can I see the room?'

'It may be occupied.'

'We could give it a try.'

He offered no further objections and I followed him along one dingy corridor and into another. It was busier here, with staff moving in every direction, some taking food and drinks out to serve to the customers, others bringing back the remains of what they had already consumed. There was nothing here that remotely resembled Mrs Croft's pie and mash.

We went through a double door and were suddenly in a different world: the hotel bar. It was lunchtime and busy – the clientele of the Metropole didn't have to wait for a bank holiday to visit Brighton. I had to blink as my eyes adjusted to the brighter light. I was reminded of what Tremaine had said about *The Time Machine*. We were Morlocks emerging into the world of the Eloi.

Coates led me out into the lobby, then raised a hand to tell me to wait. He went over to the desk and spoke to a colleague, then picked a key from the rack behind.

'It's taken,' he said as he returned to me, 'but they've left the key so they must be out.'

We went up two flights of stairs and then along a passageway to the door of room 235. He put his ear close to it and knocked softly, then louder. He looked at me. 'Seems all right,' he said.

'Is this the room O'Connor always used?' I asked.

'He had a few he liked; depended what was available.'

He turned the key and opened the door an inch, before again raising his hand, warning me to stay. Then he swung the door open and stepped boldly through.

'Housekeeping!' His voice was loud and confident. There was no response. I heard him walking about, and a few moments later his head poked out through the door. 'All clear,' he whispered.

It looked just as it had done in the photographs, with the exception of the bed in the middle of the room, which today was empty and neatly made up. The décor in the photos had been enough for me to recognize which hotel it was, but that stirred a hint of doubt. All the rooms here had the same wallpaper and a similar style of furniture and fittings. What I'd seen in the pictures could have been 235, or just as easily the room above or below. Why should Coates make it up, though, and what did it matter anyway? I doubted I'd find much evidence here.

There was a wardrobe opposite the foot of the bed – Chinese in style if not in origin. I stood with my back pressed against the its doors, looking directly at the bed.

'Think that's where he hid?' asked Coates.

I shook my head. 'No, angle's all wrong.' Beyond that, I couldn't see a wardrobe as a very good hiding place. There was too much risk that someone would want to hang their clothes in there. Or perhaps I was being naïve to imagine the man in the photos neatly placing his trousers on a hanger before leaping on to the bed to do what he had come to do. On the other hand, he was German.

I paced the room, my eyes always fixed on the bed,

watching it shift in perspective as I moved. I might have done the same if I'd been preparing to work on a painting, judging where the best viewpoint would be. But in this case I was trying to determine what had already been done; from what angle the photograph had been taken. And for that the criterion would not so much have been the best view as the best hiding place.

I stopped. I was in roughly the right position. I reached into my pocket and took out one of the larger drawings, unfolding it, hiding the contents from Coates. In this picture at least she was mine, not to be shared. But that wasn't the reason I was studying it. It was the perspective that interested me now: the position of the bed relative to the door and to the window. It all helped to reveal where the original photograph had been taken from. I was still a bit too close to the bed and too low down. I put the sketch away and took a few paces back, until I felt the wall behind me. It still wasn't quite right. I looked up: inches below the ceiling, set into the wall, was a grille.

'Pass me that chair,' I said, indicating one of two wooden seats by the table near the door. Coates brought it to me. I put it against the wall and stood on it. The grille was still a little above my eye level. I turned to face the bed, standing on tiptoe. It still wasn't quite the same point of view as in the photographs, but it left no doubt as to where the camera had been concealed. I turned back to the wall. The grille was too fine to have taken the photos through, but it would have been easy enough to remove. I looked at the screws and saw there were scratch marks on them. I imagined O'Connor in the room beyond, standing on a chair just as I was, or something a little higher. He'd have to be able to see through to judge the best time to take a shot.

'What's through there?' I asked.

'Linen cupboard,' Coates replied, without further elaboration.

'Is it the same for the other rooms O'Connor liked to

use?'

He thought for a few moments, then nodded with increasing confidence. 'Yeah, I think so. Yeah.'

He was playing dumb. He must have known exactly how O'Connor worked things. He'd have made it his job to find out – otherwise how would he be able to work out a fair price for the blind eye he so regularly turned?

I stepped back down to the floor. 'We'll take a look there once we're done in here.'

'That's a different key.' Again it was a matter of pricing, not a real objection.

'It'll be worth your while.'

'I'll go get it. Wait here.'

I doubted I'd learn very much from searching in the linen cupboard, but it would be foolish not to be thorough, both here and next door. I opened the Chinese wardrobe and took a peek inside. It looked as though a single man was currently occupying the room. There was a dinner suit and a raincoat; nothing else.

'Shit!' Coates's voice was only a whisper.

I looked round in time to see the door closing behind him as he left. I could only guess that he had seen someone. I decided to follow his lead and strode over to the door. But before I was halfway across the room, I heard a key in the lock. I glanced over at the dressing table. The key that Coates had brought with him lay there, just where he had left it. This was someone else. They fumbled for a moment, not realizing that the door was already unlocked. There was only one place to hide. I went back to the wardrobe and got inside, pulling the doors closed behind me and trying to squat down, hoping that would make it easier for me to stay quiet.

Outside I heard the door open and close. The footsteps were not loud, but sounded heavy enough to be a man's. Evidently the room's occupant had returned from lunch. I could only pray that he didn't need anything from the wardrobe. It was too early for dinner and it was a fine day, so perhaps I'd be lucky. I heard the footsteps pause for a few seconds and then begin again, this time coming towards me. I realized he might have other reasons to open the wardrobe – not to take something out but to deposit whatever he'd been wearing. He stopped again, just inches away from me. Then light flooded in on me, and a face peered close to mine.

CHAPTER 9

I recognized him at once. It was beyond the reaches of coincidence that *he* was the guest who was booked into this particular room.

'You following me, Tremaine?' I asked.

'Just following the same train of thought, I suspect,' he replied, offering me a hand to help me out of the wardrobe and on to my feet. At the door to the corridor stood a concerned-looking figure clutching a bunch of keys. I took this to be the hotel manager. Tremaine turned to him.

'I can deal with things now, thanks all the same.'

'I need to lock up.'

'The room key's there,' I said, pointing to the dressing table.

The manager glanced at it, but seemed to accept he had no power to make us – or, more specifically, Tremaine – leave. He closed the door gently behind him. Tremaine gestured me towards the chair I'd used to stand on, before himself sitting on the bed.

'So,' he said with an exaggerated grin and a raising of the eyebrows, 'this is where it all came to pass.'

'Looks like it,' I replied. Already I was considering what he'd said: that he'd followed the same line of reasoning I had. It didn't seem quite right – he didn't have the local knowledge. 'But how did *you* know?'

'My dear boy, do you really suppose I'd let a chap like Mr O'Connor have a totally free rein? I insisted he keep me abreast of everything.'

'Even down to the room number?'

Tremaine emitted a deliberate sigh to suggest his disappointment in me. 'Even down to the hotel bill, on which was written the room number.'

'So what did you expect to find here?'

He frowned. 'An interesting question, but I suspect you only ask it to distract from a rather more important issue.'

'And what would that be?'

'You asked me how I found the place, but perhaps I should be asking the same of you.'

'I saw the pictures, remember? It was obviously the Metropole.'

It was an insufficient answer, but I hoped he wouldn't notice. I was disappointed.

'Obviously room 235?'

I said nothing.

'I do hope you're not going to be troublesome. I can easily have you arrested again – and not by the local constabulary. I'm not asking you to incriminate whichever housemaid it was you slipped a few shillings to. I'm just puzzled how they knew to bring you to this precise room.'

I considered for a moment. If he thought that my dealings with the staff here were as casual as that, then I wasn't going to disabuse him. I might need Coates's help again before long. On the other hand, what else could I tell him? The drawings I'd made having seen the photos were the ultimate proof that this was the place where it had happened, but they were also my ace in the hole. And it wasn't the copies themselves that were most dangerous to me; it was the fact that I'd been able to reproduce them from memory. Paper could easily enough be crumpled and thrown on the fire. I didn't want to discover how the Security Service went about similarly eliminating any information in a man's mind.

'He was a regular here … O'Connor,' I said. 'Not necessarily this room, but ones like it. It was only last week he was here, so she didn't have any trouble remembering.'

I hoped the '*she*' would confirm Tremaine's assumption and put him off Coates's scent. He thought for a few moments, analysing what I'd said, his eyes on me, not fixed, but flickering across my face and momentarily down to my body. I almost felt he could see the folded drawings in my jacket pocket. I wondered how much O'Connor had told him about me – whether he guessed what I'd been able to do.

'And what precisely have you discovered about what he did here last week – beyond that for which we already have such unequivocal visual evidence?' It seemed like an innocent question, but still he brought things back to the photographs.

'Not much.'

'Not much, but something? You said, for example: "not necessarily this room, but ones like it." Like it in what way?'

I wasn't surprised he'd cottoned on to that, but it was better if he thought he was teasing it out of me. 'One with some kind of space next door where he could position himself. I reckon he was hiding in the linen cupboard, took the shots through that ventilator.' I pointed.

Tremaine looked around the room. 'Shame there are no mirrors,' he said.

There was one on the dressing table, but I knew what he meant. 'O'Connor wasn't stupid enough to catch his own reflection.'

'Have you looked in there?' He nodded towards the wall and the closet beyond.

I shook my head. 'Not yet, but he wasn't stupid enough to have left anything, either.'

'And of course this room will have been serviced several times since Herr … since our German friend was himself serviced here.'

I might have taken the smutty joke as an attempt to cover his near revelation of the German's name, but I knew it had been no slip-up. He was toying with me.

'You could always show the photographs around, see if anyone recognizes … our German friend.' I was rising to his bait, and it was stupid of me. It was only a small leap from the photos to my skill as an artist, and then he'd have worked it all out.

He let out an embarrassed harrumph. 'Not all that easy, I'm afraid. I have to say, I was a little annoyed with our Mr

O'Connor. For all his claimed expertise in these things, he never got a clear picture of the gentleman-in-question's face.'

I'd noticed as much myself. For a moment I was tempted to show him the more speculative drawings I'd made, to ask his opinion on how well I'd captured the likeness. But it still wasn't worth the risk.

'Just didn't have the artistic temperament, I suppose,' Tremaine continued. 'Unlike yourself.'

So O'Connor had told him that much about me, at least. As he paused, I was convinced he'd worked it out and that in a moment he would reach forward to slip his hand into my pocket and draw out my handiwork. But, as it turned out, his mind had been on a quite different tack.

'Ever thought of using your skills in the national interest?'

'Skills?'

'As a detective, operating as a servant of His Majesty's government? The fact that you got here ahead of a professional such as myself must count for something.'

'I prefer to work alone, thanks all the same.'

'You used to work with O'Connor.'

'I didn't like his kind of work.'

'But ours is quite different.'

I raised my hand, indicating our surroundings. 'It still comes down to taking dirty pictures in a hotel room, doesn't it?'

'For the greater good, unless … You're not a sympathizer with Herr Hitler, are you? It really doesn't matter. We could always find you something to do against the Bolsheviks instead. If we don't go to war with one of them, it'll be the other.' He seemed quite jolly at the prospect.

'I'll think about it,' I said.

'Do. Seriously, do. In the meantime, I don't suppose it would have much effect if I asked you again to lay off on this case.'

'That's very astute.'

'Can you at least keep me informed?'

'There hardly seems much need. The only lead I've got has brought me here – and you were only minutes behind me.'

'Even so.' He handed me a card with his name and a telephone number printed on it. It gave his rank as commander. I pocketed it. He stood up, brushing his trousers to straighten them. 'Shall we be off, then?' He picked up the keys and made for the door, while I remained seated. He looked back at me. 'I don't think the manager would be very happy if I were to leave you here on your own.'

There was no point in arguing. I'd still have liked to get a look inside the linen cupboard but that would require a different key – one which Tremaine could easily get from the hotel manager. By the time I devised a way to get in, any evidence would be well on its way to his colleagues in London.

He locked the door behind us and we headed back downstairs together. In the lobby a debate had begun as to the location of a set of room keys. I could guess which ones. The room's occupant was a tall, angry American who was beginning to raise questions as to whether it would have been better for him to stay at the Grand. Tremaine and I stood and watched for a few moments, both with a sense of amusement at the escalating row.

'I think I'd better just go and smooth things over,' said Tremaine at length, with a knowing smile.

My eyes followed him as he sauntered across to the reception desk, squeezing past the American to ask one of the staff something that I couldn't hear. I doubt anyone but me noticed the practised way that he slipped a hand – and the keys with it – into the man's coat pocket, removing it within the blink of an eye. The skills of a pickpocket could be useful in his profession, and just as useful if applied in reverse.

Tremaine walked back towards me, smirking to himself, but continued straight past me and out of the hotel. I was out in the street seconds later, but he was nowhere to be seen.

*

The following morning was that of O'Connor's funeral. It was only about a mile to the Crematorium, so I walked. I tried to make sense of anything that I'd learned about my former colleague's death, but another matter kept forcing its way into my mind: Tremaine's offer. It was tempting. He was right that it would put my skills to good use, better use than in all but a handful of the cases I'd taken on in Brighton. And it would be regular work, regular money. He was wise to appeal to my patriotism. It was obvious – at least I hoped it was – that I was no Nazi sympathizer, and however much my politics might lean to the left in British terms, I wasn't fool enough to be blind to the gulf between that and what Stalin was up to. Working for Tremaine – whoever we were against – would put me on the side of the angels.

That was if his offer was serious. What he really wanted from me was to lay off investigating O'Connor's death – to let him deal with the killer in his own way. Bringing me in to work for him might be the best compromise for all of us. At least I'd get to know what actually happened, to see that in the end this Kraut got what he deserved, even if it wasn't at the end of a British rope. But there was no rush. I'd do what I'd suggested and think about it.

I passed under the viaduct and arrived at the gates of the Extra-Mural Cemetery, built like a medieval keep with a tall round turret on one side. There remained a long trek up the hill to the chapel. A few dozen yards ahead of me, a woman was heading that way too. I could only see her back, but I was pretty sure it wasn't O'Connor's wife. There was always the chance that the girl in the photos would show up. I'd no idea how well she knew O'Connor, and if she understood why he'd died, then she'd be a fool to let her face be seen. But it was a possibility and this could be her, though for now there was no way to tell. The only thing I might recognize from behind would be her hair, and that was currently hidden by a hat.

I heard a car behind me and stepped a little further to the side of the road; there was no pavement. I turned to look as it drove past. It wasn't a hearse, just a black saloon. I caught a glimpse of a woman sitting in the back, and this was a face I recognized: Vera O'Connor. There was a man with her, an old man, perhaps her father, or perhaps even O'Connor's.

The car drove smoothly on. As it passed the woman in front of me, I hoped she might turn her head towards it and give me a chance to see her profile, but she paid no attention. Her gaze never left the ground in front of her. I was walking faster than she was, but I didn't think I'd quite catch up before we reached our destination. I didn't want to either; it was one of those situations where to overtake someone would seem like showing off. And there was no need; I'd see her face soon enough.

I reached the chapel a touch out of breath. Behind it the Downs continued to rise ever upwards, and here I could already feel it was a little colder than down in the town. Somewhere up there was the racecourse, hidden behind the elms. It was a busy day for the crematorium. A small crowd stood in silence close to the chapel door. On the other side of the building stood a similar crowd that had just emerged from the previous ceremony, and was preparing to leave. It would take them a few minutes to get things rearranged inside.

Vera O'Connor stood looking up at the chapel's tower. Her car had now gone. The man with her must have been in his seventies, and looked more like her than he did her late husband. The woman I'd been following still had her back to me but I recognized some of the other faces. One of them was a bookie I'd encountered a few times. Remick, that was his name: Percy Remick. The two men standing beside him looked familiar and presumably shared his profession, but I couldn't name them.

'Hullo, Charlie.'

I turned. It was Lottie, her distinctive red hair shrouded today in a black net. Her voice was as soft as ever. Her body seemed tiny. I couldn't recall ever seeing her standing up before.

'You got him yet?' she asked.

'I'm working on it.'

'I might have something to help you.' Just like in the pub, she didn't turn to look at me as she spoke, but here there was no mirror to help her.

Before she could say more, the door to the chapel opened and we began to file in. At the same moment another car pulled up – a police car. I wasn't surprised to see Marchant climb out and say a few brief words to the driver. He saw me and tipped his hat. I did the same.

'Later.' Lottie's voice had become even quieter than before, but she now moved away from me and into the chapel with surprising speed. She had good reasons for not wanting to associate with the police. I hung back a little, as did the inspector, so that we were the last to enter.

It wasn't a big chapel, but even so the smattering of mourners occupying the pews was insufficient to make it seem full. If O'Connor had been in his dotage it would have been a good turnout – a sign either that he was particularly popular, or that his friends were long-lived. But O'Connor had been only forty-four. His wife sat at the front, next to her father. They'd had no children, but I remembered O'Connor mentioning a brother who was in the army somewhere in the colonies. There would have been no time for him to return, even if he'd wanted to. O'Connor had spoken of him neither frequently nor with affection. The others were scattered around as if trying to make the place look fuller than it was. The woman I'd seen was sitting at the back, hoping to remain unnoticed. I could still only see her from behind.

Marchant and I walked up the aisle and found ourselves a seat at about the halfway point. As I shuffled along the wooden bench, I turned to get a better look at the mystery woman. I recognized her in an instant. It was not the girl from the photos, which was a disappointment. In truth I couldn't think how I knew her at all, but I was sure I'd seen the face before – though not recently. I'd have time to think about it. A sidesman closed the door and the service began.

We sang 'Immortal, Invisible, God Only Wise' and 'When I Survey the Wondrous Cross'. In-between, the vicar read a passage from John. It was about the resurrection of Lazarus, though it stopped short of the actual miracle, ending simply with an assurance of the general resurrection of us all. Perhaps mentioning that Lazarus himself was a special case would have seemed too pointed. The vicar also said a few words about O'Connor, but I doubted the two men had ever met. I wasn't really concentrating, too busy trying to remember who that woman was. I glanced back towards her more than once. She was in her mid-thirties, still pretty, but with the sort of good looks that fade with age. The process was already beginning and she wore too much make-up in compensation. Today it was a particular mistake because she couldn't hold back the tears. Their tracks cut through her face powder like rain on a dusty pavement. I wondered if Vera, his widow, was taking it so badly.

At last the coffin rolled away to be hidden by the curtains, and we trooped out through a different door, just like the group before us had done. Most of us stood about uncomfortably, wondering what we were supposed to do next. Marchant went over to offer his condolences to the widow, but I kept my eyes on the chapel door. The unknown woman had still not exited. As soon as the inspector was out of the way, Lottie came back over to join me. She was dabbing her eyes with a lace handkerchief. Her sorrow seemed genuine if not profound.

'Nice service,' I said, for want of anything better. There are times when platitudes are all that can be uttered.

'Vera chose the hymns. I'm not sure Al would really have cared.'

I wasn't paying much attention. The woman had just emerged from the chapel and displayed no intention of lingering. She was already heading down the hill, back the way she had come. She might have had nothing to do with O'Connor's death, but her presence here was a mystery and that was the closest thing I had to a lead. I didn't want to let her go. I grabbed Lottie's handkerchief from her hand and walked briskly after the unknown woman.

'Excuse me!' I called. 'Miss!' She must surely have heard me and realized I was talking to her, but she kept on walking. 'Excuse me!' I persisted, and finally she turned. I held up the handkerchief. 'I think you dropped this.' There must have been better ways to start a conversation, but I'd not had time to think of one.

'No, I don't think so,' she said. She held up her hand and I saw that she was clutching a handkerchief of her own. Her eyes were still wet with tears. She added nothing more and turned away, but it was already enough; I wasn't going to mistake that voice a second time. It was she that I'd spoken to on the phone both times I'd dialled the number O'Connor gave me. And now I remembered where I'd seen her before. It had been four or five years ago, when O'Connor had introduced us briefly, lying about who she was. But it had been easy enough to work out the truth: she was his mistress – had been back then and still was right up until his death. Her name, I could now recall, was Sylvia Clay. I even knew her address, or what it had been back then. With luck she'd still be living there. I walked back to Lottie and gave her back the handkerchief.

'I won't ask,' she said.

'Best not,' I replied. 'You said you've got something for me?'

She ignored the question. 'Some of us are going for a drink down at the Bear. Vera won't say anything – not to you – but she'd like you to be there.'

'You sure?'

'Makes up the numbers. And then I can tell you what I've found out.'

The black car had pulled up again and O'Connor's wife and her father were climbing back in. It drove off down the hill. Lottie walked determinedly after it, though there was no chance of keeping up. Most of the others did likewise. Soon it was only me and the inspector.

'Coming for a drink?' I asked him.

'Best not. People don't like to be reminded that their loved one's death was far from peaceful.'

'So why come at all?'

He looked at me as if he didn't understand the question. 'How's the investigation going,' he asked, changing the subject.

'Shouldn't I be asking you?'

'Then I would have to answer "What investigation?" You know I've got to leave this to the boys from London.'

'Same applies to me,' I said.

'Stinks, doesn't it?' he spoke with more passion than I would have expected. He must have seen enough crime in Brighton over the years to inure him to most things, but not to being told he wasn't allowed to do his job.

'I'll walk down with you,' I suggested.

'The car's going to be back for me soon.'

'I'll see you, then.'

I headed off on down the hill. It was easier than the journey up and once I'd emerged through the cemetery gate, the Bear was just a few yards away along Lewes Road. I doubted I'd have gone in if it wasn't for what Lottie had said. It was an attack on two fronts; an appeal to my better nature and also to my curiosity. The curiosity would have won out on its own, and I had little awareness of possessing a better nature. Why should I go in there just to show sympathy for Vera O'Connor – sympathy that had an evens chance of being thrown back in my face? But Lottie had something to tell me.

O'Connor's wife was sitting alone at a table close to the door. I took a look around quickly and spotted her father up at the bar. Then I looked back at her, aware that I had nothing to say. I tried to produce a comforting smile but didn't want to appear too happy. It seemed to do the trick.

'Thank you for coming,' she said softly.

'It was the least I could do.'

After that, neither of us could see any need for further conversation, but she could find no convenient way to dismiss me, and I could not bring myself to simply walk away. We were saved by her father, who came back to the table with a drink in each hand. He sat down and put one of them in front of her. She thanked him, glancing towards him as she did. I took the opportunity to slink away.

Lottie was sitting at the bar, just as she had been in the Royal Standard. As I reached her she was just paying for her drink.

'I'll get it,' I insisted. She offered no protest. I ordered a Harveys for myself. Again there was a mirror behind the bar in which she studied me. It was less garish than the last one, but still I avoided staring into it. The dread of an impending migraine was becoming stronger, and I didn't want to do anything to bring it on sooner than necessary. I gazed down into my beer.

'I found her,' Lottie announced.

'The girl in the drawing?'

She may have nodded but I didn't see. 'She's new in town; from London.'

'Down for the summer?' I suggested.

'Maybe. Her name's Rachael. Rachael Westby. She's

living in Hove, in Furze Croft, flat 202.'

'That new block? On Furze Hill?'

'That's it.'

'Classy. Who can afford to set her up in a place like that?'

'No one. No one round here. Supposedly she's still got a mack up in London, though he's asked Spindly to look after her while she's here.'

'Spindly?'

'Spindly Cochran.'

'Shit!' I scarcely knew Cochran but he had a reputation for being extremely protective of his girls.

'Spindly's all right. It was him that told me. And he's too scared of this fellow in London to get chummy with her – unless she asks for help.'

'Let's hope she doesn't, then.'

'You going to see her?'

'What else can I do?' There was no need for me to tell Lottie that I had another lead – in the form of Sylvia Clay.

'The girl won't know anything.' Lottie declared confidently.

'She knows O'Connor's killer.'

'Really?'

'Intimately.'

CHAPTER 10

I arrived at Furze Croft around 6 o'clock that evening. That seemed to me like a good time to pay a visit to a tom, before she got too busy. I could easily have got there earlier but I resisted the urge, knowing my interest was becoming more than professional. Instead I'd loitered around town for a few hours, but even then set off before I needed to, forcing myself to walk slowly. The building was only a couple of years old, ultramodern in its design and unashamedly intended to impress, certainly from the outside. It didn't really feel like Brighton around here, or even Hove. The area was too secluded – too suburban. There was no trade here, no shops selling their wares, no pubs, no tourists. People simply lived here, and even then not like in the tight terraces that covered the side of every other hill in the town – places like Grove Street. People lived over there because they had to. If you lived here, you wanted to. This was the realm of the Eloi. And yet some trade was done. Why else had Rachael Westby come here?

Even the doorbell exuded modernity: a polished brass plate with numbered buttons for each flat and a grille above, which I guessed hid a loudspeaker. I pressed No 202. After a few moments the speaker crackled, and then a voice spoke: 'Yes?'

'Spindly sent me,' I said.

There was a pause and then a reply. 'I've not got long.'

I hesitated to assure her that I wouldn't need long, but she didn't wait for more. The door buzzed and I pushed it open. It took me only a few minutes to find my way up to flat 202. When I got there, the door was already ajar. I knocked anyway.

'I left it open for a reason,' came her voice.

I went in, closing the door behind me. It was a big

enough living room, looking out to the south, but I didn't go over to take in the view. She reclined on a chaise longue, wearing a pink satin dressing gown, white fur trimming the lapels. This was undoubtedly the girl from the photographs, though my comparison with Claudette Colbert seemed less appropriate now I saw her in the flesh. She smiled up at me but it was not a friendly, open expression – inviting rather than welcoming, if there can be a distinction. I stood there, fingering the rim of my hat nervously, wondering if it was down to coincidence or my subconscious that I held it so that it covered my crotch.

'What's your name?' she asked. She spoke with the suggestion of a London accent, which I guessed was genuine. Overlaying that was a childlike lilt that I took to be a professional affectation.

'Charlie,' I said, 'Charlie —'

'Sit down, Charlie,' she interrupted. Evidently my surname was of no interest to her. I did as she'd asked. 'My name's Rachael,' she continued. She was a real treat for the eyes. The images of her flashed through my mind, but photographs never do a girl like that justice. I'd tried to take account of it when I drew her, but I hadn't gone far enough, not from what I could see.

'Did Spindly tell you how much?' she asked.

I wondered whether I'd been wise to mention Cochran's name. I'd met him once. The gangling frame that gave him his nickname disguised a brutal strength that he'd never been afraid to put to use. The best way to avoid his getting involved was for me to come clean.

'I didn't come here for that,' I said.

She raised an eyebrow. 'What did you come here for?'

'To talk.'

'That's nothing unusual, but I still charge.'

'Not like that.' I leaned forward, handing her my calling card. 'I want information.'

She held the card close to read it. She must have been very short-sighted, but too vain to wear eyeglasses. It didn't take her long to register my line of work.

'I think you'd better go,' she said coldly.

I tried to play it tough. 'Not until you tell me what I need to know.'

She stood up and went over to the telephone. 'It's pretty obvious Spindly didn't send you, but he'll be very happy to get rid of you.'

'If you don't talk to me, you'll just have to talk to the police.'

She didn't waver. She had the receiver to her ear and her finger on the dial. She narrowed her eyes to see it better. 'Why should the police want to talk to me?'

'Blackmail.'

Her finger paused in mid-air, as if pointing at the telephone. She thought for a moment, then began to dial. 'You've got nothing,' she said.

I reached into my bag and brought out a folded sheet of paper. I tossed it in her direction, but it hit the air and didn't get very far, landing on the carpet a few feet away from her. As a gesture, it was less dramatic than I'd intended, but it got her attention. She put the phone down and bent forward to pick up the drawing. She opened it out and peered intently, again bringing it close enough for her to focus on, but at the same time too close to take in as a whole.

'I think you're going to need your glasses.'

She glanced at me questioningly over the top of the sketch, wondering how I'd guessed her little secret, but she didn't try to pretend otherwise. She sat back down on the chaise longue and reached over to open a cigarette box that rested on the table beside it. Inside were her spectacles. She slipped them on. They looked expensive: egg-shaped lenses hung from ornately decorated gold half rims, level with her eyebrows. I could understand why she chose not to wear them. They suited her, but not her profession.

Now she held the drawing at a more comfortable

distance, able to survey the scene in its entirety. I wasn't sure which one I had given her, but from the size I knew it would be displaying the full width of the bed, not just a close-up of a face. She would be able to see her whole body and his, except where one concealed the other. She examined it for perhaps half a minute, then looked at me as she spoke.

'Did you draw this?'

I nodded.

'You're quite the artist ... in a perverted sort of way.'

'It wasn't me who took the photo.'

'No. But then a camera's just a machine. This is more intimate. Your hand created this; touched it.' It was much the same conclusion as I'd come to myself while drawing it. I enjoyed the idea of us sharing the same thought; another way that I could touch her.

'Did you know he was there?' I asked.

'Who?'

'O'Connor – taking the photographs.'

'Of course. Can't you tell?'

'Tell?'

'I'd have done it differently otherwise.'

I tried not to imagine what the difference might be. 'You know he's dead?' I remarked instead.

'What?'

'Alan O'Connor died last Saturday. Murdered. A bullet in the face.' I'd decided I'd get more out of her by shocking her.

Her eyes bulged and her hand shot to her mouth. She seemed genuinely about to vomit, but controlled herself. I instantly regretted my brutality, though I was now even more confident it would get me what I wanted. I walked over and sat beside her. She reached for my hand, squeezing it – the first time we'd touched, outside of my imagination. She let the drawing fall to the floor, from where those dark eyes of hers stared up at me.

'I'm sorry,' I said.

'Who?' she asked. 'Why?'

I was surprised she couldn't guess, but it was better that she didn't. O'Connor had been taking photographs for use in blackmail, and now he was dead. The motive was pretty obvious, as was the killer. It had to be one of the people he'd photographed, and she knew as well as I did that it wasn't her. And from there it wasn't hard to work out who the next victim might be. But I wasn't going to suggest that. She might clam up and tell me nothing.

'That's what I'm trying to find out,' I said gently. 'That's why I need your help.' I felt like a louse, manipulating her like that, but it wasn't as if I was actually lying.

'Not now,' she said softly. 'I've got a client coming, and I can't think anyway. Come back tomorrow. I'll tell you, I promise.'

I jumped on the invitation, perhaps too eagerly. 'I'll be here first thing,' I said, then realized that 'first thing' probably meant very different things to the two of us. 'What time do you get up?'

She shook her head. 'Not here.' Then she smiled – more than smiled. It was a total change in her demeanour; an opening up. 'Why don't you take me to lunch?'

The archness to the expression on her face made no secret of the fact she was somehow playing me, but to what end I couldn't guess. If this was the only way I was going to get something out of her, then so be it. And there was more to it than that. I could imagine the envious looks I'd get, sitting in a restaurant on the seafront opposite a girl like her. No one would know the reason she was there, and that I wasn't her regular companion. And only I would know what kind of girl she really was, the girl I'd seen in those photos. Only *she* and I. I remembered Lottie's offhand comment about finding me a nice girl. Maybe I didn't need her help. And maybe it wasn't a nice girl that I was after.

'You're sure?' I asked her.

'Sure about what? That I eat lunch?'

I laughed. 'I'll pick you up at noon, then.'

'I can't be back too late.'

'Half eleven?'

She gave the slightest nod of assent. 'Where are you taking me?'

'You'll find out,' I replied.

*

I got myself back home, but couldn't remember anything of the route I'd taken. I'd been trying to prepare myself for the following day – to decide what I was going to ask Rachael – but, as soon as I pictured the scene of us seated opposite one another, my mind wandered to other details of how our lunch would progress. I felt her eyes on mine, imagined the sensation of her foot against my calf beneath the table as we conversed, anticipated for how long she might let her lips touch my cheek as we said goodbye. It was better to indulge such fantasies now than tomorrow. Tomorrow I'd be brought back down to earth; I knew that.

I stepped through the front door about to hail Mrs Croft with my usual greeting, just as I did every day. But before I'd said a word I noticed the message pad that sat on the table, next to the telephone. Mrs Croft's big, childish, block capitals shouted at me.

CALL YOUR MOTHER

I already knew what it was about. Mum would be wondering about the small brown parcel that had arrived in the post, addressed to me. It was O'Connor's money – the money I'd offloaded at Victoria. Given my arrest, it had turned out to be a cuter move than I'd imagined. And there'd be no trouble collecting it, given that we'd already arranged I'd be going round there for …

'Shit!'

Thankfully I'd kept my voice low. That wasn't the usual salutation with which I assailed my landlady. I glanced around, but both her doors were firmly closed.

I had reason enough to swear. I'd already planned to go to mum's for lunch the following day, Wednesday. We'd set the date weeks ago. And now I had made a very similar appointment with Rachael. I'd have to cancel one of them, and I knew which was more important. Seeing Rachael was business: not that this was quite how it looked in my head when I contemplated the prospect, but that didn't change the truth of it. I still had a murder to investigate, though I couldn't tell mum that. But I'd find a way to appease her.

The phone rang for a good thirty seconds before she answered. As soon as I heard her voice, I knew this was going to be a tricky conversation. But within five minutes we'd sorted things out. I hung up, then tore off the sheet of paper with Mrs Croft's message and crumpled it into a ball. I'd obeyed the instruction written there, and found a solution that would keep everyone happy. I'd still be seeing Rachael tomorrow, and I could still indulge in the anticipation of how our rendezvous would unfold, though now in rather different ways from those I had imagined before.

I went up to my rooms. I could faintly hear the wireless from the floor above, and the sound of Crosby moving around. I thought about going up to talk to him, but he'd been away for a whole week and, from the little I knew of him, I reckoned he wouldn't take kindly to answering my questions. It was best left to the police. There was nothing to be done until tomorrow, but the clock told me it was too early for bed, particularly with thoughts of Rachael on my mind. In my living room the window still wasn't fixed and I felt suddenly uncomfortable, unwilling to spend the evening in the place where O'Connor had died. But neither could I go to bed. There was a simple solution. I grabbed a book and went downstairs.

It wasn't a long walk, just as far as Preston Circus, a big junction of five roads, including the main route out of Brighton. The new fire station facing on to it made the whole area look different. It had only been open a week, but I'd watched it being built, and so for me the transformation had been gradual. The pub hadn't been affected. The Hare and Hounds was a big place, which meant it never had that homely atmosphere enjoyed by some establishments. I knew a few of the regulars but, if you sat on one side of the pub and they were on the other, they might never notice you. And even if they did, they'd leave you in peace. I got my pint and sat at an empty table by the window, but I didn't look out. Instead I started to read.

'*The Road to Wigan Pier.*' The statement was filled with disdain, pretending to read the title as if that precise combination of words had never before been uttered. Even so I recognized the voice. I must have been reading for an hour or so by then. I didn't look up.

'By that socialist, isn't it?' Marchant continued. He sat down beside me, forcing me to pay him some attention.

'It's not as simple as that,' I said.

'Better that than the Nazis, I suppose.' He pronounced the 'z' of 'Nazis' in the same way as the second 's' of 'suppose'. A lot of people did. Some understood enough German to know how it should sound, but mispronounced it as a mark of deliberate disrespect. Others were just plain ignorant. It was impossible to tell which was which.

'They claim to be socialists too,' I said.

'You don't buy that, do you?' He seemed a little drunk. He cradled a Scotch in his hand, and I doubted it was his first. I'd never seen him in the Hare and Hounds before, so guessed he must be here to see me. Perhaps he'd stopped in for some Dutch courage on his way to my flat, and I'd saved him the trouble of going any further. It seemed likely that whatever he wanted was unofficial. He could easily have put a stop to my investigations into O'Connor's death, but he hadn't. That counted for something.

'It was good of you to come to the funeral,' I said.

'Sniffing for clues, really.'

'Me too.

'Find anything? No, don't tell me.' His change of mind took only an instant.

'Why not?' I asked.

'I'd have to pass it on.'

'To Tremaine?'

Marchant nodded.

'I think he's worked most of it out anyway,' I said. 'He seems pretty acute.'

Marchant let out a sharp, exasperated sigh. 'He's worked it all out, and he's not going to do anything about it.'

'He's got his reasons. Good reasons.'

'Maybe so, but that doesn't make me feel any happier. Be better if he'd just kept it all to himself.'

I turned to him. Perhaps this was why he'd sought me out. 'He's told you something else?' I asked.

'He's told me enough. How else am I supposed to make sure this Kraut doesn't get arrested, if I don't know his name?'

I said nothing. It was thrilling. My business was all about information. In almost every case, *somebody* knew who did it – somebody other than the criminal himself. It was just a matter of getting them to spill the beans. There'd never been any question that Tremaine knew the name, but he wasn't going to crack. Marchant was a different matter.

We sat in silence for over a minute. At first it had seemed quite obvious that he was going to let me in on his secret but, with each passing second, the likelihood receded. In the end there was nothing I could do but ask directly, fearful of the response I would get.

'You going to tell me?'

'Wish I could. But, as Commander Tremaine has so clearly explained, that would be tantamount to treason. He said there'll be people hanged for less, when the war comes.'

'"*When*"?'

'That's what he said, and he'd know.' The inspector downed the last dregs of his whisky and deposited the glass heavily on the table. He wiped his lips with his hand. I stood up.

'Another?' I asked.

'Please,' he answered rapidly.

I drained the remnants of my pint and went over to the bar. When I came back, I found Marchant had my book in his hands. Once he saw me, he put it down, apparently embarrassed.

'Don't let me stop you,' I said, handing him his drink.

'That's all right. My wife read *Keep the Aspidistra Flying*. She told me I'd like it, but I couldn't get into it. This looks much the same.'

'It's not,' I said. 'This isn't fiction.'

'Even less reason for me to enjoy it, then.'

We talked for a little longer, but not about O'Connor's murder. We tried literature, but obviously he wasn't much interested. Then came football, for which the same applied to me. Finally, we settled on rugger, where we had some common ground. But by then we'd almost finished our drinks. He didn't offer me another. We walked a few yards down London Road together, then I turned off into my own street. He seemed about to say something as we parted, but then thought better of it.

I made an effort to be quiet as I opened the front door and climbed the stairs to my room. It was late and Mrs Croft would have long been asleep. For my part, I wasn't tired and, once I'd changed into my pyjamas, I decided to read some more. I opened the book where I'd marked it and immediately noticed the new addition. It was right at the top of the page, above the printed text: two words, written in pencil. It could only be Marchant who had put them there, and they could mean only one thing. They comprised a name, a German name:

Ernst Metzger

CHAPTER 11

So now I had it all. I knew the killer's name and where he worked. Ernst Metzger of the German Embassy in London. Case closed.

The reality was nothing like as simple as that. This was nothing remarkable. It was news to me, certainly, but Tremaine had been aware of it from the start, and had refused to act. Now I shared his knowledge, and I *couldn't* act. And, anyway, I wasn't certain. Metzger was the prime suspect, but there was no proof. Yet even if I could never bring him to justice, I could still take him a few steps closer to it.

The following morning, I rang the German Embassy. I didn't know the number but the operator looked it up and quickly connected me.

'Good morning. I'd like to speak to Herr Metzger, please. Herr Ernst Metzger.' It occurred to me, even as I spoke, that he might have a military rank, but I had no way of establishing it.

There was a moment of silence, then the woman's voice replied. 'I'll put you through.'

I heard the clicking of the exchange, and then a man's voice – young.

'*Reichskirchenministerium.*'

I tried to break it down using the little German that I had. It meant something like 'Ministry of Churches'. It didn't matter.

'Is that Herr Metzger?' I asked.

'Herr Metzger is out of the office. May I be of assistance?'

'Do you know when he'll be back?'

'His hours of work are between 10:00 and 19:00. You may call him between these times.'

'Thank you, then. I will.' I said.

'Thank you. Good day.'

I put down the receiver and turned to go upstairs. At the end of the hall, framed by the kitchen door, stood Mrs Croft, eyeing me suspiciously.

'You finally got around to calling your mother, then?'

I'd already called mum the previous evening, but there was no need to complicate matters. 'That's right,' I said.

I continued upstairs. It was about a quarter past nine but there was no need for me to wait and try calling Metzger again, not now I knew his working hours. I considered what I'd learned. Firstly, I'd established that there certainly was an Ernst Metzger at the embassy. I hadn't doubted Marchant's word, but Tremaine could easily have made up a name to put the policeman off the scent. It seemed unlikely that Tremaine would have much to gain by blackmailing someone from the Ministry of Religion, though, on the other hand, it might mean he had more to lose than most if the content of those photographs was revealed. And the department he was assigned to might just be a ruse. If he was a spy, he'd hardly announce it. It would explain his unconventional working hours, too, though not why his colleague should be so happy to convey them to me. Perhaps Metzger's true role was unknown even to those who worked alongside him.

I went into the bathroom and shaved, then came back to my rooms and put on my best suit for the second day in a row. Yesterday I'd worn it for a funeral, but this was something different. I chose a more colourful necktie than the black of the day before, emphasizing the distinction. I hoped she'd like it. I even pictured what *she* might look like wearing it – wearing *only* it. It was easy to make that slight alteration to the images of her I held in my mind. I could even make the same alterations to the drawings too, if I chose. And perhaps, by the end of the day, I'd need neither artistry nor imagination to see all that I wanted. But no, not today. Perhaps in the future but not today. I splashed cold water from the sink on to my face, but it didn't help much.

I walked back to Furze Croft, arriving a few minutes earlier than promised. My hand had been forced by circumstances, but now I could only see my plan as madness. And yet I couldn't back out – nor could I allow my fears to become apparent to either of the ladies involved. I pressed the button on the intercom again, but this time I was not given entry.

'Wait there,' she said.

She was more punctual than most women I'd known. I was only left standing for a couple of minutes before the door opened and she emerged.

'So,' she asked, 'where are we going?'

'Rottingdean,' I said.

'What's that?'

I'd forgotten she'd not lived in Brighton long. 'It's a village, out to the east.'

'How are we getting there?' She was like an inquisitive child.

'We'll take the bus,' I said. 'My treat.'

We walked down into town without much conversation. Summer was really starting to take hold now and I felt warm in my suit. If it stayed like this, then the town would be overflowing with tourists come the bank holiday weekend. That meant I'd be able to make good money on the pier.

I glanced furtively at Rachael, though why I should feel guilty about looking at the girl I was taking to lunch, I didn't quite know. Her outfit was more appropriate to today's weather than mine – a chocolate-brown dress decorated with posies of yellow flowers. They looked like Black-Eyed Susan, but I doubted the designer had been too worried about botanical accuracy. I hadn't advised her as to the sort of thing to wear, but it was a suitable choice for the occasion. I felt my concerns begin to ease. Over the dress was a white knee-length coat which she hadn't bothered to button up. On her head she wore a broad, white sunhat. The only item that might lack modesty were the red patent-leather shoes, striking enough to distract even my eye from the curve of her stockinged calves. I remembered that like me – like so many other Morlocks – she would make good money from a busy weekend, but I pushed the thought into the darker recesses of my mind.

We boarded the bus on Western Road and I watched her as she made her way to a seat towards the back. Heads turned to follow her – both male and female. In part it was because she seemed so out of place, at least in terms of her clothes and her style. But as she sat down, and then slid over to make room for me, she displayed no hint of feeling uncomfortable there.

The bus rolled down to Old Steine and then up on to Marine Parade, and before long we were out in the countryside. Whether deliberately or not, she had chosen the right-hand side of the bus, so we were able to look out over the Channel, calm and wide and blue.

'So you want me to tell you about O'Connor?' she asked. 'Or wait till lunch?'

I glanced around. The bus was quiet, but not empty. A woman and her daughter were sitting two rows behind us, and there were two men up towards the front. 'Maybe *after* lunch,' I said. 'When we're alone.'

'So we're not having lunch on our own, then? I might have guessed.'

We sat in silence, her eyes gazing out across the sea. After a few minutes she reached into her handbag and took out her spectacles. She kept them on for only a few moments, just long enough to confirm that the focused reality of what she saw was the same as she imagined it to be. Without them her view of the world must have been like an Impressionist painting. But I didn't see that world at all – my eyes were fixed only on her. She took them off, about to return them to her bag, but I put my hand on her arm.

'No, leave them on.'

She looked at me momentarily, then perched them back on her nose. 'So where *are* we going?' she asked.

I explained.

*

From where the bus dropped us on Rottingdean's picturesque High Street, it was a short walk to my mother's house – more than half of it taken up by the driveway. Mrs Wilkinson, the housekeeper, opened the door. She'd only worked for mum a few years, and I hardly knew her. She was wearing an apron with stains on it that might well have been blood. We'd evidently interrupted her in the middle of cooking. It was for her culinary skills that mum had employed her, not for her welcoming nature. She looked Rachael up and down, and then turned to me.

'She's in the conservatory,' was all she said before standing back to let us through the doorway. I'd taken off my hat before ringing the bell and now I handed it to her to take from me. She jerked her head towards the coatstand on the far side of the hallway. I went over and hung my hat on it, noting how easily, on returning home, I'd fallen back into the habit of expecting to have done for me what I could easily do myself. I took Rachael's coat and hung it there too, enjoying how natural the action seemed – the act of undressing her. By the time I'd finished, Mrs Wilkinson had disappeared back into the kitchen.

'This way,' I said, leading Rachael to the door that led to the back of the house. We passed through the dining room, and then the room we'd always called the snug. From there a door led to the conservatory. I went in first.

Mum was seated in a wicker armchair, gazing out across the garden. She must have heard us, because she turned. Her eyes rested on Rachael for only a moment, taking her in, before she looked to me and smiled.

'Hello, mum,' I said. 'This is Rachael.'

'Delighted to meet you,' she replied. Her accent seemed stronger than when we had last spoken, and that had been on the telephone only the previous night. I'd always suspected that she emphasized it a little for the benefit of strangers. 'Please, do sit.' She indicated two chairs opposite her. 'Lunch won't be long. Why don't you pour us all a sherry?' This last remark was addressed to me.

Rachael sat down and I went over to the table where a bottle and three glasses stood waiting. I rushed the operation, fearful of leaving the two women to talk alone, and yet excited by it too. I spilled some and mopped it up with my handkerchief, then handed out the glasses and finally sat down. I took my first sip quickly. Rachael eyed the pale liquid with some suspicion, then imitated me almost exactly in drinking it. Mum clasped hers in her hands, staring benignly at Rachael. Eventually she spoke.

'I'm afraid I haven't heard very much about you, my dear.'

'There's not much to tell.' In contrast to mum's, Rachael's own accent seemed almost to have vanished.

'Carol only mentioned your name to me last night.'

Rachael frowned. 'Carol? Who's she?'

Mum's face formed a similar expression. 'My son – Carol.' It was a pretence on her part. She knew perfectly well she was the only person on the planet who called me that. Even dad had avoided it, once I'd grown old enough to express a preference.

'Everybody calls me "Charlie", mum.'

'That's not true,' she replied with an air of assurance. 'Some people call you "Big-Bad".'

I grinned. She only knew it because I'd told her, and I remembered how she'd laughed. Even so, her mentioning of the name reminded me of O'Connor.

'I think Carol's a nice name,' said Rachael. 'Polish, isn't it?'

'Romanian,' mum corrected, though with less scornfulness than I heard her employ in confronting the same mistake in the past. 'It was my father's name.'

'You were born there?'

'I left in 1904, when I became engaged to Carol's father. He brought me back here, to his home.'

'It must have been terrible for you when he died.'

I saw mum bristle. As we'd travelled here, I'd had time to tell Rachael the fundamentals of my life story, but not to warn her how sensitive an area dad's death still was.

'He died fighting for his country,' she said simply.

I decided to change the subject. 'Did a parcel come for me?'

'It arrived on Monday,' she replied, pointing back at the door we had come through. I got up and went inside quickly, not wanting to leave them alone for too long. The packet was on the table in the snug. I picked it up. It didn't seem to have been interfered with in any way. I went back to find Rachael laughing, and mum with a smile on her face. They looked up at me and fell silent, then both began laughing again.

'I was just explaining to Rachael how it's beyond my understanding why you send packages to yourself at my address. And even more so why you try to disguise your handwriting when you do.'

I sat back down and finished my drink. If my evident embarrassment helped to make things go smoothly, then all the better. Rachael reached up and tugged at a large hatpin in her hat, freeing it before putting it down on the table beside her. It seemed she was relaxing, though I wasn't convinced she had ever been nervous.

We were interrupted by Mrs Wilkinson. 'Lunch is served, ma'am,' she said, directing the words solely to my mother. She didn't wait for a reply and mum began to push herself shakily out of her chair. I moved to help her, but she brushed me aside. 'You lead the way, Carol.' Rachael had also stepped forward to assist, and in her case the aid was accepted. We made our way back to the dining room, with Rachael taking my mother's weight on her arm.

*

After lunch I suggested I show Rachael around the garden. Mum stayed in the conservatory and watched us, but we were far enough away to be unheard.

'Some kind of con trick, is it?' Rachael asked.

'What?' I genuinely had no idea what she meant.

'Something to do with the inheritance. You only get it if you're married? I'm quite happy to pretend, if you are.'

I laughed. 'No, it's not that.'

'There don't have to be kids, do there? I'm not faking that.' I could tell she wasn't serious.

'It's nothing to do with any inheritance.'

'Just trying to prove you're not a ponce, then?'

'Just trying to make her happy,' I said. 'It worked.'

She took a moment to respond 'Most men would have denied it – being queer, I mean.'

'And the fact that I didn't proves I am? Or that I'm not?'

'Proves you don't care what I think, which is *very* flattering.'

Of all the impressions I might want to give her, that was the furthest from the truth. But it would be clumsy to tell her – to show her – how much I actually cared for her. 'I don't think you need me to help form your opinions,' I replied instead.

We were in the arbour now. It felt cooler in the shade. She was staring intently at the grass beneath her feet.

'Penny for them?' I asked.

'I wouldn't have said you were, judging by that drawing you did of me.' She looked up at me. 'You should do more.' I felt my heart begin to pound, and she must have noticed my reaction. Whether her words had genuinely been intended to tease or were just a slip of the tongue, I couldn't tell, but she soon clarified the matter. 'Drawing, I mean. You're talented.'

I pointed ahead of us, probably too quickly, eager to seize the more innocent interpretation of her words. 'You see that tree over there; the ash?' She nodded. 'That's the first thing I ever remember drawing.'

'I'd like to see it.'

'You have. It's in the dining room, behind where mum was sitting.'

I reached into my pocket and drew out two sheets of paper. 'Speaking of drawing, take a look at these.'

She realized at once what they were. 'Do I have to?'

'There's nothing sordid in them. Just his face.'

She examined them, but not for long. 'What do you want me to say?'

'Is that him?' In one sense, it was a stupid question

'Who else would it be? The profile's better than the other one, but they're not bad, either of them.'

It was good to have my guesswork confirmed by someone who had actually seen Metzger in person. 'You want to tell me what happened?'

'I got a call from Spindly. Said he'd got a client who was into taking pictures. It's not unusual. More money for less work to be honest, or it is sometimes, if he just wants pictures of you on your own. This was different.'

'And this client was O'Connor.'

'That's right. Said he was a detective. Said he was working for this fellow's wife, trying to prove he was more interested in toms than he was in her. But he'd been having trouble getting any evidence.'

'Did he say how the wife knew all this?'

'I didn't ask. But I got the impression O'Connor didn't know much either – like somebody else was pulling the strings. I went to the Metropole with him. He said this bloke always met the girls there, and liked a new one every time. Said I should wait in the lounge with a book on the table with a carnation in it, so I'd be recognized. Then he went off upstairs to hide.'

'Hide where?' I asked.

'In the cupboard next door. He put the camera in a ventilator, up on the wall, opposite the bed. He told me where so I could make sure he got a good view of things. You know me – with my eyesight I wouldn't have spotted it otherwise.'

I remembered how in the photographs she often seemed to be looking directly into the camera, deliberately posing. 'Did your ... friend spot it?'

'Don't think so. Why would he be looking?'

'Did you have to wait long for him, in the lounge?'

'Half an hour? Long enough for a cuppa. And then he walked up to me. He'd obviously spotted the book and the flower. He didn't say much. We just went upstairs and ... well, you saw the pictures.'

'Did he give you a name?' I gave no credence to the 'Blenkinsop' that he'd checked in with.

'He told me to call him Ernie.'

Ernst Metzger – Ernie. It made sense of a sort. 'Did he tell you anything else about himself,' I asked.

'No. He was – you know – concentrating on the job. I don't think he said more than a few words once we got up there. It's not unusual.'

'Was he suspicious?'

'Suspicious?'

'He didn't guess O'Connor was there, taking pictures?'

'Why should he? Al didn't make a sound.'

'And you didn't do anything that might have given the game away?'

'Like what?'

I shrugged and tried not to imagine – but not imagining is one of those things where the more you try, the more you fail. 'And he paid you afterwards?'

'No, he'd already paid.'

'Paid *you*?'

'No, paid the girl he was expecting – or her pander at least, since he obviously hadn't met her.'

'And what happened to her?'

'Al caught her on her way to the hotel. Recognized her by the carnation and the book. Paid her off, and then paid me to stand in for her – and to make sure he got some good snaps.'

'You must have known him quite well – to call him Al.'

'In my line of business, people like to stick with Christian names. They're less traceable ... Carol.'

'Carol!' Rachael's use of my name coincided almost exactly with my mother calling it out across the garden.

'Yes, mum?'

'Do you want coffee?'

I turned back to Rachael. 'Coffee?'

She nodded. She linked her arm around mine and we went back inside.

*

It was approaching mid-afternoon when we got back to Brighton. Rachael's presence had made the whole occasion rather more pleasant than many a lunch with my mother, in that it cut off one regular topic of conversation: the question of when I was going to find myself a nice girl. And for me Rachael was pleasant company in herself, whatever her effect on mum might be.

That had still left one line of attack open to mum: when was I going to get myself a proper job? It was, apparently, an even more pressing matter now that I had a young lady to look after - didn't Rachael agree? To my annoyance, Rachael *did* agree, and took evident pleasure in doing so. We could only leave once I had promised mum that I would get in touch with my great-uncle Graham, who knew everybody in Whitehall and would easily find me gainful employment – if not on his home turf in the War Office then in any one of a dozen other departments. It was the second proposal of a career in the civil service I'd received that week. I probably would call Uncle Graham, but only because he told good stories and paid for dinner. I pictured the scene, and pictured Rachael there too, charming him. But I knew that was unlikely to happen. Today had been a one-off; a departure from the reality to which I had to return.

I walked with her back to Furze Croft. The return journey was uphill, and it was warmer now, too, but Rachael didn't seem to display the physical effects of either. At the flats she unlocked the front door and held it open for me. I hadn't been planning on going up to her apartment – I had things to do – but the gesture was so natural that I'd stepped inside before I'd even had the chance to think about it. Upstairs her flat was just as it had been the previous day, and we took the same seats as before, though she now sat rather than reclined on the chaise longue. I put the parcel that I'd picked up at mum's on the floor beside me.

'What's in there?' Rachael asked.

'It doesn't matter.'

Suddenly she lunged forward and grabbed it. 'Let me guess.'

She started to squeeze it, like a child with a Christmas present. She grinned. 'It's money, isn't it? Ten-bob notes, I reckon. There must be twenty-five quid in there.'

She'd judged the thickness precisely, but got the denomination wrong. I held out my hand but she ignored me. She knelt on the floor in front of me, clutching it to her chest. 'You got all this money and you made us take the bus?'

'It's not my money,' I said. 'It's just passing through my hands.'

'I know what you mean.' Still she kept hold of it.

'It's for O'Connor ... for Al. Or for his widow, at least.' Some of it was, anyway.

'Oh,' she said meekly. She handed it back.

'I ought to get over there now,' I said. I looked at my watch: it was past 3 o'clock.

'You sure you don't want to spend a little of that money?' she asked, fixing me directly in the eye. Her voice dropped to a murmur. 'On something just for you?'

I understood exactly what she meant. I had fifty pounds in my hand that I could easily call my own, and a beautiful woman kneeling in front of me, offering herself. And of course it wouldn't come to anything like fifty pounds – though in truth I had no idea what her price might be. A crown – the same as charged for a drawing on the pier? More than that, surely, but how was I supposed to go about asking her?

And, with that thought, the moment was broken. Perhaps my entire perception of her was broken too – or reconstructed to something resembling the truth. Much as I wanted her it could never be like that, never as a customer – not with any girl. I could pay for their dinner; I could pay for their clothes; as an artist I could even pay them to strip naked and model for me. But somehow I just couldn't bring myself to pay for the act itself.

'Like I said, I need to go and see his widow.' I stood up, and so did she. She looked a little disappointed. 'I'm sorry,' I mumbled. 'It's not ... you.'

'I should think not!' she laughed, her mood suddenly changing. It was a façade. She walked over to the door and I followed.

'Anything else at all you remember about this Ernie chap?' I asked. 'Nothing distinctive?'

She thought for a moment, then shook her head. 'Nothing really ... apart from the accent.'

'But nothing you could say about that, except that he was German?' It was absurd to hope that she'd be able to distinguish the intonation of a Bavarian from a Prussian.

'German? No, he wasn't German.'

'But you said the accent.'

'He had an accent all right, but not German. He was a Geordie.'

CHAPTER 12

It wasn't a long distance down from Furze Hill to Eaton Villas, and I walked quickly, trying to drive from my mind the activities that I might have been enjoying instead, but for my own pig-headedness. I pulled the bell and then looked sideways to the bay window, expecting her face to appear, but it didn't. I heard footsteps in the hall, and then the door opened. It was the man I'd seen at the funeral, whom I'd taken to be Mrs O'Connor's father. He peered at me, recognizing my face but unable to place it.

'How do you do?' I said. 'My name's Woolf. We saw each other at the funeral yesterday.'

He smiled and nodded, offering his hand. 'Baxter,' he said. 'Gerald Baxter. Vera's father. I expect you've come to see her.'

He led me back through the hallway. The ginger cat sat halfway up the stairs, watching us as we passed. We went into the living room and Baxter indicated I should sit down on the sofa. 'I'll go and find her,' he said.

He left the door leading on to the hall open, but I heard another open and shut beyond. There were voices: his slow and soft against hers, which was raised and coming in short bursts. The nature of their conversation was quite evident, even though I couldn't make out a single recognizable word. Then there was silence, followed by the same opening and closing of a door, and Baxter returned.

'I'm afraid Vera's not really feeling up to seeing visitors. You'll understand, I'm sure, with the funeral only yesterday.'

'That's quite all right,' I said, standing. This didn't have to be done in person. It might be better if it wasn't. I reached into my pocket.

'She mentioned that you used to work with Alan,'

Baxter continued. 'A while ago.'

'I did.'

'And that your flat was where he was killed.' There was no hint of having drawn any conclusion to accompany those words. He simply conveyed the facts.

'I'm afraid so.'

'That can't have been very pleasant for you.'

I was about to point out that it was less pleasant for O'Connor, but it would have sounded like a joke. 'It was a shock,' I said simply. We stood for a few more moments, facing each other uncomfortably.

'Was there anything you'd like me to tell Vera?' he asked.

I pulled the money out of my pocket: twenty one-pound notes, held in a roll by an elastic band. I'd split up the fifty pounds as I walked down from Rachael's: ten for me, twenty here, twenty at my next port of call.

'Just give her this,' I said. He took the money, but gave it no examination. 'We were working together on something … when he died,' I explained. 'That's his share.'

'I'll see she gets it.'

I wondered if there was some etiquette for the situation. Even to offer the money was to suggest it was some recompense for O'Connor's death. But it had been his money, and now it should go to the woman he loved – to the women. Baxter showed me to the door.

I headed west, crossing Sackville Road and on into the neat grid plan of streets that made up Poets' Corner. I wasn't sure how many poets lived there, but the streets themselves were each named after some historic master of English verse. Sylvia Clay lived – or had once lived – in the street that took its name from William Cowper. It had been pure chance that I'd been walking along here four years previously, and seen O'Connor kissing a woman at the door of a basement flat, then trotting briskly up the steps to the street. It was at that point he'd caught sight of me. He didn't know how much I'd seen, but he tried to bluff his way through. He introduced us. I was his business partner, which at the time was entirely the truth. The woman, still at the door, was a potential client. The two of us walked on together and he invented some details of the case she wanted us to investigate – something about a dispute over which side of a family had rightful ownership of some inherited jewellery – but I knew he was lying and I didn't bother to listen. About a week later I asked him whether we were taking on the case, just to tease him, but he said the situation had been resolved amicably, and I didn't press it. I'd had no idea how serious their relationship was, or how long-lasting, until I'd seen her at his funeral four years later.

'I thought you might turn up,' she said, as soon as she opened the door. She'd recognized me as easily as I her.

'May I come in?'

She said nothing, but turned away and walked back into the flat. I assumed I should follow. Her living room was at the front of the house. It faced north and of the little sunlight that managed to shine on this side of the street, even less made it down below the level of the pavement and through her window. But the place was immaculate, the furniture only a few years old, if that; stylishly modern. If she was a kept woman, she was well kept.

'You've got a good memory,' she said, sitting down in an armchair. She took a cigarette from a box on the table beside her and lit it, but didn't offer me one.

'You, too,' I replied. I tried to fathom what it was that O'Connor had seen in her. She was younger than his wife but, once that was taken into account, probably not as good-looking. But, then, maybe I was being shallow. O'Connor might have loved her for other reasons. She certainly had good taste.

'Was it you who telephoned?' she asked.

'When?'

'On Sunday, to tell me he was dead.'

'That's not why I called but, yes, it was me. Me who

called on Saturday, too, while he was here. He gave me the number.'

She nodded. 'I thought so. I didn't know what had happened to him till then – Sunday, I mean. After that I bought the paper and it was all in there.'

'I'm sorry I broke it to you like that.'

'Better that you did. I wouldn't have wanted to miss the funeral.'

'Can you tell me what happened … on Saturday?'

'He came here around 4 o'clock. We … we spent a few hours together. Once you'd telephoned, he said he'd have to go out. I made him some tea first. Then he grabbed his bag and left.'

'What time was that?'

'Half past seven?'

That fitted in with him meeting me at the station. I still didn't know whether he'd gone straight from there to my rooms afterwards. 'Did he come back later?'

She held back a tear. 'That was the last time I ever saw him.'

'But you *were* expecting him? He wasn't planning to go … home.' It seemed a cruel word to use in the circumstances.

'He said he'd come back here, to leave his things. I was hoping he'd stay the night.'

'Did *you* go anywhere, after he'd left?'

She gave a curt laugh. 'You think I did it?'

I didn't think so for a moment, but that didn't matter. O'Connor had taught me the process: the questions you had to go through were pretty much the same, whatever you thought. You might confirm something you already knew; you might learn something you didn't.

'Somebody did,' I replied simply.

'Why would I? I've lost everything.'

'Everything?' I held up my hand, indicating the room around us. 'You still have this?'

'For another month. Al paid the rent but I can't afford

it. She'll get it all in his will.'

'You're sure?'

'He told me. He said he didn't want to upset her; said he'd make other arrangements for me, but there was no rush.'

I reached into my pocket and drew out the remaining roll of pound notes. I leaned across and handed it to her. 'I owed him this,' I said. 'I think he'd have wanted you to have it.' In some way it seemed more insulting to give the money to O'Connor's mistress, who needed it, than to his wife, who didn't. If I'd known earlier, I would have given Sylvia the whole forty pounds. I could still have given her my own ten, but I didn't. The twenty might help keep her going for a few more months, but it would only be delaying the inevitable.

She took the rubber band off the roll and counted the notes. 'He said he had some money coming in. I assumed he meant more than this.'

It didn't sound like she was questioning my honesty. 'I think this was supposed to be just the first of much more,' I said.

'And that's why he was killed?'

'Seems like it.' There was no point in hiding it from her. I changed the subject. 'Have the police been here?'

She shook her head. 'You're the only person who knows about me.'

I remembered what had happened at O'Connor's office, just a few minutes' walk from here. 'No one been hanging around? No one tried to break in?'

'You think they would?'

'You said he left things here. There might be something that would incriminate the killer.'

'There's not much.'

'May I look?'

She thought about it for a few moments, then nodded. 'Better you than someone else,' she decided, rising to her feet. She took me to the rear of the flat, to a tiny room lit only by high, narrow windows that peeped into the garden of the house above. 'This is where he kept all his stuff,' she said. 'Mind if I leave you to it?'

She didn't wait for an answer, and a moment later I was on my own. There wasn't that much to go through: a desk and a chair, and on the opposite wall some wooden shelves, but they weren't full. The desk itself was bare apart from a lamp, which I switched on. Then I turned and examined the shelves.

My eyes were drawn straight away to the camera. I picked it up. It was a complex-looking thing. I'd had to use cameras in my work more than once, but I wasn't fascinated by them like O'Connor was. He was always reading about them, always keen to buy the latest model – usually made in Germany. This one had the word 'Exacta' etched on its front, above the lens. Below that were 'Jhagee' and 'Dresden'. I wound it on and could feel, from the lack of resistance, that there was no film inside. I pressed the shutter release. Nothing happened. I wound it on and pressed again. This time I heard something – almost imperceptible, but there was the faintest click as the shutter slid across. Even the sound of the wind-on was quieter than I'd have expected. Perhaps O'Connor had chosen this model specifically because of its silent mechanism, or perhaps he'd made some adjustments of his own. Either way, it was an essential feature for the use he had been putting it to. I opened it up but, as I already knew, it was empty.

I put the camera back where I'd found it and heard the clank of it knocking into some other fragment of metal. I reached right to the back of the shelf and brought out what I found. It was a rectangular piece of brass, about the size and shape of a letterbox. It was pierced by narrow slats, stacked up in four columns. I'd seen something very like it just a couple of days before, though this was a little different. Towards one end, a neat circular hole at been cut out, breaking through the pattern of slats. I picked the camera up again and fitted the two of them together. The lens nestled snugly in the hole. It wouldn't have been much effort for O'Connor to replace the Metropole's ventilator cover with his own version, allowing him take his pictures while the camera remained unseen. Metzger wouldn't have noticed anything amiss.

I put them both back where I'd found them and glanced up at the spines of the books on the shelf above, but there was nothing of immediate interest. Mostly they were about photography; a couple about fishing. There was a fair bit of fiction there, too. Leaning against them all at one end of the shelf was a black leather-bound volume with nothing inscribed on the spine. I picked it off the shelf and looked at it, but there were no words on the cover either. A strip of elastic held it closed. I sat down at the desk, to see better in the lamplight, and opened it up.

As I'd suspected, it was a notebook; the one O'Connor had with him when we'd spoken in the Albion. It was about half full of his writing. The first entry was dated 4 December 1937. I glanced at my watch, realising I didn't have time to read the whole thing now. I flipped through to the most recent entries. The last one read simply 'Tremaine. Eccleston Square, 28 May, 10pm.' It was an appointment I'd kept in O'Connor's place. On the previous page was scribbled my address. It fitted with what I'd already concluded: O'Connor had got me out the way so he could search my rooms. After that I could see the traces of a page having been ripped out, but that wasn't too suspicious. I remembered the moment O'Connor had done it as he handed me Sylvia Clay's telephone number. I decided I'd read the rest later. I slipped the notebook into my pocket and stood up again.

On the very top shelf sat a cardboard box. I had to stand on the chair to reach it, which wasn't easy as the thing was on castors. The box was very light, suggesting little, if anything, inside. I brought it down on to the desk. There was a piece of black cord attached to it at both ends, not so much to hold it closed, rather to provide a strap by which it could be carried. I opened it to look inside, but it was empty. There was printing on the underside of the lid, enough to tell me what had once been stored within.

PACKING OF RESPIRATOR
The Respirator should be placed in box with …

I didn't read all the details. This was where O'Connor had kept his gas mask. The box didn't look at all dog-eared, so I guessed it was a new acquisition. The mask itself had been in no state to examine for wear and tear when I'd last seen it, strapped to O'Connor's dead face as he lay on that slab in the morgue beneath Brighton nick.

There was nothing else to examine on the shelves, so I began to go through the desk drawers. But they were mostly empty. A few contained bits of stationery: pencils, blank paper, a stapler. In the bottom right drawer was a pile of brown envelopes of a style that was instantly familiar. It was one such that O'Connor had handed me to take to Tremaine in London; and one very similar that I'd bought for myself as a replacement, to conceal the fact that I'd opened the first and examined its contents.

I picked up the pile to see if there was anything underneath, and noticed a certain stiffness to it, more than I'd expect from a stack of mere paper. I flicked through them. All were empty except one, nestling between the others. I'd no doubt as to what I would find inside. I looked over my shoulder – I didn't want Sylvia to witness the truth of what her lover had done for a living – but the door was still closed. This time the envelope wasn't sealed. I tipped it up and let the contents spill over the desk.

It was as I'd expected: a second set of prints of the photos O'Connor had taken of Rachael and Metzger, if it really was Metzger. That Geordie accent threw the whole thing into question. It was unsurprising that he should keep copies – who could tell how many times over he might be able to sell the same images? I looked inside the envelope but there was no sign of the negatives. Perhaps O'Connor had kept them at his office, and they'd been taken in the burglary. He'd been wise to keep these separate.

I looked through them, one at a time, though I wasn't sure I needed a reminder. I'd seen them before and had remembered them well enough to reproduce them on paper. But, since then, I'd met Rachael. We'd spoken. I might almost have considered her a friend, and she'd offered me more than that – or perhaps less. Looking at the pictures meant something quite different now, something wrong, and all the more exciting for it. But I didn't stop. Now what I was looking at was real, more real than the first time I'd seen them, more real even than when I'd drawn them. Since then I'd been close to that body, touched it, if only on the hand and the arm. What I could now see in front of me had been hidden then only by the weft and warp of the thinnest cotton.

And, on top of all that, these images constituted evidence. They had to be examined thoroughly for anything that might lead to O'Connor's killer. It was a good job that this last excuse lurked somewhere at the back of my mind, because I did notice something. Some of the photographs were unfamiliar to me, even though they were all much of a muchness. There were in total perhaps five distinct poses of the two bodies, and for each one several images with only slight variation in the position of a head, or a limb, or some other body part. It was as if O'Connor had waited and then taken a cluster of shots in tight succession. But, in terms of those slight variations, some of the pictures were new to me.

I counted them: there were twenty-five in all. That meant nine more than I'd taken up to London, which posed several questions. Was twenty-five the full set, or might there be still others that O'Connor had taken? And were there only two sets of prints: this and the one I'd given to Tremaine? And – which intrigued me most, though I had no hint of an answer – what had happened to those other nine from the first set?

I looked through the pictures again, sorting them into the ones I'd seen before and the new ones – trying to discern precisely which those extra nine were. It wasn't too difficult; my memories were clear, reinforced by repeated recollection. Then I examined the nine in detail, to see what was different about them, what clues there might be that I'd not seen before, and most of all to determine just *why* they had been excluded. Moments earlier my focus had been solely on the image of Rachael, but now I concentrated more on her bedfellow. As I'd noted before, Rachael had a tendency to look straight at the camera, as if she was well aware of its presence. I'd since established that she was. And that was when I noticed what was different about these nine. In the others, Metzger's face had been in profile or sometimes obscured completely. Tremaine himself had complained on that score. In these, however, he could be seen from the front – fully recognizable to anyone who knew him. It made no sense. Why would O'Connor exclude the images that best depicted the target of the blackmail? They would be the first that Tremaine wanted, so that he could show them to Metzger and leave no doubt as to the strength of evidence against him. Or perhaps that was what had already happened. I hadn't entered this story at the very beginning. Perhaps mine was not the first delivery that O'Connor had made to Tremaine.

There was a knock at the door behind me. I quickly gathered the photos together and slipped them back into the envelope. Sylvia entered a moment later, but she had no chance to see them.

'I was wondering if you wanted a cup of tea or something,' she said.

I looked at my watch, remembering I had a train to catch. I stood up. 'No, I've got to be going.' I held the envelope up in front of me, not wanting to make any suggestion that she should take a look at it. 'Is it all right if I take this away with me?' I didn't bother to mention the notebook in my pocket. It was too small for her to notice, anyway.

'Please do,' she replied, with a hint of vehemence. 'I don't want to see them again.'

I felt my cheeks turn crimson. She *knew* what was in the envelope. She had seen them. It hardly mattered whether that had been while O'Connor was still alive, or after he had not returned, and she'd begun searching for some clue as to his whereabouts. Perhaps he'd even shown them to her, to add spice to their relationship. Somehow I doubted it. But, whatever had happened, she and I had both seen the pictures and we each knew that the other had. They might as well have been laid out on the desk for both of us to admire. For want of anything to cause a distraction, I reached into my pocket and handed her my card.

'Call me,' I said, 'if anyone comes round asking questions. Or … if you need anything.'

She took the card, but I knew she wouldn't call.

CHAPTER 13

I was in London again. This time I'd travelled up from Hove Station, just a few minutes' walk from Sylvia Clay's flat. It still brought me into Victoria. Once again I'd spent the journey clutching an envelope full of dirty photographs. It was a risk, but not a huge one. There was even a thrill to it, the sensation of how close I was to public humiliation if anyone were to discover what I was carrying; much the same thrill you get from taking a tart to see your mother and pretending she's your sweetheart. And, anyway, there'd been no time for me to go home and get rid of them. Just like the preceding Saturday, I had an appointment to keep: a little earlier this time, at 7 o'clock. The big difference was that the man I was meeting tonight was quite unaware that I was coming.

I knew what he looked like now – Metzger. I'd got clear pictures of his face. The guesses I'd made from my drawings hadn't been too bad – I'd learned that from what Rachael had told me – but, based on what I'd sketched, you could have walked past the man in the street and missed him. And I needed to recognize him when I saw him. *If* I saw him.

More troubling was what he sounded like. Rachael could have been mistaken about his having a Geordie accent, but she'd seemed confident about it. I certainly couldn't imagine how she could have mistaken German for that. The simple explanation was that he'd been disguising his voice but, if so, it was an obscure accent to choose. Perhaps it had just been some awful attempt to speak like a native Englishman, and the best sense that Rachael's ear could make of it was to interpret it as Geordie. On the other hand, Metzger might not be a simple diplomat; he could well be a spy. That could mean he had been trained to mimic the voices of a dozen different British regions. I would soon find out.

On the train I'd read through O'Connor's notebook, working backwards on the presumption that recent entries would be of the greatest significance. It wasn't much help, though. He'd not imagined it was going to be read by anyone else, and so it mostly recorded fragments of information too detailed for him to trust to his own memory: engagements, addresses, telephone numbers and the like. There were a few meetings with Tremaine listed, in advance of the one I had kept, but that was no surprise. I'd heard from Tremaine himself that he and O'Connor had been in contact for some time, arranging to put Metzger in the frame. The earliest mention of him occurred about a month before. '*Call Ralph Tremaine*' followed by a telephone number. Next to it O'Connor had added a note: '*Gilbert case? Lt Cdr?*' O'Connor had remembered him in the same way I did. There was one final note beneath that; in different shade of ink, so presumably added later: '*Dudley?*'

All I knew of it was that it was a town in Worcestershire. I'd never been there, nor could I imagine any connection with the Gilbert case. But then I came across the word again a few pages earlier, and realized it could signify something else. It was included in a list, a list of what seemed like surnames – nineteen of them in all. Dudley was the sixth one down. In that context it made far more sense as the name of a person than of a place. Some of the entries on the list had ticks against them, others crosses. Dudley had a tick. The last four had no mark at all. There was another name I recognized there: Remick. I immediately thought of Percy Remick, the bookie who'd come to O'Connor's funeral. It might be a simple coincidence, but it wasn't that common a surname. On O'Connor's list Remick had a tick. Come to think of it, some of the other names on the list could have been bookies as well. There was one I recognized called Reece, and a Corbett too. Both of them worked at the Brighton track. They were just surnames, but with three out of the nineteen having the connection, the odds were that it was down to more than mere chance. And who better to ask about odds?

But that wasn't for today, and I wasn't even sure it was worth following up at all. It was a tenuous link, even if the two Dudleys were connected. From Victoria I walked up Buckingham Palace Road, past the palace itself and into the Mall. It was a longish trek but there was no direct Tube route, and I didn't know the busses well enough to be bothered with them. When I was almost at Trafalgar Square, I saw the Duke of York Steps rising to the left, crowned at the top by a column commemorating the said duke. I went up them and found myself at my destination: Carlton House Terrace. It didn't take me long to find number 9, the German Embassy.

It was a quarter to seven. If Metzger stuck to the timetable his colleague had given me that morning, then he should be leaving work soon. It wouldn't be dark for another couple of hours, so I'd have no trouble in recognizing him, not now that I knew what he really looked like. Across the road from the embassy was a little park reminding me of Eccleston Square. I couldn't see a way in and suspected it might be private, belonging to the big houses beyond. Even so, after a quick glance around, I leapt over the fence and took up position in the bushes. From there I had a clear view of the embassy's front door. There must have been other doors too, but I could only watch one at a time. If he didn't come out this way tonight, I'd try a different exit another day.

I had only a few minutes to wait, but the time passed slowly. Finally, I heard a clock somewhere beginning to chime, and counted the full seven strokes of the hour. A couple of minutes later the door opened and two women emerged. Chatting to each other, they headed away down the Duke of York Steps. After that, out came a man on his own but he was far too short to be the one I was after. Then two more men appeared. The one on the right was too old, but the other must surely be Metzger. At that distance I couldn't see his face clearly, and besides, he had his hat pulled down low, but I felt confident it was him. He paused to light a cigarette and do the same for his colleague, then the two of them descended the steps to the pavement. I was half-expecting to witness the curtly raised arms of the Nazi salute and an automatous '*Heil Hitler!*', but instead they exchanged nothing more than a cheery '*Auf Wiedersehen*' and set off in opposite directions.

I followed Metzger, who was heading north, towards Regent Street. The area wasn't crowded, but there were enough people travelling in both directions that I could keep track of him without the risk of raising his suspicions. At Piccadilly Circus he went into the Tube station. I saw him heading down to the Piccadilly line, but then lost sight of him as I bought my ticket. I had to guess which direction he was taking – and got it wrong. He was nowhere to be seen on the eastbound platform. Thankfully, it was only a short dash through to the westbound side and I made it just in time to see him boarding a train. I managed to jump on a couple of carriages further along. The train trundled west, eventually emerging from the tunnels into the evening sunlight. He finally got off at Barons Court and walked a few hundred yards to reach a street that would have fitted in just as well in parts of Brighton as it did here in London. He stopped at a large house, presumably split into flats, and reached into his pocket for a key.

I continued walking towards him, not knowing what I would do next. If I timed it right, I'd reach the door just as he opened it. I could have taken him by surprise, bundled him inside, and perhaps forced him to confess. But that would be a preposterous risk. It would be better, for now at least, to talk to him, to discover what he was prepared to tell me before trying to extract what he was not. He'd found his key and was halfway up the steps to the front door when I came level with him.

'Herr Metzger?' I said. 'Herr Ernst Metzger?'

He turned and looked at me. 'That is correct.' He spoke English but his German accent was clear. It was certainly not the Geordie that Rachael had mentioned. 'How might I help you?'

I didn't reply. It was the first time, since he'd emerged from the German Embassy, that I'd managed to get a clear look at his features. I could feel my jaw hanging open and I knew I must look like a fool, but I could think of nothing to say. Whatever his accent and whatever his name, this was not the man in the photographs.

*

The train journey back home gave me time to think, but I came to no conclusions. I'd managed to regain the power of speech and begin a conversation with Metzger, but only to confirm what I already knew. He was Ernst Metzger and he worked as a representative of the *Reichskirchenministerium* in the German Embassy. That could still be a cover for espionage work, but what did it matter now? Metzger had not been with Rachael in room 235 of the Metropole Hotel. Metzger was not the victim of blackmail. Metzger had nothing to do with any of it. And, if that was the case, why had I come to London to find him?

Inspector Marchant had given me the name. He'd pretended to be doing so as an act of conscience because he couldn't stand seeing a murderer go unpunished, but that might have been a ruse. He could just have made the name up. No, that didn't work. There *was* a Metzger working at the embassy; Marchant couldn't simply have guessed that. He'd have needed to do some research – detailed research. Metzger wasn't just any old name plucked from the telephone directory. Moreover, he had a passing resemblance to the man in the photos: the age, the build, the height, the hair. That would have taken more investigation than Marchant could have found time to do. The name must have come, just as Marchant claimed, from Tremaine.

Perhaps Marchant had been aware he was lying to me, perhaps not. It didn't matter. Clearly Tremaine had the resources to know every face in the German Embassy, and so to pick Metzger's as the one that best matched the photographs. He'd then made sure the name got passed on to me. As to why, I couldn't guess. He must have assumed, correctly, that I'd go and find Metzger. Was Tremaine hoping I'd do his dirty work for him, and kill Metzger in vengeance for the death of my former partner? It would be a ridiculous gamble and, anyway, it would fail as soon as I saw Metzger close up and – as was the case – recognized that it wasn't him in the photos with Rachael.

Except, of course, that neither Tremaine nor Marchant knew I'd seen the full set of images – the extra ones that I'd found at Sylvia's flat and was still carrying with me. None of the photos I'd originally couriered to London featured a clear shot of Metzger's face – or not Metzger's but somebody else's, as I'd so recently discovered. If I'd seen only that first set, would I have still thought it was Metzger in them when I encountered him face to face? I went through the images in my mind. It was plausible; in profile, the two faces were alike enough. The drawings I'd done to try and extrapolate the entire face from what I'd seen were closer to the extra photos than to the real Metzger, but I'd have dismissed that as a mistake on my part.

And then it hit me: I'd been looking at this whole thing arse about face. I hadn't been given Metzger's name because he had a passing resemblance to the Mr X of the photographs. Metzger had come first. He *was* a German spy, and Tremaine was trying to blackmail him for the good of the nation. But something had gone wrong and they hadn't been able to catch him in the act. Perhaps he wasn't even a philanderer at all. So they'd found someone who looked sufficiently like him – this Mr X – and got him to pose with Rachael, then selected only the pictures that showed his face at an angle from which it could be mistaken for Metzger's.

But what would be the point? Could they really hope to blackmail a German spy with pictures that he would immediately recognize as being of someone else? The photos might have fooled me, but not his wife – presuming he had one – nor his masters in Berlin. What could they hope to achieve? But, then, who were the *they* in question? Not the Security Service. Not Tremaine and O'Connor in collaboration. The simplest solution was the best: the deception was O'Connor's alone. For whatever reason, he'd been unable to lure Metzger to the rendezvous at the Metropole, so he'd found a passable substitute, and then removed any photographs that showed him clearly enough to reveal that he wasn't Metzger.

It was a plausible line of reasoning, but the truth was it had little connection to O'Connor's murder. Metzger was now an unlikely suspect. He might have had motive enough if O'Connor had really captured him in the photographs, but to him the pictures would be so clearly phoney that he'd hardly have wasted time laughing at them. Tremaine would be the person most aggrieved by such a fraud, having paid £50 for pictures that, when he presented them to Metzger, would prove to be worth nothing. But that was hardly motive for murder and, with the Security Service behind him, Tremaine could have found much better ways to have O'Connor dealt with. And, anyway, he couldn't have known quite so soon that the pictures were fake. He might not even know it now. I smiled to myself at the prospect of telling him, but I'd have to be careful. If I was hoping to take up that offer of work, I'd do well not to show him up.

And what of Mr X himself as a suspect? Again the motive was weak. Given that O'Connor had found him specifically for the job, he might well have been aware he was being photographed. And if he *didn't* know it at the time, how would he have found out since? Unless O'Connor had resorted to a second strand of blackmail. It was possible, but there was also a more depressing interpretation of the evidence: that O'Connor's murder had nothing to do with the photographs whatsoever and that the motive was something quite different, something regarding which I had no clues at all.

But that was untrue. I had two possible lines of enquiry. One was the list of bookies I'd found in O'Connor's notebook, and the other was Rachael. Her comment about Mr X being a Geordie had seemed incongruous at first, but now it was one of the few leads I had. Perhaps there was more she might be able to remember, if she tried. I looked at my watch. It would be after 11 o'clock by the time the train got in; too late to visit her. Or would it be? It was more likely that she'd be too busy to see me than that she'd have retired for the night. But if I was prepared to pay, then why shouldn't she let me take up an hour of her time just as she did with any other client?

The train rolled along and I let my mind wander. What would she be doing now, at home in her flat? It was easy enough to picture her curled up on the chaise longue, reading a book. And who was I to assume that she wasn't? But it seemed unlikely. The image in my mind transformed to something more akin to what I'd seen in those photographs, but with myself taking the place of Mr X. I pushed such thoughts away and gazed out of the window at the dark Sussex landscape rolling past. But still the concept lingered somewhere deep in my mind, as a possibility, not a reality. And yet I knew that one could become the other – she'd made that very clear.

By the time the train pulled into the station, I'd already

made up my mind that I was going to see her. I was going to ask her a few more questions, and if something else happened, well so be it. But the more I thought about it, the less I could think of what to ask her, and the more I just wanted to go and visit her. I still had the £10, despite my earlier reluctance to pay. And it wouldn't cost that much. Some part of me – some egotistical voice – hoped it would cost nothing. But each time I thought of her, that voice spoke more softly.

I'd travelled up from Hove, but taken the train back to Brighton. The guards didn't seem to mind much which route you took – it was all the same railway company. Furze Croft was about halfway between the two stations. It took me ten minutes to get there, but it wasn't the effort of the walk I'd just taken that made my heart beat so fast as I arrived.

The block of flats had a crescent-shaped driveway. Just as I turned off the pavement, a man began to exit through the front door about ten yards ahead of me. I continued walking, but it struck me how similar the present scene was to one I'd witnessed earlier tonight as I'd watched Metzger emerge from the embassy. This fellow fitted the same general description: about six feet, with neat dark hair and a small chin. It was a description that could fit a hundred men in Brighton alone, and I began to wonder just how difficult it would really have been for O'Connor to find so approximate a lookalike for the German after all. The figure remained still as I approached, occupied – as Metzger had been – in lighting a cigarette. Seeing me come towards him he caught the door and held it for me. The light from the hallway within spilled on to him and it was as I took the door from him that I looked him squarely in the face and knew for sure.

This was no chance match for a description – six feet, dark hair, mid-thirties. This was the man himself. Those eyes had stared blankly into O'Connor's camera and moments later stared down on to Rachael's supine body.

Those lips had tasted the saliva on her tongue, the sweat on her skin, and so much more. In London I'd stared into Metzger's face and known with absolute certainty that he was not the man I was looking for. Now I looked into another face and knew quite the reverse.

This was Mr X.

CHAPTER 14

He walked away, leaving me standing in the porch holding open the front door. For a foolish moment I'd been afraid that he would recognize me just as I had him, but it was in a photograph, not a mirror that I'd seen him – a strictly one-way means of identification. I had two options. The first was to rush up to Rachael's flat and confront her. She clearly knew more about this man than she was telling. But Rachael would still be there tomorrow – whereas this might be my only chance to follow Mr X. I let him get a little further away, heading in the opposite direction along the crescent of the drive from the way I'd come. It was late and the streets were empty, so he'd easily spot me if I followed too close. He was getting near to the main road before I started to move. When he reached it, he turned right and was blocked from view by the building itself. I quickened my pace, no longer worried about being seen and keen to reach that same corner and discover where he was going. But, even as I walked briskly over the tarmacadam, I heard the sound of a car door slamming and then an engine turning over. I broke into a run, but already knew it was too late. Before I reached the gateway, I heard the car driving off. I ran out across the pavement and on to the roadway, just in time to see a dark vehicle turn left on to Lansdowne Road. I couldn't make out its number plate but I was pretty sure that it was an Austin.

I considered going back to see Rachael but decided it was wiser not to. The passion I'd felt for her moments before had dispersed. She had lied to me – that was part of it. There were dozens of flats in the block, to be sure, but for him not to have been visiting hers would have been an absurd coincidence. And what sickened me more was to consider just why he might have been visiting her, at this time of night. I could have questioned her there and then.

She'd have been surprised to see me so soon after his visit and might more easily have made a mistake. But I was feeling emotions far stronger than surprise, and might have done the same myself. It was safer for me to go home.

*

I didn't go to see her the next day either. There was a race meeting on and, considering I had a list of nineteen bookies that I wanted to talk to, it would be convenient to catch them all in the same place. I went by tram, jumping on an M at Preston Circus, then changing to an E. The motor groaned as it pulled us up the steep incline of Elm Grove, and I could smell ozone and burning oil. Race Hill was the end of the line, but the tram was still almost full. Everyone disembarked and began walking towards the track. It was nearly an hour until the first race of the day, but there was plenty of betting to be done beforehand. I didn't think the bookies would be at their most talkative if it meant losing business.

The crowd was quite a mixture: from boys as young as ten, mostly accompanied by their fathers, to shrivelled, stooped figures, with lips and cheeks caved in to the hollows where their teeth once had been. The only segment of society that was not represented was women. There was a buzz in the air and a babble of voices, as men discussed their expectations for the day with friends and with strangers. Cutting through it all was the sound of bookies touting for business and of hustlers selling their wares.

'Dark Traveller. 15-2. Best price on the course.'

'Lucky heather, just a penny! Certain to bring you good fortune.'

'Cigarettes! Two shillings for 20.'

I paused. None of it was of much interest to me but

still I couldn't ignore it. Two shillings for a packet of fags? I looked over. The high prices weren't affecting the man's trade. I realized what was up. The punters would be handed their smokes, but they'd get a free gift as well: a little note with a recommendation for one of today's races. It was illegal for a tipster to charge for his services, but giving advice away as a free gift with a packet of overpriced cigarettes was fine. And it was advice worth far more than a couple of bob, if the horse won. If.

I walked on through to the field bordering the track where most of the bookmakers plied their trade. The shouts continued, but now it was purely to advertise the odds. Beyond the noise other levels of communication were being employed. Hands made shapes against one another or touched heads and faces as the odds were transmitted across the course using ticktack. For more complex messages, runners traversed the ground. Everywhere, money was changing hands – both notes and coins. For now it was in a single direction: from the punters to the bookies. After the first race, and every race, the flow would be reversed, but they'd rarely pay out quite as much as they took in – just as long as they got the odds right. They were the epitome of the Morlocks in Brighton, but it wasn't just the Eloi that they exploited. At a guess, half the men betting were locals, some spending the last pennies they had on a desperate gamble. Morlock fed on Morlock.

I took O'Connor's notebook from my pocket and glanced inside at the listed names, some ticked, some crossed, some unmarked. Presumably he hadn't got around to speaking to the unmarked ones. If they really were all bookies, then they'd be easy to find – even the ones I didn't know – from the names on the noticeboards they used to mark their pitches. I could only guess that the ticks indicated those with whom O'Connor had had some success in whatever he was doing, so I'd start with them. And within that group I'd start with a name I knew: Percy

Remick. I could see him not too far away, perched on a soapbox, bending forward to hand over a betting slip. More than most, he needed something to stand on to be seen above the crowd. It wasn't so much that he was short; he was simply diminutive, tiny in every respect, wizened and insignificant. Maybe that was an asset in his trade. I hovered nearby until there was no one waiting for his attention. He turned to one side and spoke to a boy of about fourteen, who bore an unmistakable similarity to him. The boy ran off across the grass.

I looked up at Remick and caught his eye. He gave a little jerk of his head in acknowledgement, but didn't greet me.

'Good of you to come to the funeral the other day,' I said.

'It was no effort. Al would have done the same for me.'

He seemed more confident of the suggestion than I would have been, but I didn't question it. 'You were close, then?' I asked.

'Close as any two men who sometimes have a Scotch together. That doesn't mean you tell each other your life stories.'

'Was he close to Corbett too? And Reece?'

He eyed me suspiciously, unsure as to what I was getting at. 'He knew a lot of people round here.'

'Dudley?'

'Frank Dudley?'

I nodded, though I'd not known the Christian name.

'Maybe,' said Remick, 'but I'd be surprised. Frank's from London, just comes down here on race days.'

'His name's next to yours.'

'What?'

I held up the book and showed him. 'What do all those ticks mean, Percy?'

He tried to snatch the book but I tugged it away. I'd made a copy of the list, anyway, but it was better to have the original.

'Go to Hell!' he said, leaning close to me, his voice low.
'Or what?'

He laughed throatily. 'You trying to pick up where he left off, are you? Well you know what happened to him.'

I tried to hide my surprise. 'It was because of this?'

Remick shrugged. 'Who knows? Someone was bound to get him.'

'You going to tell me what it was all about?'

'Like I said, go to Hell. I know how to take a hint.'

He stood up straight again and began signalling to a bookie about twenty yards away, who in turn forwarded the ticktack to another. It looked to me as though Remick was just using the exchange as an excuse to stop talking to me, though I couldn't help but wonder if he was sending others a message to do likewise.

I meandered through the crowds, looking for further faces I recognized. I found Jerry Corbett and went through a similar line of questioning. When I showed him his name in the book, he had a better response.

'Al liked a flutter, so what? It was never much. He spread it around, amongst the bookies. Looks like he ticked the ones that gave him best odds.'

It sounded like Corbett had had time to prepare. Perhaps I'd been right in my suspicion about Remick warning them all. Taffy Reece just told me to sod off. I was getting nowhere. I moved on to some of the names I didn't recognize. The first was Carter, but he just played ignorant, telling me he'd never heard of O'Connor even after I showed him the list. I was getting bored.

'Do you know where Frank Dudley's pitch is?' I asked Carter before moving on.

'Over there.' He pointed. 'Right next to the Tattersall stand.'

I went over. It was a good place for Dudley to work from, with quite a flow of punters passing by in both directions. Dudley's business seemed better funded than the others I'd visited. Like Remick, he was a small man but a couple of heavies, one on each side of him, made up for that.

'Frank Dudley?' I asked.

'That's the name on the sign.'

'You hear about what happened to Al O'Connor?'

He glanced surreptitiously from side to side, then nodded. 'I heard.'

'Did he ask you about Tremaine?'

'Who?'

'Ralph Tremaine? He said he was going to.' It was a long shot, but it was the only sense I could make of that brief note in O'Connor's book.

'Well, he didn't, and it wouldn't have helped him if he had.'

'Why not?'

'Because I don't know any Ralph fucking Tremaine. Did he tell you I did?'

'He told me plenty. Told me about you and Remick and Corbett and the rest. He wrote it all down.'

'He wasn't that stupid.'

I held up the black notebook and waved it at him, but instantly realized I'd gone too far. Dudley flicked his fingers and the thug on his left took a step forwards. I didn't quite run, but I moved off pretty swiftly through the crowd. After half a minute I looked back, and could see the thickset figure searching for me. His eyes locked on mine and he began to move again, as did I. The next time I looked, there was no sign of him. I was up against the rail now, just yards from the track itself. It was still a good few minutes before the first race but I could see the runners and riders beginning to assemble at the starting gate, far away down the track.

I wasn't too worried about Dudley or his henchman. They wanted to see what was in the notebook and I'd overplayed my hand. If they got hold of it and saw what was in it, they'd realize I knew nothing. As to his denial of knowing Tremaine, I believed him – but I could easily have been mistaken. I wasn't getting anywhere. The ticks on the list clearly didn't indicate anything as simple as who had been cooperative. Or perhaps they did, and the fact that they'd cooperated with O'Connor meant that they *weren't* going to with me. It was time to move on to the crosses.

The first of those was Mullender. I asked around and soon found out why I'd not heard of him before. His business had previously been owned and run by a chap called Thompson. On the occasions I'd met Thompson he'd lived up to his reputation. He was probably one of the five biggest bookmakers in the town and Mullender had been his lieutenant. But Thompson had retired, retired suddenly, left his house and his business and gone to live a comfortable life in Oxfordshire. That was one of the problems of living in Brighton – you couldn't say you were retiring to go and live by the sea. As to the truth of it, there were various possibilities. He might have been killed and his body dealt with so that it would never be found. He might have been frightened into his retirement. It might even have been his genuine desire. But all that was a different case from the one I was working on.

Whatever his newfound seniority, it seemed Mullender still liked to do business in person. Just like all the others, he had a soapbox to stand on and a blackboard on which he chalked the odds. He was stocky, a bit like the man that Dudley had sent after me, but his eyes showed he was intelligent too.

'Roy Mullender?' I said, holding out my hand to him.

'Who wants to know?'

'Woolf. Charlie Woolf.'

He blew air into his cheeks and raised his eyebrows, making it clear that the name meant nothing to him. I hadn't expected it to.

'I used to work with Alan O'Connor.'

He stepped down to the ground so that his eyes were level with mine. 'That's hardly likely to impress me. And with Al everything's 'used to' these days isn't it?'

'We went our separate ways a few years ago,' I explained. If Mullender hadn't seen O'Connor as a friend, then it might do better to emphasize my own differences with him. 'I didn't agree with his methods.'

'Very wise of you. So why are you talking to me?'

'He had your name in his notebook.'

'Just mine?'

'There was a list. All of them work here at the races.' There was no point in not telling him the whole story. 'Some have ticks against them; others have crosses. You've got a cross.'

Mullender chuckled. 'That's a very restrained way for him to express it. What I actually told him was that he should go shove his head up his arse, and if he came near me again I'd make sure he did. I do hope I'm not going to have to do the same with you.'

'What did he want from you?'

He cocked his head to one side, insofar as a man with such a thick neck could, and narrowed his eyes. 'No harm in telling, I suppose. He wanted a list of my punters.'

'All of them?'

He shook his head. 'Just the losers.'

'There must be a few of those,' I observed.

'The *real* losers. The ones who lose and lose again and keep coming back. The ones you know would lie or steal or kill just to get hold of a few bob they could put on a nag.'

'Why did he want them?'

Mullender snorted. 'Don't be green.'

'And what did he do when you wouldn't tell him?'

'How many names on that list of yours?'

'About twenty.'

'And how many are ticked?'

'More than half.'

'Then he obviously tried it with the others – and succeeded, too. All the better for me.'

'How come?'

He turned his head to take in the crowd before explaining. 'A man and his bookmaker, it's something special, something private. It's like with his doctor or his lawyer. If people can trust me to keep my mouth shut – more than they can trust the others – that's business that comes my way.'

'So you told everyone what O'Connor was up to?'

'Not everyone, just the ones he was trying to do the dirty on. Just the losers.'

I was about to ask the obvious question but stopped myself. If O'Connor had managed to get the information he was after from another bookie, then any one of those losers might have had a very good reason to kill him. And so if Mullender could give me those names, it would make a list of very likely suspects. But I remembered his response to O'Connor himself asking the very same question.

'Anyway,' said Mullender, 'what you done to piss off Frank Dudley so much?'

I looked at him questioningly. He nodded over my shoulder and I turned to see Dudley's flunky a few yards off, uncertain of whether to approach. 'Ah!' I said.

'Any reason I shouldn't just let Frank's colleague there deal with you?'

'Dudley had a tick by his name.'

Mullender considered this for a moment, then grinned. 'In that case our interests would seem to coincide. Make sure you don't dilly-dally.' He walked straight past me and I turned to watch as he shook Dudley's man firmly by the hand and placed the other hand on his shoulder. I stepped back a few paces and saw the thug's eyes following me, but he was unable to move, either through actual physical restraint on Mullender's part or merely out of fear of him. I didn't wait to see how long the bookie's hold over him would last. I made myself scarce.

The crowd had compacted itself now, half a dozen

bodies deep and pressing close to the rail. The first race was about to begin. Behind them, the bookies were left alone at their pitches. Soon they would be paying out for whichever horses had won or placed – hoping the winner would be an outsider. I felt the ground begin to shake and then heard shouting from the crowd as the pack approached. The racing itself was of no interest to me, but I was always fascinated to see the excitement on the faces of the punters – expressions I could never create in my own imagination, but which I could store in my memory to reproduce on paper or canvas at some later time. Not that I often got to draw anything other than those cheap portraits on the pier.

But then I spotted a face I knew – or a profile at least. It was Tremaine. His appearance was as dapper as ever, putting him out of place here – more suited to the members' enclosure. My first assumption was that he had come here to see me; to find out what I was doing. But I couldn't fathom how he'd got on to me so quickly, unless he'd simply been following me – or had had me followed. But that assumption was a little arrogant of me. It was just as likely that his own enquiries had brought him here quite independently. It had happened before at the hotel. For the moment, however, his attention was concentrated entirely on the race – just like any of the punters around him. His look of intense passion surprised me, but I didn't want to let myself be distracted. I knew I had to get finished here. Remick's stand was not far away. Although I'd got nothing out of him before, things were different now.

'What do you want?' he asked aggressively, as I approached. He was smoking a pipe; during the actual races was probably one of the few times he got the chance. 'I told you to get stuffed.'

'Yeah, but that's not what you told O'Connor, is it?'

'What do you mean?'

'Did he offer you a lump sum – or a cut of the profits?'

'What for?' Remick's voice showed he was afraid.

'For the list. The list of your customers. Your least successful customers.'

'You're guessing.'

I was guessing about the payment, but Mullender had explained enough about the rest. And either way his face told me I was right. 'They'd all have something to hide, wouldn't they?' I continued. 'They'd all have lied or stolen or worse. They'd want all that kept secret. They'd pay to have it kept secret.'

Remick began talking quickly. 'He didn't tell me why he wanted the names, and I didn't ask. He just paid me: a guinea a name. Easy money. For all I know, he might have been planning to help them out.'

I laughed. It didn't sound like O'Connor. 'Well, maybe I should help them out, too. Why don't you give *me* their names?'

'Don't be a mug, Woolf. You won't get a thing out of me.'

'In that case I'll just have to tell everyone, won't I?'

'What?'

'Well, if you're not going to tell me precisely who you sold out to O'Connor, all I can do is warn *all* your punters.' I turned to face the crowd beside the track, cupping my hands to my mouth. 'Roll up! Roll up!' I shouted, though there was no chance they would hear me. 'Come and learn —'

I felt the feeble blow of Remick's fist on my back, but it was no effort for me to turn and knock him aside. He fell to the grass. He wasn't a big man like Mullender, and couldn't afford muscle, like Dudley employed. Even if the boy I'd seen earlier was still around, he wouldn't have been much help. The son was even punier than the father. I didn't like to play the bully, but sometimes it got results.

'You'd better tell me then, hadn't you,' I said, deliberately standing over him.

'Not here.' He seemed genuinely afraid, and it was

more than just my doing. 'I'll telephone.'

'You do that.' I reached into my pocket and took out one of my calling cards. I flicked it towards him and watched it spin through the air, landing neatly in the centre of his chest. Nine times out of ten it would have missed him completely, but today I was lucky. I knew it would help reinforce his impression of me – make it even more likely he would contact me with the names. But I'd learned enough up here on the Race Hill. It was time to go. With a smile on my face I turned away.

CHAPTER 15

The fist caught me right in the middle of the belly. The pain was indescribable. I doubled up and began to retch, but that only made the agony in my stomach muscles worse. The fist came down again, this time on the back of my head and I fell to the ground. A foot came in at the side of my ribs, kicking me over on to my back. I looked up, raising a hand to block out the high sun, though it must have looked like I was trying to defend myself. Perhaps that would have been wiser. I recognized the face; I shouldn't have been in any doubt. It was Dudley's flunky. I might have managed to lose him twice, but he hadn't given up the chase. He held out a fat, meaty paw.

'The notebook,' he said.

'What notebook?' I've no idea why I bothered to lie. It seemed like the right thing to do, even though he'd seen it in my hand less than an hour before.

He kicked me again, this time in the thigh, then reached into the side pocket of his jacket and brought out something long and thin, the colour of tortoiseshell. He flicked his wrist to reveal the blade. It was the favoured weapon at racecourses up and down the country: a straight-razor – easy to conceal and with a variety of uses. You could inflict pain, you could scar, you could kill. And more than that, the very sight of it would scare most adversaries into doing just what you wanted them to. It worked on me. I fumbled in my pocket and brought out the black notebook, proffering it to him from my position on the ground. He took hold of it but, either out of fear or stupidity, my fingers didn't release. He raised the blade and slashed at them, without much force, but the sudden movement returned me to my senses and I let go before the razor's edge could connect. It cut harmlessly through the air.

His broad figure loomed over me, considering what to do next, then suddenly his attitude changed. He quickly slipped the notebook and the razor into his pocket and reached out towards me, as if offering to help me stand up. I wasn't fool enough to respond to the gesture, and moments later I understood what he was up to. We were surrounded now by hordes of stampeding feet, migrating away from the track and back to the bookies' stands. The race was over; the result known. Some were returning to collect their winnings, others to place their next bet. They might have done something about my prostrate figure and the man standing over it, but if one was seen helping the other, it could be regarded as someone else's problem.

Once the crowd had enveloped us, however, the thug's mood changed again. We were now screened by the mass of bodies. He grinned and reached for the razor once more, opening it slowly with one hand, keeping it tight against the side of his leg so no one would see. He leaned forward and raised his hand to the side, not very far, but he wouldn't need much of a swing for the blade to prove effective. I tried to work out where he was aiming, raising my hands to cover my face – though I wasn't certain as to which I valued more. But, as I peeked between my fingers, his expression changed again. His eyes widened and his mouth opened to emit a low grunt. His free hand reached behind him to press against his kidney as he straightened and turned. I saw the face of the man who had punched him. It was Tremaine.

The heavy lifted his blade high this time, but Tremaine was too quick for him, bringing the back of his clenched fist down hard against his opponent's wrist. The thug's fingers snapped open and the razor fell to the ground. In the same movement Tremaine's other fist hit him hard in the stomach. It wasn't a boxer's punch. Given his line of work, Tremaine would have been trained in unarmed combat, and I suspected the influence of the oriental martial arts. There was no sense of gentlemanly fisticuffs to his actions. The flunkey had doubled up and Tremaine clasped his hands together and brought them down on the back of the fellow's head. A fraction of a second later he raised his knee. The thug's face bounced off it and his body fell to one side, his hands covering his bloodied nose. Tremaine took a moment to brush his trouser leg where it had made contact. Somehow he retained his usual rakishness. He squatted down and hauled me to my feet.

'You damned fool!' he muttered. I was upright now, but staggering to one side. 'Are you all right?' he asked with genuine concern.

His vanquished foe was just beginning to stand up, whereupon Tremaine gave him a light kick to the backside He stumbled forwards but managed to transform the action into a staggering run. He disappeared into the crowd.

Tremaine led me out of the enclosure with considerable force, his hand gripping my upper arm firmly. He knew what he was doing. I was dazed from the attack, even though my injuries didn't feel too serious. Once we were out from among the crowd, I began to feel better, and could walk alongside him unaided. We didn't speak. He seemed to know where he was going and soon we were entering a little pub that I'd not been aware existed. He sat me down and went over to the bar, quickly returning with three Scotches, two of which he put in front of me. I downed one immediately, then began the second at a more reasonable pace. I was the first to speak.

'I never took you for a racing type.'

He assumed an expression of mock offence. 'Me? One of the Eloi?'

'So you didn't bet?'

He looked me in the eye, evaluating me. It had been an offhand remark on my part, but when I'd first caught sight of him up at the track, as the horses raced past, I'd seen the look of excitement on his face. It wasn't the expression of a disinterested onlooker.

'I had a flutter,' he conceded. He brought his hand out of his pocket and showed me a crumpled betting slip, before tossing it into the ashtray between us. 'She came in seventh,' he added.

'So why were you really there?'

'Well, obviously I was following you.'

It was much as I'd suspected. He certainly hadn't been on either of the trams I'd taken. But if he had a car, or had hired a taxi, it wouldn't have been difficult.

'You been following me all week?' I asked.

'What would be the point?'

'Then why now?'

He leaned forward and spoke a little more softly. 'Look, when a chap telephones the London embassy of a major power, someone in Whitehall inevitably gets to hear about it. When a chap rings the German Embassy, then my organization hears about it. And if this chap asks to speak to Herr Ernst Metzger of the *Reichskirchenministerium*, then *I* hear about it. And it doesn't take long to find out where the call came from, and the name of the chap who was calling.'

'I see,' I said, embarrassed at my own stupidity.

'So question number one is: how did you know?'

'That he works at the embassy? You told me yourself.' I felt like I was cheeking a teacher – gaining a small, temporary victory.

'I told you that much,' Tremaine confirmed steadily, 'but I didn't tell you his name.'

It wouldn't have been any real problem to reveal the truth – that the information came from Marchant – but that would hardly be fair. And it would ensure that Marchant never confided in me again. 'I got hold of O'Connor's notebook,' I explained instead. 'He'd written it down.'

He raised an eyebrow and I realized the potential mistake I'd made. I couldn't be sure that Tremaine had ever given the name to O'Connor. But he didn't question what I'd said.

'A notebook?' he asked. 'Where did you find that?'

'I'd rather not say.'

His nostrils flared briefly, but he contained his anger. 'Professional confidentiality?' he said. I nodded. 'And does that confidentiality extend to you allowing me to have a look at this notebook.'

'I don't have it any more,' I confessed.

'Oh, come on! You don't have to lie to me.'

'That bloke with the razor, he took it. Thanks, by the way.' Up until that point I'd failed to display any gratitude for Tremaine's actions.

'You'd have done the same,' he said dismissively. I wasn't sure I'd even have tried, but I certainly wouldn't have been as successful as he was. 'I take it you can remember what else was in the notebook.'

'Some of it.'

'And it relates to Metzger?'

'Not really, no.'

'Oh!' He sounded disappointed.

'Let me ask *you* a question,' I said. 'You ever heard of a man named Dudley? Frank Dudley?' It occurred to me that I'd read O'Connor's note the wrong way round. It might not be that Dudley knew something about Tremaine, but the reverse.

He looked thoughtful for a moment, but shook his head, at first slowly, then faster. 'Should I?'

'He's a bookie. He was up at the races. It was his man beating me up.'

He looked at me blankly. 'I still don't see how he fits in.'

'I'll level with you,' I said. 'I don't think Metzger killed O'Connor.'

He laughed but his heart wasn't in it. 'Why ever not?'

'Because it's not Metzger in the photographs.'

'Don't be a fool. I've seen them … and him. There's no mistake.'

'Have you shown them to Metzger yet? Sprung your trap?'

He downed the last of his Scotch, then leaned back in his chair, rubbing his chin and lips and eyeing me warily. 'Not as such, no.'

'When you show him those photos, he'll laugh in your face.' I told him the details of what I'd discovered. I described the additional photographs – though not where I'd found them – and my trip to London, and finally the confrontation with Metzger. 'I think O'Connor was trying to put one over on you,' I concluded.

'So O'Connor found a lookalike? But … why? Metzger's an old dog. He'd jump into the sack with anyone, certainly a cutie like … well, like that.'

'I don't know – and I'm not sure I care. What it means is, Metzger had no reason to kill him. Metzger was never at the Metropole. I doubt he even knows of O'Connor's existence.'

'And you think O'Connor's death is to do with something else, then? Something up at the races?' I nodded. Tremaine sat in pensive silence for several seconds. Then abruptly he switched on a smile. 'Not my case then. I should leave you to it. All previous embargoes lifted.'

'You should tell that to Marchant, too,' I said.

His smile became more natural. 'But you'd prefer it if I didn't.'

I hadn't thought about it, but he was right. I felt I was getting close to something. I could tell Marchant when I needed his help. 'For the time being, maybe,' I said.

'But there is something I need from you. Those photos.'

'Not much use to you are they, given the chap in them isn't Metzger?'

'Still more my side of things than yours, though.'

I shrugged. He was right. 'They're at home.'

'I'll give you a lift.'

I'd finished my drink now and couldn't find any other excuse not to go. We walked back up towards the racetrack until he stopped at a car parked at the roadside. It was a J-Type Midget, white with red leather seats. The weather was good enough for it to have the top down. He vaulted into the driver's seat without opening the door. The car suited him and I liked to think it would have suited me, if I'd been able to afford one, but I was probably kidding myself. I climbed in more conventionally on the other side. The engine sprang to life and we were off.

'You'll have to let me know the way,' he said cheerily.

'Head back down into town.'

'Righto!'

We turned on to Elm Grove, where the gradient that had caused the tram such effort in bringing me up the hill now had the reverse effect. The car speeded up without any impetus from Tremaine's right foot. He changed down a gear.

'I find it best to keep her in second along here,' he shouted over the noise of the wind and the engine.

I gave him further directions, but it was an easy enough journey home: a slight kink at the bottom of the hill, then across the Level, another kink and on to Rose Hill Terrace. Tremaine stayed in his car while I went up to my rooms. I got the envelope from my filing cabinet, realising I didn't have long. I'd not told him exactly how many pictures the full set contained. I could keep perhaps two and he'd be none the wiser, but I'd have to choose quickly. I was about to empty them out on to my desk when I heard the creak of a foot on the stair. I turned and a moment later, Tremaine appeared in the doorway.

'Just thought I'd take a look at where poor old Al died,' he explained. 'May I?'

'Please come in,' I replied nervously. He must have been suspicious even to come up after me. My guilty reaction would only have reinforced his misgivings.

'Those the piccies?' He held out his hand. There was nothing I could do but give him the envelope and all the photographs it contained.

'They found him through there,' I said, pointing to the living room door. He went in first and I followed. I was pleased to see that Jack had finally fixed the window. 'He was lying against the wall, beside the chair.'

Tremaine nodded slowly. 'Gruesome,' he said. He looked around. 'Not sure what I was really expecting to see,' he announced at last. He went back out and downstairs to the front door, with me close behind him.

'I suppose this is goodbye, then,' he said, offering me his hand.

I took it. 'I suppose so. Though you said you might be able to find some work for me ... your department.'

He smiled unpleasantly. 'I think we both know that that was just to try to keep you off Metzger's scent. It didn't even achieve that.'

He tipped his hat and walked down the steps to the pavement. Moments later he had driven away. I went back up to my room. I wasn't too surprised to learn that Tremaine's job offer had been bogus. It didn't matter. Even if I wanted a job in London, I'd prefer to get it through Uncle Graham. But there were still leads to be followed, and the most important was Remick. He was supposed to be calling me here, so I'd have to wait around. Besides, I had plenty to be getting on with. It would have been better to have kept hold of one or two of those photographs, but it wasn't essential. I'd recreated them from memory before, and I could do so again. But I'd be more accurate if the memory was fresh. I reached for my pad and pencils and began to draw the face of Mr X as I now knew it to be.

But his wasn't the only face I drew that afternoon.

CHAPTER 16

It was 8 o'clock and Remick still hadn't called. He'd seemed scared enough, though maybe it wasn't me he was scared of. But I knew his haunts. I walked up to the Queen's Road and stuck my head through the door of every pub along there, and a few off it. There were a lot of them. Lottie was sitting at the bar of the Royal Standard, just where I'd found her earlier in the week. She saw my face in the mirror.

'Hello, lover,' she said absentmindedly. She was more than a little tipsy.

'Evening.' I tried to look at her in the mirror, but immediately the reflected angular patterns began to dance. I stared down at the bar. They could bring on the aura and then the headache would almost certainly follow. I squeezed my eyes shut, but the colours persisted on the inside of my eyelids. At last they faded. I was all right again for now.

'You not well?' asked Lottie.

'I'll be fine.'

'You need a drink.' She called across to the barman. 'Get him a pint. And I'll have a Mackeson's.' When the drinks came, she made no attempt to pay for them. The barman looked at me wearily and I felt obliged to cough up. It could have been a routine the two of them had worked out between them.

'You talk to that girl, then?'

'Rachael, you mean?' I knew perfectly well who she meant, but it was pleasant to feel the name on my lips.

Lottie shrugged, uninterested in the detail.

'I found her. She was very helpful.' I kept my eyes on the frothy head of my drink as I spoke.

She emitted a slight chuckle. '"Helpful"? Just as long as you didn't help yourself.' It was only down to chance – or to my own stupidity – that I hadn't, but I said nothing. She interpreted my silence as a yes. 'You didn't? You want to be careful. You don't want to get on the wrong side of Spindly Cochran.'

'I didn't,' I assured her, 'and I won't.'

'So you found out who did for Al?'

'I found out who didn't.'

'That's something, I suppose.'

A thought hit me. I'd found no clues to point to it, but it was an obvious solution. 'You don't think Cochran could have done it?'

'What?'

'If he didn't like what O'Connor had done with Rachael – didn't like her having her photos taken, at least not without getting a cut himself.'

She turned to face me, which was rare in itself, and placed a hand on my arm. She spoke in a hiss. 'Don't you go saying that sort of thing about Spindly. He doesn't like having lies told about him.'

'But it makes sense.'

'It makes *no* sense. Spindly would *never* kill a man, not if it was easier to shake him down. Did Al strike you as the kind who'd want to do things the hard way?'

I couldn't speak for Cochran, but her view of matters fitted O'Connor to a T. And what evidence I had so far indicated elsewhere. But it was a possibility I shouldn't have overlooked.

'So is that the best you've got?' she asked.

'Percy Remick knows something. I've been trying to find him.'

'Percy? You saw him on Monday, at the funeral.'

'I saw him today as well, at the races.'

'He's no murderer. Mind you, he must know a few.'

'Exactly. That's what he's supposed to be telling me.' I drained my pint quickly. I knew I was wasting time sitting here.

'Well, he's not been in here tonight. Have a look in the Evening Star.'

'Been there.'
'Maybe the Butchers?'
'I'll give it a try.'

He wasn't in the Three Jolly Butchers, but I eventually found him in the Quadrant. I almost didn't notice him but, as I was about to leave, his son came in – the one I'd seen up at the track. The boy gave me a fearful look, then turned and left, but it was enough to tell me his father was in there somewhere. I took a second glance around, more carefully this time and there he was, huddled in a corner. He looked terrible. As far as I knew he was in his forties, but now seemed around three decades older than when I'd seen him up at the track, just a few hours before. He sat as though deliberately trying to go unnoticed, pathetic and small, with his legs crossed and his arms tucked against his body. His head was lowered, but that didn't hide a livid bruise to his right eye. His lips sucked at the tiniest stub of a hand-rolled cigarette, which he held delicately between the tips of his index finger and thumb. His hand was bandaged, including each of his four fingers. Blood seeped through the dirty white linen.

Without asking, I bought him a Scotch from the bar, but I didn't feel like anything more myself. When I put the glass down in front of him, it took a moment for him to notice it. He reached for it with his other hand and I saw that it was bandaged, too, but in this case the bloodstains showed on the palm, not the back. Then he looked up and saw me. He snatched his hand away from the glass as though it was hot.

'I hope you're proud of yourself,' he said.

I sat down next to him. 'What did *I* do?'

'You asked questions.'

'You answered them.'

'I fucking didn't. And don't you tell anyone I did.'

'You were going to.'

'No, I wasn't.' He spoke loudly, making sure the whole bar would hear. 'I only said that to get rid of you.'

'It didn't work, did it? Here I am.'

'And the sooner you get lost, the better.' There was nothing more he could get from his roll-up and he threw it to the floor. I offered him one of my Player's. He eyed it suspiciously, then took it. I lit it, and one for myself.

'Don't forget your drink,' I said. He gave it that same wary look, then quickly raised the glass to his mouth and knocked back half of it. The blood on his bandages glistened, still wet. It was the unmistakable mark of a razor – the hands instinctively go up to protect the face but with nothing to protect themselves. It could have been me if Tremaine hadn't shown up. Perhaps we shared the same attacker, Remick punished doubly to balance the failure in dealing with me. 'Was it Dudley's man?' I asked.

'Don't be stupid. Why would *he* care about what O'Connor was up to? And, besides, Dudley ...' He came to a sudden halt, realizing he was being too helpful. He swallowed the rest of his drink. 'Like I say, just get lost.'

I looked at him. I didn't know him that well but I had some idea of the sort of man he was. When he'd said he call me with the names, he'd meant it. He'd been scared by me, by my pathetic attempt at bullying. But now he'd encountered a professional, and there was nothing I could do to make him more afraid than he was. Nothing I was prepared to do, anyway. I reached into my pocket and laid my sketches out on the table in front of him, straightening them up so he could examine the faces.

'You don't have to say anything,' I said. 'Just point.'

With a groan he lifted his head back. I could see another bruise on his jaw, and the thin line of a shallow razor cut across his neck – a deliberate reminder of what might happen next time. He produced a hawking sound in his throat and then his head shot forward as he spat on to the table. It hit one of the drawings, catching Mr X square on the cheek and slowly spreading into a tiny puddle. I wiped it clean with the sleeve of my overcoat, then collected it together with the others and stood up.

'Thanks!' I said bitterly.

'Pleasure.'

I was back on Queen's Road before it occurred to me that my sarcasm might not have been in order. I'd asked him to point, but perhaps he'd chosen to be more subtle, indicating who'd attacked him in a quite different way. I dismissed the thought; no one could have aimed that well. I walked back up the hill towards the station.

'Mister!'

I turned. A figure was standing in the shadows of Air Street, on the far side of the pub. It sounded like a woman's voice. Whoever it was had a slight build. I wondered if it might be someone in the same line of business as Rachael but without her own cosy flat to work from. After all, we weren't so very far from West Street.

'Who's there?' I asked. I kept on the main road, under a streetlamp that hung from the side of the building. This girl could easily be the bait for a trap.

'My name's Ronald … Ronald Remick. You were just talking to my dad.' He stepped forward. It was the boy I'd seen at the races and, not long before, when I first went into the pub.

'I'm sorry about what happened to him,' I said.

Ronald sniffed and wiped his nose with his sleeve. 'I was there. The bloke said he'd do the same for me next time. That's what really scared dad.'

'Who did? Who was it?'

He shook his head. His eyes were wet. 'Why should I tell you? I saw you, too. You pushed him over. He's not well.'

'I didn't mean to. I'm sorry. But it's not the same as that, is it?' I nodded my head in the direction of where I'd left his father. 'Sometimes you've got to be tough to do the right thing. You know that. You've seen it in the talkies, haven't you?'

'Suppose.'

'And you can look at me and look at him, and you can

tell which one's the bad guy and which one's the good guy.'

'Still doesn't mean you can help.'

'I can't do anything if I don't know. Had you seen him before?'

A shake of the head.

'But you'd recognize him again.'

'Course.'

I took a step forward, trying not to startle him, like you'd approach a stray cat, but he didn't move. I pulled out the drawings again and showed him the first. 'Is that him?'

'No, that's Teddy Granger,' He spoke quickly, which made him sound unconvincing. 'He works for Frank Dudley.' The second part of it was true, as I already knew to my cost. I'd not had long to study his face, but I'd seen it very close up and so made a reasonable stab at a good likeness. Perhaps Ronald's gabbling was a sign of fear, not deceit.

I showed him the second drawing but he shook his head, then the third. 'That's him. He came round our house today, after the races.'

'Do you know his name?'

'Like I said, I never saw him before. But he's nothing. Just muscle.' From a boy of his age, it was an astute understanding of how the world worked.

'So who's his boss?' I asked. 'Who pulls the strings?'

'How should I know?'

'There'd be no point this fellow coming to see your dad, and not saying who sent him, would there?'

'I heard him say a name, his boss's name. It's … It's …' Finally, he blurted out the word: 'Holsworth.' He took a step back into the shadows, as if cowering from the revenge that might be meted out to him even for mentioning that name.

To me it was a disappointment. The boy had given it a good build-up, as if sensing my eagerness, my hope, that with this one revelation everything would fall into place. But the name meant nothing. An entirely new suspect, and perhaps not a suspect at all, not one for O'Connor's murder. It certainly wasn't on that list of bookies; it might have been somewhere else in O'Connor's notebook, but it didn't ring a bell. It was a shame I couldn't check anymore.

'So what does this Holsworth do?' I asked. 'Is he another bookie? Is he in the rackets?'

'He's not a bookie, for sure. I don't know about the rest of it. I just heard the name.'

'That'll be enough. You've been a good lad.' I reached into my pocket and found a two-bob bit. I held it out to him. He stepped away.

'I don't want that. That's blood money, that is. They told us about it in Sunday school.'

I couldn't quite see the connection, but I didn't press it. 'How about a fag, then?' I asked, holding out the packet. 'They mention those in the Bible?'

'S'pose not.' He reached out towards the carton. It seemed like a pathetic reward, given how much he'd told me. 'Take the whole pack,' I said. It was about half full.

He grabbed it with a subdued 'Thanks, Mister,' then made to disappear along the twitten than ran behind the shops, parallel to Queen's Road.

'One more thing,' I called after him. He stopped and turned, eyeing the cigarettes in his hand, keen to savour his reward. 'The bloke that did that to your dad – did he have an accent?'

'Yeah, he did. A funny one. Northern – but not Yorkshire.'

'Geordie?'

'What's that?'

I considered trying to give a rendition, but it would have been laughable. Anyway, there was no need. 'Never mind,' I said. He ran off and I began to make my way home.

I didn't need to know the accent. I was certain now

that it wasn't German. But Ronald Remick had identified the man quite definitely from my sketch of him. Perhaps his father, Percy, really had been intent on doing the same with his well-aimed expectoration. I could see no way to make the pieces fit, but I had no doubt as to what I'd discovered. The man who'd slashed Remick senior's hands, who'd punched him in the face and God-knew-what-else was the same man that O'Connor had photographed screwing Rachael at the Metropole Hotel, the same man I'd seen leaving her flat the previous night.

But still I didn't know his name. To me he remained Mr X.

CHAPTER 17

I awoke early, though it was already light. I'd asked Mrs Croft often enough, but she never got around to putting up thicker curtains, or telling Jack to. If it came to a war, she might have to. I gazed at the ceiling, trying to make sense of it all. Only yesterday Tremaine and I had agreed that there were two separate matters here: O'Connor's murder and the attempt to blackmail Metzger. I hadn't really believed it, and I doubt Tremaine did either. But yesterday it had been simply a gut feeling. Now there was a link: Mr X. He was the man in O'Connor's photographs and, the moment I started to investigate O'Connor's list of names, he appeared and beat up the one person who'd had even half a mind to give me information.

Clearly O'Connor and Mr X had been working together. I could only guess that O'Connor was the brains within the team. He'd have planned it all. He took the pictures while Mr X did the hard work – if that was an appropriate term for it. And then O'Connor had another blackmail scheme going: collecting the names of punters on a losing streak so he could squeeze them for a little more, rather than let their wives or their employers or their bank managers know what was going on. He might need muscle for that, too. If O'Connor had still been alive, then it would have made perfect sense that, as soon as I started asking Remick questions, the bookie would be persuaded to shut up. O'Connor would have sent Mr X round to do it. So what did it signify that Mr X had done so of his own volition? Was he carrying on O'Connor's operation for himself? Not on his own, he wasn't. He was working for this chap Holsworth. Obviously Holsworth was taking over O'Connor's business. And to do that, he'd first have to get rid of O'Connor. And why do that himself? Why not get someone else to do it, someone like Mr X?

And so I was back where I started. *Plus ça change.* The man in the photographs was the man who had killed O'Connor. I'd been wrong about who he was, and wrong about why he'd done it, but everything else remained the same.

But there could still be more to it than that. Tremaine wasn't levelling with me, any more than I was with him. He must have spotted, long before I told him, that the photographs were duds. Perhaps he'd already confronted Metzger with them. He was trying to find out what O'Connor had been up to, just as much as I was. That's why he'd been up there at the races. His story about tailing me was bull. If he'd followed me all the way from my place, how come he needed to ask me for directions to get back there? It was a stupid mistake for a professional.

And there was one other thing that nagged at me. If O'Connor had hired Mr X to go up to that room in the Metropole, and if both of them – Rachael and Mr X – had known they were being photographed, then why did O'Connor need to go to the effort of concealing himself. It was almost as though he was the only one who *didn't* know what was going on. And yet all the evidence indicated that he himself had planned it.

The only useful question was: what next? Who could I talk to that I'd not already tried, and either been told what they knew, or told to get lost. There were only two candidates, a face without a name and a name without a face: Mr X and Holsworth. Could they be one and the same? It was conceivable. I only had the name from young Ronald Remick and he could have been confused.

But I was looking at things the wrong way. I didn't need to speak to anyone new. When you're trying to solve a crossword puzzle, you don't go through the clues just once and then give up. The discovery of one word gives you letters to help with other words that you previously hadn't been able to guess. So you go round again and again until the whole thing's solved – or until you reach deadlock. It was the same here. I'd go and talk to people again, armed with the new information I'd since received from others. I already knew where to start: Mullender.

*

Mullender had taken over Thompson's business, and when he wasn't up at the track, Thompson worked out of a house just east of the Old Steine, in Devonshire Place. I'd been there once and it was somewhere to start looking. It was mid-morning when I rapped the heavy brass knocker against the door. It opened quickly, as though someone had been waiting behind it. I recalled Thompson telling me it always paid to keep a man on the door; it looked good in front of the callers you wanted to see, and gave you an extra few seconds to escape out the back from those you didn't.

The boy who opened the door was unfeasibly thin, with a pencil moustache and a straw panama that was jammed down on to his curly hair. He was only about twenty. He looked at me but said nothing.

I spoke instead. 'Mullender in?'

'Who wants to know?'

It was exactly the question Mullender himself had asked me when we first met. 'Tell him it's Charlie Woolf, O'Connor's friend.'

The door closed in my face and I waited. The sun hadn't hit this side of the street yet, but it was already warm. Glancing south, I could make out a little patch of sea glittering blue, scarcely distinguishable from the sky above it. It would be Saturday tomorrow, Whit Sunday the day after, and then the bank holiday. It would be a busy time for Mullender, who made his money from more than just racing. It would be a busy time for everyone in Brighton, when the trains from London spilled out their passengers on to the Queen's Road, pockets and purses brimming with cash, and we all would try to make sure just a few shillings of it came our way.

The door opened again. 'He's not in.' The response had taken far too long for it to be true.

'Tell him I know who did Percy Remick over.'

The door closed again, but this time I didn't have nearly so long to wait. 'Come in.' It was a grudging invitation. I followed the skinny figure up a flight of stairs and then to the back of the house. He knocked on a door, which was opened from the inside, but didn't enter. Instead he indicated that I should go on in alone. The man who had opened this door was older, and far better dressed. He wore a pair of pince-nez, which gave him an air of respectability, as though he were a lawyer or an accountant. A man in Mullender's position would require the services of both.

'Mr Mullender will see you on the terrace,' he said. He pointed to a pair of French windows that stood open. Beyond I could just see Mullender enjoying the fresh air while he read a newspaper spread out on the wrought-iron table in front of him. As I went out he folded up the paper and put it to one side, then indicated I should sit opposite him in a chair that matched the table.

'Percy Remick deserved everything he got,' he announced.

'For talking to O'Connor?'

'For talking to you.'

'He didn't. He might have done, but he changed his mind.'

'That was wise of him. Like I told you yesterday, it's a very intimate relationship a bookie has with his clients. Percy just had to be reminded of it.'

I suddenly wondered if I might have got things very wrong. Mullender was talking like he approved of what had happened to Remick. Approving was only a step away from instigating.

But Mullender had more to say. 'Even so, it's not up to the punters to start enforcing the rules.'

'How do you mean?'

'We've got a code, all of us in this business.' He must have caught my sceptical expression. 'Oh, I'm sure it doesn't match up to *your* high and mighty standards, but it stops this town descending into anarchy. And if one of us breaches it, then it's up to *us* to deal with that. Otherwise it just turns into a free-for-all.'

I felt a little safer now and decided to push my luck. 'So you don't approve of what Holsworth did?'

Mullender eyed me, suspecting, quite correctly, that I was bluffing, but I held his gaze. 'If he'd asked, I'd have had a word with Percy. It didn't need to come to that.'

'So Holsworth's one of the "losers"?' My mind was racing, but it seemed like a good guess, based on what little I'd heard. I had to convince Mullender that he was telling me what I already knew.

Mullender let out a brief laugh. 'Oh, he's a loser, but not like that. I mean he loses money – just can't pick a winner. If he backs a horse, then I'll *lengthen* the odds. But he's loaded – I don't know where from. I think they call it a private income. However much he spends at the track, it doesn't put a dent in it.'

Private income. It was the same phrase Lottie had used to brush over how she made ends meet, but for her it meant something quite different.

'Not a good mark for O'Connor, then?'

'You can't blackmail a man who doesn't care. What is it they say: "Publish and be damned."?' He chuckled, proud of his erudition, though I didn't ask him who he thought he was quoting.

'But then why bother with Remick?'

Mullender shrugged. 'Pride, I suppose. Who knows?'

Once again I reached into my pocket and drew out three of the drawings I'd made, laying them on the table between us. There was a slight breeze, so I kept my fingers on them, splayed out to keep a firm hold on all three. 'Recognize any of these?' I asked.

He scoffed. 'You know I do,' he said, though he'd scarcely looked at them.

'Care to give me names?'

He leaned back, putting his hands behind his head and laughing openly now. 'What's your game, Charlie? You trying to play me or something?' He gestured with his hand. 'Look, you obviously know about Holsworth, but you're not getting anything from me. If you're worried about Percy, don't be. He's learned his lesson. And you should learn yours. So sod off!'

He said it light-heartedly, but there was a threat in his eyes. As he spoke, the man in the pince-nez appeared at the open doors. It was time for me to leave. And I'd learned enough. I was led back downstairs and to the front door. Then I was back out on the street. I was in something of a daze, just like I'd been after my beating at the racetrack, but this time there was no physical cause. The shock now was purely mental. I made my way down to the Old Steine, without really thinking, then found a bench where I could sit and take it all in.

I tried to replay the scene in my mind, wondering if I might have been mistaken, but there was no question about it. The action had been subconscious on Mullender's part, but still definite and unmistakable. At the same moment that he was saying, 'You obviously know about Holsworth,' his hand had flicked out at the three drawings I'd put on the table – at one of them specifically. It could have meant nothing other than that he was indicating Holsworth's picture. He thought I already knew, so he'd been incautious.

I'd shown him three drawings. One was of Frank Dudley's henchman, Teddy Granger, but it wasn't that one he'd pointed to, and I'd never expected it to be. The second had been of Mr X. If Mullender had indicated him, then I wouldn't have been too surprised. Only that morning I'd speculated that Holsworth and Mr X might be one and the same. But they were not.

Mullender had pointed towards my third sketch. I wasn't even sure why I'd shown it to him, or even why I'd drawn it, but I suppose I'd become suspicious up at the racetrack the previous day. If anyone was going to be able to tell me whether a face seen in the enclosure was a regular punter or just a one-off visitor it would be someone like Mullender. But I hadn't expected to learn so much – to learn who Holsworth was. But then I already knew Holsworth quite well, albeit by another name.

The name I knew was Ralph Tremaine.

CHAPTER 18

I marched up the hill and into Hove. It still didn't fit together. So Tremaine went by the name of Holsworth. There was nothing so surprising in that. He was a spy, so of course he had aliases. But what was there for him to spy on up at Brighton races? There could be a million answers to that, or a thousand at least. The men who gambled their money up there on race days – the Eloi – came from every walk of life. Some of them might be German, some might be Bolsheviks, or at least work for them. Again it hit me that Tremaine had been lying when he described the two sides of this case as separate. They were both about the same type of crime: blackmail. O'Connor's scheme of getting lists of big losers from bookies such as Remick was – just like his photographs at the Metropole – carried out at Tremaine's behest. Perhaps he had a suspect in mind; perhaps he was just fishing. Either way, gambling was as good a vice as sex when it came to persuading someone to betray their country.

As to Tremaine himself being a gambler – and a loser – that could be genuine or it could be part of the same operation. It would be much easier to uncover and befriend punters with heavy losses if you're one of them. Even if the ponies really were a hobby for Tremaine, like Mullender had said, he could afford it. He was one of the sort who could always fall back on his family for money. I was, too, though I chose not to.

But there was still one piece that didn't fit: Mr X. If he was working for Tremaine, then Tremaine must have recognized him in the photographs. So how could he *ever* have hoped to fool Metzger with them? There was still one person who might have the solution, and I was on my way to visit her now. Even so, none of it got close to answering the main question, the only real question: who killed Alan O'Connor?

LATE WHITSUN

I stood at the door, my thumb hovering over the button. It would be the first time we'd seen each other since my rejection of her. The previous time I'd come this way, it had been with the intent of correcting that mistake, but now I pushed such ideas from my mind. I pressed the bell.

'Yes?' The voice was familiar even through the speaker.

'It's Charlie. Charlie Woolf.'

'I don't know any Charlie Woolf. I know a Carol Woolf.'

'Just open the door, will you?' I instantly regretted saying it. There was time enough to indulge her flirting. The pause seemed timed to convey her annoyance, but then the lock buzzed and I entered. When I got up to her flat, the door was open, just as before. I went inside. Once again she was wearing a dressing gown, but not the showy satin number of earlier in the week. This was long and practical. She had her spectacles on, but no make-up. I could only assume she'd not long been out of bed. Even like that, she was still beguiling.

I got straight to the point. 'I came to see you on Wednesday.'

'I know you did, sweetheart. We went to see your mum, remember?' She sounded quite natural, as though she had nothing to hide – as though she could never be afflicted by a guilty conscience.

'After that. Late. Getting on for midnight.'

She averted her eyes, but still she didn't cotton on. 'I hoped you would. But if I don't answer the door, it means I'm busy.' Then her eyes were on me. 'I'm not busy now. Not for hours.'

'I saw him leave.'

'Who?' Then she realized. 'Oh.'

'What's his name?'

'I can't tell you a trick's name.' She reminded me of Mullender and the other bookies. It was the code of the Morlocks.

'You bloody well will tell me.' My anger was entirely fake, but I was surprised by how much I enjoyed expressing even synthetic emotion to her. I was evidently convincing.

'He's called Ingram. Vince Ingram.'

At last I had it. A name for Mr X. That's if it was genuine. He could have been lying ... or she could. 'Not "Ernie"?' I asked.

'No, not Ernie.'

'Why didn't you tell me before?'

'I didn't know before, did I? Not till he came round on Wednesday.'

'He came round? Just like that?'

'He called first, but I was free. I'd told him how to get in touch the first time. I'm not going to miss a chance for business. He said he'd enjoyed it last time. Wanted to do it again, you know, normally.'

'And that's when he told you his name?' She nodded. 'And did you believe him?'

She laughed. 'More than I did when he said he was called Ernie.'

'You know anything more? An address?'

'You don't ask that sort of thing.'

'You got a telephone directory?'

She nodded her head towards the table near the window, where the telephone sat. 'But I already looked,' she said. 'He's not there.'

I went over to the phone. 'I thought you said you didn't ask that sort of thing.'

'You don't ask, but you still try to find out.'

'Why?'

'It's safer that way.'

I didn't press the point. It was easy to forget how precarious her existence – the existence of any girl in her line of work – could be. However vile men like Spindly Cochran were for taking their cut, they still might save a brass's life once in a while. The directory was sitting on a shelf under the table. I scanned its pages anyway, but she was right. There was no V. Ingram in there. No Ingram at all.

'Satisfied?' she asked.

'Not really.' I wondered what else I could get out of her. I still needed to show her my drawings but, if she recognized one face in particular, she'd clam up. There was something she'd said earlier that I'd tried to ignore, but I knew I had to follow it up, however sordid the response might turn out to be.

'What did you mean, *normally*?'

'What?'

'You said when he came to see you again he wanted to do it normally.' I spoke the word with a strange revulsion.

'Well, you know. Just the two of us.'

I felt my face redden. Images began to push their way into my mind, but they didn't distract me from the inconsistency of what she'd implied. 'It was just you two at the Metropole, wasn't it?'

'And Al. He was in the linen cupboard, remember?' She giggled. Was it really so everyday to her?

'So Ingram knew O'Connor was there? Knew he was taking photographs?'

'I didn't guess it at the time, but something was up.'

'And when you saw him again, he admitted it?'

Little wrinkles formed between her eyebrows, just above the bridge of her glasses. 'I'm not sure. He never really said. But that must have been what he meant ... I mean afterwards, on Wednesday. He said he'd preferred it – no, said he "did better" – when he'd known he was putting on a show.'

I should have pressed her for even more, but I doubted I could stomach the details. 'So, if you both knew he was there, what was the point of O'Connor hiding next door?'

'I don't know. You're the detective.'

I'd already come up with some kind of answer, but I moved on. I got out of my chair and sat beside her on the chaise longue, close enough that our legs touched, not because it would help me find out anything else, just because it felt nice. I put three sketches on the table in front of us, though not quite the same trio I'd shown Mullender. This time, I didn't bother with Dudley's flunky; he wasn't relevant. I kept my eyes on her throughout, looking for the slenderest hint of a reaction. 'Recognize any of these?'

She pointed. 'That's Ingram. It's a better likeness than the one you showed me before.'

'What about that one?' I pointed to the drawing I'd done of Metzger, based on my brief glimpse of him near Barons Court.

She shook her head. 'He looks a bit like Ingram, though, don't you think?'

I gave a brief laugh, which must have sounded bitter. 'Yeah, a bit. And that one?'

'Never seen him before.'

She sounded entirely convincing and I'd no reason to doubt she was telling the truth. I gave it one more try. It had worked, however accidentally, with Mullender; maybe it would again. 'The name Holsworth mean anything to you?' She shook her head. 'What about Tremaine?' She considered for a moment longer this time, but ultimately her response was the same. If she did recognize either name, then she was hiding it better than Mullender had done.

My next question was, 'Did you tell Ingram that I was asking after him? That O'Connor was dead?'

She stood up abruptly, turning her back to me. 'Look, I've got a fellow coming soon. You don't want to meet him, any more than he does you. And, anyway, I've got to get myself ready.'

'But —'

'Please. Maybe another time – we'll talk some more.' She paused and gave half a smile. 'Or not talk.'

She went over to the door and held it open for me.

There was nothing more I could do. As I stepped past her, I stopped to tip my hat, but at the same moment she stretched up on tiptoe and I felt her lips briefly touch mine. 'Another time,' she said softly. 'Really.'

I remained still for a moment, hoping the kiss would last just a little longer, but it didn't. I left. There was more on my mind than the faint trace of her saliva on my lips. She'd behaved just as I'd expected – that one last action aside. Whether it was the drawings themselves that had done it, or the names … but something had made her panic, however gracefully. One moment she'd had hours to spend with me, the next there was a client due. It showed she knew something. If it was the sketches, I doubted it was the one of Metzger; there was no reason she should ever have seen him. I was pretty sure by now that Herr Ernst Metzger had very little to do with any of this.

Back out on the road outside, I looked up at her window. I could just make out her figure through the nets, standing roughly where I had been as I looked in her phone book. Unsurprisingly, she was in no rush to get ready. I raised my hand and waved, and saw the vague movement of her waving back. She didn't turn away, and so eventually I had to. I headed off down the hill.

*

I walked back into Brighton. I needed to think and I needed to eat. I made for the Sussex Grill, on Ship Street. It wasn't bad there; you could get a good idea of the menu just by reading the name of the place. It could be expensive, but not if you knew what to order. I had sausages with mash, and a cup of tea. It came quickly but I lingered over it. I'd realised there was one very simple way I could find out about Ingram, but it felt like an admission of defeat. Another cup of tea stretched my lunch to over an hour, but then I had to get moving. It wasn't a long journey. I cut through Black Lion Lane, a passageway between the buildings so narrow that two people couldn't pass each other without turning sideways, and soon I was outside the Town Hall. I asked for Marchant and it took him only a couple of minutes to show up.

We sat in the same room as before, in the bowels of Brighton nick. I decided it was better not to mention that he'd given me the name Metzger, not even to thank him. He'd wanted to keep his action secret, and I knew now that Metzger had nothing to do with the case anyway.

'Making progress?' he asked me.

'Plenty.' I was making plenty of something, but I wasn't sure it was progress.

'But now you need some m... some help.' He caught himself before admitting he'd helped me already. 'Why else come to me?'

'I need to find someone.'

'You know I can't help you. This is Tremaine's business.'

'What, you mean because the chap in the photographs is a Nazi agent?' That much was allowed. Tremaine had told us both about the supposed connection to the German Embassy.

'Exactly.'

'And what if I told you that the man in the photos is a Geordie hoodlum by the name of Vince Ingram?'

Marchant raised an eyebrow so high that I wondered if it might be one of his Masonic signals. 'You're sure?' he asked. His voice hinted of repressed excitement at this newfound freedom to investigate the case.

'I might have been lied to. One thing I'm sure of – it's no German.'

'And this Vince Ingram,' – he wrote the name down on a pad as he spoke – 'is he local?'

'Like I say, he's a Geordie, but I think he's been down

here a while. Nobody would bother hiring muscle that didn't know the turf.'

'Description?'

'You saw the photos.'

'Not for a while.'

I sighed. I hadn't intended to lay down all my cards just yet. In future he'd be wary, not letting anything pass under my nose for even a second, for fear I'd memorize it and reproduce it. But I needed to find Ingram, and this disclosure would surely help. I handed over my sketch.

Marchant chuckled. 'Your work I take it? Very clever. Anything else?'

'He drives a dark Austin; black or blue I'd guess. I don't know the model or number.'

Marchant scribbled those last details down, then tore the sheet off the pad. He took it, along with my drawing, over to the door and out of the room, reappearing moments later. 'If he's got form down here, we'll soon find him.'

'Thanks.'

'You think he did it? Killed O'Connor?'

'To be honest, no. But I think he was working with O'Connor, so he might know something.' Even as I spoke, I knew I was regurgitating my theories of a few hours before. It was O'Connor who had been the victim of some preposterous hoax, convincing him that he was photographing a couple who wanted to keep their actions secret. Ingram was undeniably one of the perpetrators of that hoax. If he was collaborating with anyone, it was with Rachael, not O'Connor. But it didn't change the basic fact that he must know something.

'You work out anything more about the missing files? Yours or O'Connor's?'

'The Peeping Tom on Grove Street? Can't see how that fits in at all. You never told me what they took from O'Connor's office.'

'Didn't I?' He flipped through his notes. 'Right, well

according to what you told us about his referencing system, there were actually two files missing. One was marked "Metropole" and the other was marked ... hang on, can't read my own writing. Looks like ... "Painters"?'

'"Punters,"' I said confidently.

'"Punters", that's it. How did you know?'

'O'Connor was doing some work up at the racetrack. Seems it involved Ingram.' I took care not to mention Tremaine.

'I suppose you're going to tell me next what was actually in the file.' He laughed, but it had an expectant ring to it.

'A list of names. People who were making big losses. People he might be able to shake down.'

'And we both know what happened at the Metropole.'

'That file probably contained the negatives. Maybe some extra prints.'

'More pictures of this Ingram character. I'm becoming keener to speak to him by the minute.'

The door reopened and Sergeant Purvis walked in, holding a sheaf of papers fastened with a staple. 'We got him, Governor.' He handed the bundle to the inspector, but then was kind enough to summarize for us both. 'Been in Brighton about five years. Four arrests for various kinds of assault. Got off when the witnesses failed to show up. One arrest for obscenity.'

'Obscenity?'

'Caught with a suitcase full of dirty postcards. They were seized and burned. He got a fine.'

'Was he *in* any of them?' asked Marchant.

Purvis looked bemused. 'I don't think it says, Governor.' He leaned over to look.

'I take it there's an address?' I interrupted.

'Absolutely. On Grenville Place.'

I was already on my feet. 'Right, I'm off.'

'I think we'll all go, shall we?' said Marchant, somewhat more calmly. 'I, for one, would very much like to meet this

LATE WHITSUN

Mr Ingram. And, besides, it'll be quicker if we take a car.'

*

It was only half a mile, but travelling in the black Wolseley gave our journey a sense of urgency. I half hoped that they'd start ringing the bell, but evidently that was not justified by the circumstances. Marchant plainly had the bit between his teeth. Having sat inactive for a week under Tremaine's prohibition, he was pleased to get to work at last.

It was a rundown area, just a block south of Western Road, not far from the pub where I'd found Remick the previous night. I doubted he had any idea how close he was to his attacker's home. A couple of streets nearby were already in the process of being demolished to make way for some new shopping arcade. From the look of it, Grenville Place would follow soon.

Ingram's flat was above a tailor's shop. The black Austin 10/4 outside was undoubtedly the one I'd seen driving away from Furze Croft two nights before. The flat was accessible via a door opening on to the pavement between two shop fronts: the tailor and a greengrocer's. Marchant hammered on it with the flat of his hand, but didn't wait very long for a response. He stepped back out into the roadway and looked up at the window. He raised his hands to his mouth and took a deep breath, as if about to give a shout. Then his arms fell to his sides and a single word escaped his lips; a whisper rather than a yell. 'Shit!' I took a step back and looked up towards the window, shielding my eyes against the reflected sunlight, but I couldn't see anything. Marchant strode over to the door of the tailor's shop, but the owner had already emerged.

'What's going on?' The voice was clipped and shrill, like an old woman's, but there was a strength to it, too, particularly considering the four of us who stood around him, each at least a foot taller.

'Do you have a key to upstairs?' Marchant asked him.

'Of course I do, but why should I give it to you?'

Our driver's police uniform should have revealed who we were, but the man can't have registered it. Marchant briskly produced his warrant card. 'I'm Detective Inspector Marchant of the Brighton Borough Police. Now give me the key.' The tailor reached into his trouser pocket and brought out a whole bunch attached to his belt by a chain. He searched through them until he found the right one, then offered it to the inspector. Marchant grabbed it and headed back to the door, unhindered by the tailor who was forced by the taut chain to keep pace with him. Soon he had the door open and was bounding up the stairs beyond. I was right behind him, with Purvis and the driver in tow. The tailor showed little inclination to follow.

'What did you see?' I shouted up at Marchant, as we climbed, but he didn't respond. Soon we were on a small landing, with room only for me and the inspector. The other two queued behind us on the stairs. There was only one door. Marchant tried it but it was locked.

'I'll get the other key,' said Purvis, as he turned and went back down. We couldn't see what was happening, but heard the jangling of keys once again.

'Sod this,' grumbled Marchant. He put his hands up to my chest and firmly pushed me as far away from him as possible, then he barrelled along the short landing and charged the door with his shoulder. I saw almost an inch of light appear between the door and the frame as it bent open, but it didn't break. A second attempt was more successful. The sound of splintering wood filled my ears, and Marchant fell through the gap he had created, only just managing to regain his balance and stay upright. I followed him into the room and sensed the police driver right behind me. I heard Purvis running up the stairs.

We were in a room at the front, with a bay window

looking out on to the street, right above the shop. I don't know how Marchant had managed to see it from down there. Perhaps he'd witnessed such things often enough in the past, so that just a slight silhouette told him all he needed to know. The body was hanging by a short length of rope, which itself was tied to the cable for the light; an unshaded bulb was angled inappropriately to one side, as though to mimic the attitude of the head suspended below it. It was an odd thing to do in the circumstances, but I took a moment to be surprised how the light fitting could support such a weight.

For a moment the corpse remained anonymous, facing out towards the street and so with its back to us. But as we watched the tension in the rope caused it to twist, turning slowly round, as though it had heard us enter and was looking to see who had burst in so rudely and unannounced. This was Ingram's flat and my guess was it must be Ingram's body, but soon we would see his face and we would know for sure.

'Jesus Christ!' It was spoken as a whisper, and I don't know which one of us said it. It could have been me. It certainly expressed my feelings.

The body was facing us now, and already beginning to turn away again, but still we could not tell who it was, because we could not see a face at all. Once more I was gazing into the snout-like nose and dead, round, glassy eyes of a gas mask.

CHAPTER 19

I rushed forwards and grabbed his legs, pushing them upwards in an attempt to take the weight off his neck, but even by the feel of him I could tell he was already dead. Marchant pulled a table over and climbed on to it, taking out a pocket knife to work at the cord. Purvis came over to help me, while the driver hovered beneath Marchant ready to catch him if he fell. When finally the rope snapped, we felt the full weight, demonstrating just how little of it we'd been supporting. We laid him out on the threadbare carpet. Marchant lifted up the head and began fumbling behind it. I thought he was trying to undo the straps of the gas mask, but he clearly had a better sense of priorities than I did. Moments later he had the rope loose and pulled it away. Only then did he begin work on removing the mask. It took him just seconds. He rested the head gently back on the carpet and put his fingers to its neck to feel for a pulse. He tried again on the other side, then leaned over and listened at the chest, but finally he got to his feet, grimly shaking his head.

'That him?' he asked. 'That Ingram?'

I nodded, but then realized he wasn't looking at me. Purvis went through his papers and found the sketch I'd drawn. He showed it to the inspector, who looked at it, then at the corpse and then back again. 'No question,' he said at last.

'It could be Metzger,' I suggested, forgetting that I wasn't supposed even to know that name. In life the two men were similar but distinguishable, but in the discoloured stillness of death – and with such scant familiarity with either of them – we might have been fooled.

Marchant scowled at me. 'What would a representative of the glorious Third Reich be doing in a rat hole like this?'

I didn't respond but reserved judgement on the issue.

I'd been jumping to conclusions about the identities of the two men enough already.

Marchant turned to the driver. 'Get back to the station,' he snapped. 'Tell them what's happened. Tell them to get a team up here.' The officer hurried out of the room. 'Let's take a look around,' the inspector continued. He looked at me and I thought he was about to tell me to clear out but, in the end, he settled for, 'Don't touch anything. Prints, remember?' He produced a pair of leather gloves from his pocket and put them on, then turned and walked across the room. It would have sounded authoritative, but for Purvis's keen eyes.

'What's that on your foot, Governor?'

'What?' Marchant looked down. A scrap of white paper was stuck to the sole of his shoe. He bent his leg behind him and plucked it off. He looked at it. Even from where I was standing, I could make out handwriting on it. 'Shit!' muttered the inspector.

'What is it?' I asked.

'Suicide note, by the looks of it.'

'It must have been on the table,' said Purvis. 'Not your fault, Gov. You had to do something.'

I was more concerned with what Ingram had written. 'What does it say?'

Marchant held it out for me. It wasn't a full sheet of paper – just a slip big enough only to fit the words scrawled on it.

Sorry things had to end like this, but after O'Connor I just can't see any other way out for me.

Vince.

Marchant gave me a moment to take it in. 'Speaks for itself, don't you think?'

'Really?'

'"After O'Connor." He's confessing that he killed

...r. And he'd have been hanged for that, so he did ...lf, instead.'

...ho's he writing to?' I asked.

'What?'

'"Sorry." Who's he apologizing to? It's very personal sounding. "Vince," not "Vince Ingram,' or "Vincent Ingram." If you were leaving a note for some stranger to find, would you sign it like that?'

'There's no guidebook for writing suicide notes. And, believe me, I've seen dozens. People don't think straight. Anyway, who says he expected a stranger to find him. He didn't know we were coming. Perhaps he had a sweetheart who had a key. Or maybe he thought the bloke downstairs would find him.'

I tried another tack, glancing up towards the ceiling. 'How did he get himself up there?'

Marchant was ahead of me on that. He pointed to a wooden chair, lying overturned in the corner. 'Climbed up on that.'

'Long way away.'

'A man kicks out when he's dangling,' explained Purvis morbidly. It was probably true. Even if this wasn't suicide, then whoever had set it up would have left the chair where it chanced to fall.

'Let's just take a look around,' said Marchant.

There were only two rooms; the one we'd entered and a small bedroom at the rear. Downstairs I'd noticed another door leading out back. The communal WC would no doubt be through there, either inside or outside; there might even be a bathroom somewhere. Purvis went into the bedroom, leaving me and the inspector out front. There wasn't much to search through; no shelves, no desk. In one corner sat a couple of cardboard grocery boxes stuffed with papers.

'We'll go through one each,' I suggested.

'Fingerprints!'

I reached into my coat pocket and pulled out a pair of

gloves; wool rather than leather but just as effective. 'It's my job as much as yours, you know.' That was an exaggeration, but he didn't raise any further objections. As I pulled them on, I spotted a hole had worn through at the tip of the right ring finger. I twisted it round so that the skin of my fingertip was covered, and hoped he wouldn't notice.

There wasn't much of interest: racecards from Brighton and elsewhere, copies of *The Sporting Life*. I shook out each of the newspapers in turn in case there was anything hidden within their pages. With the third one, something was revealed. Half a dozen postcards fell out and landed in a pile on the floor. I picked one up and examined it.

'Looks like you missed some of them last time,' I said, handing it to Marchant.

He gave it a brief glance and muttered a single word. 'Filth!'

It seemed an overreaction. They were very tame; just pictures of girls, naked or semi naked. None of them was as pretty as Rachael, none so shameless. By the look of the clothes and the hairstyles, the photographs must have been taken twenty years ago. Fashions had moved on since then. I continued trawling through the box.

'Grove Street mean anything to you?' Purvis's voice came through the bedroom door.

Marchant was on his feet in an instant. 'You know bloody well it does.' We went into the bedroom. Purvis was standing proudly, his hands on his hips, looking down at the bed on which lay two files of the type that hang in a cabinet drawer. One was brown, the other green. I always used brown, so the other file must have belonged to O'Connor.

'Found these under the mattress,' Purvis explained.

'They don't look very crumpled,' I said, but neither of the detectives responded.

'Care to do the honours?' said Marchant, looking towards me. I picked up my file. The words '*Grove Street*' were clearly written on the tab. I opened it up and flicked through. It was mostly statements from the people who lived in the street, some in their own handwriting, others that I'd copied down as they spoke. I didn't bother to read through them in detail. There were a couple of newspaper clippings in there too, both from the *Argus*. One was very short, just a mention of the Peeping Tom when he had first been reported, before the coppers gave up on it and the residents had called me in. The second one contained a story about a fight over at the dog track in Hove. There was a pencilled circle ringing part of it, centred on the name of one of the men arrested: Vincent Ingram. I showed it to Marchant.

'Not on your list of charges,' I observed.

'Hove matter. But it explains why he stole the file from you.'

'It does?' I still wasn't convinced that it was Ingram who had taken the file.

'Obviously you had him earmarked as a suspect for this.'

'Apparently.'

'What do you mean by that?'

'I mean, I can see it's here in the file, but I don't remember the name, or the clipping.'

'It was a long time ago.'

Marchant was right. I didn't remember the details of all the cases I'd ever been involved with. But I knew how I worked. If I had suspected Ingram, why did I just leave things at that? I'd have followed it up.

But Marchant seemed convinced. 'I bet, when we go through all those statements in detail, we'll find some other mention of him.'

Not in any of the ones in *my* handwriting, I thought. But I couldn't be sure. Like the inspector had said, it was a long time ago. So long that I wondered why anyone, Ingram included, would still care. 'What's in the other file?' I asked.

Purvis had been going through O'Connor's file as we spoke. 'This one's marked "Punters",' he said. 'There's about a dozen pages in it, ripped out of a notebook. Each one's got a name at the top, then a description: profession, family life ... how much money he's lost and how much extra he's paid.' He handed the papers to the inspector.

'Lost to who?' asked Marchant, leafing through the sheets. 'Paid who?'

'Bookies, I reckon,' Purvis explained. 'It's all broken down, but it doesn't say who the extras went to.'

'To O'Connor,' I said. 'He'd got it all worked out. Get hold of the names of punters who were losing more than they should, who'd like the fact kept secret, and then squeeze them for all you can get.'

'Nice motive for murder,' responded Marchant. He handed me the pages. I flicked through them, looking only at the names which headed each page, but I didn't see the one I was after. 'I already looked,' said the inspector. 'He's not there.'

'Who's not there?' I knew the answer to my own question. My voice must have revealed my annoyance that he was a step ahead of me.

'Ingram, of course. But you should be looking at the bottom of the pages, not the top.'

I did as he suggested. He was sharp. The leaves came from a notebook with printed page numbers. They were sequential, but there was one missing. 'He took it out,' I said.

'If we're lucky, it may still be lying somewhere around here, but I doubt it. We'll find what's left of it in the fire grate.'

It was conceivable, but why didn't Ingram burn the whole lot? And why remove evidence about the blackmail, but not about him being a Peeping Tom. Maybe even he had realized how flimsy a case that was. But Marchant wasn't stupid. He'd be entertaining the same doubts. Like me, he was keeping them to himself for now. 'What about the Metropole?' I asked.

'What?'

'O'Connor's other file.'

Marchant looked at Purvis, who shrugged. 'Just these two so far, Governor.'

'Well, keep looking.'

We went back out to the other room and continued going through the boxes, still with little success. We worked for a few minutes in silence, which Marchant eventually broke.

'This mean anything to you?' he handed me a calling card that he'd found amongst the paperwork.

Miss Rachael Westby, 202 Furze Croft, Furze Hill, Hove.

I shook my head. 'Not a thing.' I regretted the lie straight away. They'd go and talk to her, and she'd mention that she knew me, and what would I have gained? But it was too late now. Soon Purvis returned to the room. He leaned against the doorframe, staring at the body that still lay in the centre of the carpet, with the gas mask just beside it, like a second head growing out of its shoulder.

'Why the mask?' he asked at length. 'Why wear a gas mask to hang yourself?'

'Guilty conscience,' said Marchant, as if that explained it all. 'He remembers it on O'Connor's face, as he shot him.'

'And he just happened to have one of his own?' I asked.

'They're not hard to come by. But it's one more thing to link him to O'Connor's death. Who would know that O'Connor was wearing a gas mask, apart from the killer? It was held back from the newspapers. I knew. A few others down the nick. You, of course.'

'And —' My attempt to suggest one final name was interrupted.

'And me, Inspector. Don't forget me.' Tremaine stood

in the doorway with smile of greeting on his face. But as he stepped forward, his eyes fell on Ingram's corpse and the smile collapsed. He instinctively took off his hat. 'Good God, the poor fellow.'

Marchant was up on his feet in an instant. 'How did you get here?'

'I was at the station, trying to find you, when the news came in. I drove straight here. Your lads can't be far behind me. Who is he?'

'Don't you recognize him?' I asked.

Tremaine took a few more steps across the room until he was standing directly above the body. 'He looks a bit like …' He stopped himself, maintaining the pretence that the name was secret. '… like our German friend. But that can't be.' Then he snapped his fingers and pointed at me. 'This must be the chap you told me about; the one O'Connor got to pose for the photographs instead.'

'It's him,' I confirmed. 'His name's Ingram. Vince Ingram.'

'Looks like him and O'Connor fell out over something,' said Marchant, 'and that's why he killed him.'

'That would explain why he has a gas mask,' added Tremaine.

'*How* does it explain the mask?' I asked.

Tremaine looked at me. 'I mean, if the two were working together – burgling your office together – then it's hardly likely that one would wear a mask and the other wouldn't.'

Marchant picked up the story. 'And, once there, they fell out over something and Ingram killed O'Connor.'

The image of it filled my head: two men, faceless in their masks, gazing blankly at each other, one backing away in fear, or already sprawled on the floor, the other holding a gun, firing … the glass of the eyepiece shattering, and blood coursing out.

'More likely he planned it in advance.' Tremaine's voice interrupted my thoughts. 'Why would he suddenly decide to do it there in Woolf's rooms?'

'Something they found together in the files?' said Marchant. Tremaine raised an eyebrow. The inspector nodded towards the bedroom. 'We found the file that was missing. And one from O'Connor's office too. Both incriminate Ingram.'

'Not in anything that would be a reason for murder,' I said. I chose not to point out the fact that only one of the files even mentioned Ingram.

'A man being blackmailed over his gambling debts?' asked Marchant. 'You'd be surprised what people are capable of.'

Tremaine shook his head. 'I have to agree with our friend here. It doesn't sound like much of a motive.' I didn't warm to being referred to as 'our friend'.

Tremaine walked back over to the body, gazing down at it for a moment, without emotion. He poked the gas mask with the toe of his shoe. A look of surprised understanding came over his face. 'I say, he wasn't actually wearing this, was he?'

'He was,' Marchant confirmed.

Tremaine bent forwards and picked it up. He stared into its face, then turned it over to look inside. 'Must have been out of guilt, I suppose.' He made to hand it to the inspector, but I was closer and took it from him. He grasped it tightly for a moment, as if reluctant to let me take charge of it, but then yielded. I peered inside it, as he had done, holding it close to my face.

'You working with the police now, then?' Tremaine's question was light-hearted, but it had more effect on Marchant than on me. He plucked the gas mask from my fingers, just as I was noticing something odd about it: a smell – something chemical, but not the rubber of the mask itself. It was familiar, a bit like the turps I used to thin paint. But I only caught a hint of it.

'It was information from Mr Woolf that brought us here,' explained the inspector.

Tremaine looked at me, his head cocked to one side. 'And when you got here, you found this? Quite a coincidence – particularly on top of the fact that O'Connor was killed in your rooms. If I hadn't seen you with my own eyes in London last week, you might be my number-one suspect.'

'So you don't think that this was suicide?' I asked. 'Or that Ingram killed O'Connor?'

'I think that's for the police to decide, not us.' He turned to Marchant. 'Though I'd love to hear your conclusions in the fullness of time.' It sounded as though he was about to leave, but he didn't. Instead he wandered across to the bedroom, looking all around him as he went, as though searching for clues. Marchant followed, explaining what we had found so far. Whether he was trying to demonstrate his grasp of proceedings, or appear subservient to the man from London, was unclear. I returned to searching through the box of papers.

I didn't get long to do it. Only moments later I heard the ringing bells and screeching tyres of reinforcements arriving in the street below. But to me they sounded far distant. The whole of my attention was taken by the sheet of paper in my hands, one that I'd found almost at the bottom of the pile. It explained everything.

Booted feet began to thud up the stairs. Tremaine emerged from the bedroom, with Marchant close behind. I just managed to slip the piece of paper into my pocket. Tremaine must have noticed, though the inspector didn't.

'Find something?' Tremaine asked.

'No, why?'

I watched him as he decided upon an answer, trying to guess the chain of thought that he must be pursuing. If he told the inspector that he had seen me, then that might demonstrate I was quite wrong in my conclusions. But he didn't tell.

'Just saw you eagerly hunched over those papers.'

'I asked him to help.' Marchant sounded embarrassed.

He shouldn't have allowed a civilian like me anywhere near the scene of a crime. 'But I think we can handle things from here.'

I was dismissed, though I had no desire to hang around anyway. 'Let me know if you find anything.' I stood upright and made for the door, though I had to wait while four uniformed constables spilled into the room.

'I think I'll make tracks too,' said Tremaine. 'This place is becoming altogether crowded. Can I offer you a lift?'

It was the last thing I wanted. 'Has the inspector told you about Ingram's previous?' I asked.

'Is there much to tell?' Tremaine's question was addressed to me, but I looked over his shoulder to Marchant. Tremaine turned as Marchant began to explain.

It was distraction enough. I was out through the door and down the stairs in moments. Tremaine meanwhile was stuck. He wouldn't want to appear too keen to catch up with me, not in front of the inspector.

Even so I took a circuitous route home, making certain no one followed me. It was a superfluous precaution. A week before, I'd evaded a young detective in the dark streets of Brighton, only to discover he knew where I lived anyway. The same was true of Tremaine. But if I could act quickly enough, it wouldn't matter.

The place was quiet when I got back home. The kitchen door was closed and there was no sound from behind it, neither of Mrs Croft's cooking nor of her singing. I got up to my room to find a note from her: she and Jack had gone to Worthing for the evening and she'd left a cold plate for me in the kitchen. I had no appetite, and didn't have time for food even if I'd been hungry. I sat at my desk and drew the fragment of paper from my pocket.

It looked like typing paper. The drawing was in pencil, though I'm not sure if 'drawing' was exactly the right word. It was simply a design. It was flat, with no concept of perspective, intended to convey reality without emulating it. But it was very familiar, not just in what it represented but the design itself. It was an anchor. I'd seen just the same image not a week before, when it had been inscribed not on paper but on human skin.

*

I left my rooms again about an hour later and took a tram into town, getting off just before we reached the Old Steine. I walked up North Road until I reached the Post Office building. There was a postbox set into the wall. It was the last one they collected from each day, taking the letters to be sorted just inside. I looked at the envelope for a moment, then slipped it through the black, gaping mouth. It hadn't taken me too long, putting together every bit of information I knew. I'd written it all down quickly, almost unable to stop, seeing with utter clarity how it fitted together in a way that I hadn't been able to fathom before. I should have realized what my excitement actually meant, but I was too wrapped up in the case. There wasn't much concrete evidence: the drawing of the anchor; my own sketches. O'Connor's notebook would have been handy, but Dudley still had that. None of it mattered, though. In fact it was an advantage. It was all spread around quite thinly in the hands and minds of Dudley, Mullender, Remick, Sylvia Clay and a few others. One of those others was Rachael; if not, things might have been different between us. And no one could silence them all, or even track them all down, not without a lot of manpower behind them. That was if they didn't just treat the whole thing as a joke. Even I wasn't sure. No, that was a lie. I was sure I was right; I just wasn't certain I had the evidence to convince anyone else. That's why I wasn't presenting it face to face.

I carried on up the hill and into familiar territory. A

little beyond the sorting office was the Three Jolly Butchers, where I'd looked for Remick just the night before. Tonight there was no one I recognized inside, but I felt safer here than I would at home.

CHAPTER 20

I knew as soon as I awoke that a migraine was coming. I'd downed a few at the Butchers before I'd headed home, but that wasn't the problem. There was no headache yet, no aura, but I felt the stiffness in my muscles that was always a sign. And, worse than that, I felt on top of the world. If migraine was God's invention, it proved He had a sense of humour. For some sufferers an attack was preceded by a mood of depression. That was reasonable, given what was to come, but it tended to make them fear the onslaught more than was necessary. For me it was just the reverse. I should have guessed it from my feeling of excitement the previous evening as I put my ideas down on paper. Leading up to an attack I would be so optimistic, so bright about the prospects for the day before me, that I wouldn't take proper precautions. I'd embark upon activities that, if thinking rationally, I would have known I'd be unable to complete once the headache inevitably struck. I'd feel invincible, and that could never be a good thing.

In the drawer of my bedside table sat a packet of ergotamine. The euphoric side of me told me I didn't need them, but I'd been here often enough to mistrust that voice. I grabbed two of them before heading along the landing to the bathroom. I swallowed them, then brushed my teeth and shaved. I didn't notice any immediate change to my mood, or to my aches, but that wasn't the point. The attack would still come; it just wouldn't be quite so disabling.

The sun shone brightly through the windows, making it warm inside. The town would already be crowded, down by the seafront at least. I imagined them pouring out of the station and along Queen's Road towards the beach. The trains would bring them in in pulses, but frequently enough so that the arriving bodies merged into a single stream filling the pavements. Some would be here just for the day, others for the whole of the bank holiday weekend. Whether this evening, tomorrow or on Whit Monday, they would make the journey back up the hill and on to the trains, many of them glowing a bright pink after too much of the sun. By then the Morlocks of Brighton would have taken all they could.

And I knew I should be one of them. There would be rich pickings on the Palace Pier for a sketch artist. I'd played detective for a week; now I should return to what I was trained for. Eventually the migraine would come and I'd be unable to work anymore, but by then I could have made at least a pound or two. I'd have to force myself to stop when the time came; I could produce some extremely strange images under the influence of an attack, things my customers wouldn't appreciate. I'd been expecting the events at Ingram's flat, the day before, to elicit some kind of reaction, but why should I sit at home and wait for it? Anyone with a little nous would be able to find me on the pier.

I dressed quickly in the usual get-up I chose for the tourists: a blue blazer and a cravat – neat but not too formal. They had to see me as an artist. Then I grabbed my two folding seats, my easel, my pad and my drawing box, and headed out. As I opened the door from my rooms, I could hear the telephone ringing. Mrs Croft had reached it before I was even halfway down the stairs. I paused, somehow guessing it was for me.

'I'll just go and find him,' she said, after listening for a moment. She looked up at me and held out the receiver. There was a smirk on her face.

I took it from her with a brief 'Thanks', and then waited for her to get back into the kitchen before speaking. 'Hullo?'

'Charlie?' I recognized the voice immediately. It explained Mrs Croft's arch expression.

'That's me.'

'It's Rachael. Rachael Westby.' She sounded nervous – unnatural. Did she really think I needed to be told her surname? 'I need to talk.'

'Fire away.'

'Not on the phone. I need to see you. It's about Vince.'

'Do you want me to come round to your place?'

'No!' The response was sudden and insistent. 'What about the cinema? The Duke of York's? That's near you, isn't it?'

It was – very near – and I wondered for a moment how she knew that. But then I remembered giving her my business card the first time we met. 'All right, the Duke of York's. What time?'

'As soon as I can get ready. Say 11 o'clock.' There was a brief pause. 'Back row of the stalls.' She produced an unconvincing giggle. 'But keep your hands to yourself.' She hung up before I could say anything more. It wasn't quite what I'd been expecting, but I knew I had to go and meet her. I felt a certain anxiety at her choice of rendezvous, but how could she know? Most of the time the flickering silver screen wasn't a problem for me, but on a day like today, with a migraine pending, it could only make things worse. Even if she did know that much about me, how could she guess that an attack would strike today? I hadn't known it myself until I woke up. I blinked and looked out through the glass of the front door, not in search of anything real, but to check whether the usual patterns had begun to permeate my field of vision. There was nothing, though; not yet.

I turned away and caught sight of myself in the long mirror next to the phone, weighed down by the paraphernalia I would have needed for the pier. That would have to wait. Sunday and Monday would be just as busy as today, if I was still around. I made my burdened way back up the stairs.

*

The Duke of York's Picture House really was nearby. I turned out of Rose Hill Terrace on to London Road, walked past the Hare and Hounds, crossed Viaduct Road, passed the fire station and there I was. The clock high on the pediment told me it was five minutes to eleven. I'd not wasted any time. I'd had a phone call to make, but that didn't take more than a few minutes. It would be a longer journey for Rachael, so I guessed she would turn up late. I went in through the arched porch and bought myself a ticket for the stalls, then stepped into the darkness of the auditorium. The flickering light of the screen was enough to see by. The place wasn't anywhere close to full. It was early in the day, certainly for locals, and this was off the beaten track for trippers who were more likely to head for the big screens in the centre of town, like the Regent or the Savoy. There was just one couple already in the back row. I kept away from them, but still it felt odd sitting there alone.

I lit up and watched the film, realizing I'd come in halfway through. I recognized the girl – I'd seen her in *The Man Who Knew Too Much* – but I couldn't name her. This looked like Hitchcock too. Basil Radford was another familiar face, though it wasn't much of a part for him. The plot seemed to swing on a box of matches from the Grand Hotel – not *our* Grand Hotel, though. It was a good deal more savoury than the clues that had led me to the Metropole. That all seemed like a long time ago now, and it was as much a piece of play-acting as the story being projected on to the screen in front of me. The question had always been over the matter of the intended audience. Were those pictures taken for me to see? For Metzger? Once I realized that whole show was really put on for O'Connor's benefit, it all began to make sense. It didn't matter that he was the photographer, he was still being duped. It was as if Hitchcock had become the victim in one of his own movies.

After ten minutes, Rachael still hadn't arrived, but it

was then that I began to notice something else on the screen, something other than the picture itself. It started out in the bottom left-hand corner – nothing you'd discern if you weren't looking for it, but I was. It was an arc, not big to start with and not smooth. It was jagged, forming into triangles, but even where the straight edge of a triangle emerged, that too shattered into smaller zigzagging lines. The first time I'd seen it, decades before, I'd been more fascinated than afraid. Now I knew it for what it was, the migraine aura, but I also knew the pain that it portended. It would only be a matter of hours now, if that.

The pattern grew and spread, propagating itself as each sharp point punctured my field of vision and caused splintering cracks to spread through it. Is wasn't fast but was possessed of an inexorable purpose. Soon it filled almost a quarter of the screen, though in its wake my sight was beginning to clear. I tried to look away from it, but knew I would not succeed. It was not on the screen, or in the air, or even in my eyes. It was in my brain – a fault of my brain. It was inescapable.

I sensed someone sitting down beside me, to my left, where I could see almost nothing. Even so I could tell that it wasn't Rachael. It wasn't a woman at all. I turned, having to look a little behind him to get a clear view. I momentarily expected to see again the blank emptiness of a gas mask, but for once I was confronted with a simple human face; Tremaine's face. I'd expected it but hoped otherwise, especially now when I could barely see, and when I knew that soon a crippling headache would make me incapable even of thinking coherently.

'*Young and Innocent*,' he said.

'What?' My only thought was that he was talking about Rachael – and what he might have done to coerce her into luring me here.

'The film. It's called *Young and Innocent*. I saw it when it first came out. Not one of his best. It turns out the drummer did it, though you'd never work it out.' He paused. 'Well, perhaps *you* would.'

I kept my eyes fixed on the screen. If I looked him in the face I knew he'd be able to tell that I wasn't myself. Now was not the time to show weakness. 'I can never make sense of any of these things,' I said.

'But you made sense of what happened to O'Connor.'

'That Ingram killed him, you mean?'

'Don't be silly.' He sat forward a little in his seat, staring eagerly at the screen. 'Now this is the good bit: this continuous shot cutting through the dancers in the ballroom, finally focusing on the killer.' We watched in silence for a few moments, until he spoke again. 'What always strikes me as wrong with these stories is the way they think you can point a gun at someone and make him do exactly what you want.'

'Fear of death seems like a pretty good motivation to me.'

He tutted wearily. 'Not if you know you're going to die anyway. The villain lures the hero to a public place where he'd never dare shoot him because of all the witnesses. But then, by threatening him with the gun, he persuades him to go somewhere quiet, where he can kill him whatever way he likes. So unconvincing.'

'So that's not how you persuaded Ingram to climb on a chair and put a noose around his neck?'

'As if I'd do such a thing.' There wasn't even an attempt at sincerity in his words, or at a true denial.

'But you had to persuade him to put on the gas mask.'

'I just told him I needed a photograph of someone wearing it. He didn't even bother to ask what the picture was for, though I'm sure I could have made something up. He was like that, trusting. Shame to lose him.'

'And what had you put in it? Ether?'

'Ah, you noticed that, did you? I thought you might have. Chloroform actually.'

'Didn't he smell it?'

'I was behind him, helping to do up the straps. There

was nothing he could do.'

'Was it that that killed him?'

'I do hope not. The doctors would spot that easily. I let him come round before I removed the chair.'

'They might still find something.'

'Only if they bother to look. Marchant thinks he's got it all wrapped up. You're the only one who harbours any doubts about Ingram at all. Which reminds me, grab hold of this would you?' He reached across and pushed something into my hand. The terror I felt at the prospect of the oncoming migraine was all-consuming, so much so that I could scarcely think about what was happening. I instinctively took it from him and at the same moment felt what it was: a revolver. Before I'd even tried to think why he should hand me such an object, I'd curled my finger around the trigger, though I'd not the least intention of firing.

I turned to face him. 'Why give me this?' The jagged lines cut across him. One eye peeped at me through them as they seemed deliberately to separate around it.

'Because you're not likely to put on a gas mask if I ask to take a picture of you in it.'

'What?'

'What I mean is, I need to solve that problem they so often have in the movies. If I were to simply point *this* gun at you,' – he moved his hand towards me and I felt something hard pressing against my ribs – 'and asked you to take a walk with me to somewhere nice and quiet, you'd just say, "No, shoot me here, if you dare." At least you would if you had any sense.'

'So why won't I now?'

'Because now I've got the perfect reason to shoot you. I'm a member of His Majesty's Security Service and you're pointing a gun at me. I've every right to defend myself. How was I to know your gun wasn't loaded? And, with a bit of luck, it would be by the time the lads from the Borough Constabulary arrived. So come on.' He pushed the muzzle of his gun harder against me. 'Let's go for a little walk. Unless you want to wait till the end of the film.'

'I still don't see what's in it for me. Die here or die somewhere else? Why don't I just let you get on with it?'

He answered with a single word. 'Hope.'

I considered for a moment, then stood up and headed out into the daylight.

CHAPTER 21

We crossed Preston Circus and walked up New England Hill. Tremaine kept a few paces behind me, his gun hidden in his pocket. He'd not taken the other revolver from me, and I kept it similarly concealed. I took him at his word that it wasn't loaded, but it still might come in handy to whack him with. We didn't talk, except for him directing me where to go. Out in the sunlight, the patterns that played before my eyes seemed almost tangible, but they'd now crossed over to the right-hand side of my vision. Once they began to fade, the pain would come. Still Tremaine suspected nothing of my affliction, but I knew it would be impossible for me to hide the agony when it reached its peak. And yet I had to remain utterly lucid in order to convince him of the pointlessness of killing me.

We passed under the bridge carrying the goods line and then the much wider viaduct for the tracks out to London and to Lewes, and continued walking. It was a steep hill but I pressed on quickly, in part because exercise tended to lessen the pain of the migraine, in part with the hope of tiring Tremaine. To the latter end it was proving ineffective. He was older than me, but in good shape. He kept up the pace without trouble. We crossed the road and continued on the other side of it, until he issued another instruction.

'Turn in here.' I didn't know the name of the street, but we didn't proceed along it more than a few paces before he spoke again: 'Stop.' He looked around, checking that we were alone. 'Now over that wall.'

I did as I was told. It wasn't a difficult climb and, before my feet had even landed on the other side, he was coming over as well, too quickly for me to be able to take advantage of our brief separation. We were in a tract of derelict land behind the terrace of houses which stretched up the hill. Not far to the left, the ground dropped precipitously down to the railway line heading out to Hove. It was a reflection of the steepness of the terrain that only a few minutes before we had passed under a set of tracks, supported far above our heads by brick and steel, and now we stood looking down at another nestling in a groove gouged out of the earth. And yet within less than a mile, at the Brighton terminus, the two lines were at the same level.

Now that we were off the public roads, Tremaine had his gun out again.

'I don't suppose you'd turn out your pockets for me, would you?' he asked. 'It would make things ever so much easier.'

It was a question to which only one answer would be accepted. I reached inside my jacket, where I kept my wallet on the left-hand side, and offered it to him.

'Just pop everything on the ground between us; that's the ticket.' He gestured with his gun as he spoke.

On the other side of my jacket were a few folded sheets of crisp, white paper from my sketch pad. I put them on the dry earth, next to my wallet.

'And the gun.'

I complied.

He tilted his head towards the railway cutting behind me. 'Down there.'

'On to the track?'

He nodded.

'So it's going to be an accident rather than a shooting, is it?'

'Or suicide.'

'And why should I commit suicide?' As I spoke, I knew for sure that the headache had finally begun. The pain had been lurking there all morning, but now it was becoming concrete. As usual, my vision was almost clear again. The cycle was quite predictable.

'Over Rachael.'

The implication hit me immediately. 'Is she —?'

He didn't allow me to finish the question. 'She broke your heart.'

'Perhaps now is a good moment for me to refuse.'

He took a step forward. 'A hefty push should do just as well.' I looked behind me. The fall would probably kill me before the trains had a chance. 'Just get down there,' he said.

There was nothing I could do but comply. I turned and began to climb down. Tremaine took the opportunity to retrieve my possessions from where I'd left them. In places the cutting was almost as steep as a cliff. I scrabbled to find handholds in the smooth chalk, a reminder that we were in the foothills of the Downs. When I was about halfway, a train passed right beneath me, heading towards Brighton, but still moving at quite a lick, despite the curve in the track it was about to encounter as it turned towards the station. I pressed myself against the hard stone and clung on, feeling everything around me shake. Once it had passed I continued down and soon I was at the level of the track. The pain was stronger now, but still nothing compared to what I knew would come.

Tremaine found himself a ledge to perch on, so that his feet were a little above my head. Bushes and trees clung to the slope of the cutting, much as I had just moments before, acting as camouflage for us both. I doubted anyone on a passing train would notice us. The tracks were only a few feet away from me, the traditional ones that kept the trains' wheels on course, and then those third rails that carried the electricity. Perhaps that was the means by which Tremaine planned my death; electrocution rather than a simple collision. In one direction the tracks continued under a bridge on New England Hill. In the other, towards Hove, the steep, hewn sides deepened further as the hill rose, before finally the engineers had given up on the idea of a cutting and instead the tracks disappeared into a tunnel. Light penetrated a little way into its black mouth, but I couldn't see far.

'What gave it away?'

I looked up at Tremaine. Evidently he wanted to quiz me before I died, to find out how much I knew – what loose ends he'd need to tidy up. I was more than happy to tell him. Once he knew everything, there'd be no point in killing me. Except I wasn't sure he needed there to be a point.

'Your face. At the races. You tried to pass it off as just a "flutter", but I saw your expression as the pack came past. That was a gambler's face. More than that, it was a loser's face – just the kind of loser that O'Connor had been looking for.'

'All that from one glimpse of my expression?'

I couldn't keep my neck craned like that to look at him. I let my head drop. 'I remembered your little speech at the Hollywood Hotel, about the Morlocks and the Eloi. You were trying to sound urbane, detached but looking back, there was just a little too much bitterness in there. It didn't mean anything till I discovered you like the ponies.'

'A shame, though, you turning up at the track just when I was there.'

'So you had no reason to be there, but for the racing?'

He shrugged. 'I made up that story about following you there. I thought it would do.'

'But then you confused yourself, overcompensated. You asked me for directions back home, where you'd supposedly just followed me from, because you knew you had to pretend you'd not been there with O'Connor.'

He clicked his tongue. 'And I'm supposed to be a spy. I realized my mistake, of course, as soon as I spoke. I could only hope you wouldn't spot it.'

'I did.'

'But that was ...' – he thought for a moment – 'Thursday. By Friday you were at Ingram's flat. Didn't take you long.'

'Once I'd found out that you and Holsworth were one

and the same, the rest was easy.'

'And how could you possibly do that?'

'I showed people your picture.'

'My picture? How the devil did you —?' He cut himself short. He must finally have understood.

'Photography was O'Connor's thing,' I said. 'You emptied my pockets. At least take a look at what you found.'

He reached to one side of his jacket and took out both my wallet and the drawings. 'Remind me to give these back to you. Wouldn't quite fit with the suicide story if you'd been stripped of your possessions.'

Maybe it was bravura, but it seemed to me he really didn't understand that the game was up. He unfolded the pages. I couldn't tell which was which but he raised his eyebrows at two of them.

'I should have taken your artistic background more seriously. Did you copy the pictures that O'Connor took, too?'

I nodded and then winced at the stabbing pain that it induced.

'You weren't supposed to get a good enough look at them to be able to recognize Vince. No one was. Even so, if I'd not sent him to shut Remick up, you'd never have made the connection.'

'It would have taken a little longer. If I'd been quicker, Ingram might still be alive.'

'He had to go.' He said something else, but I didn't catch it. The pain was becoming a distraction. I raised my fingers to my temples and rubbed them, but it provided only slight relief.

'What?' I asked.

'There had to be a scapegoat for O'Connor's murder,' Tremaine said, making it clear he didn't enjoy having to repeat himself. 'I say, are you all right?'

His fake concern was enough to make me smile. 'I'm fine. Wasn't Metzger any good as a scapegoat?'

'That was the first line of defence, but I never wanted him arrested.'

'Killing the goose that laid the golden eggs?'

'Exactly. And anyway, once you'd found the rest of the pictures, showing so clearly it wasn't him, that turned into a non-starter. Where *did* you get them, by the by?'

'You'll find out. I thought *I* was the first line of defence. Your first patsy.'

'Goodness, no. You were my alibi. And therefore I had to be yours.'

'So it was Ingram I met in Eccleston Square?' I didn't need to phrase it as a question – I was pretty sure now. My only niggling doubt was that I hadn't spotted his accent, but Tremaine would have told him to disguise it, and his voice was muffled behind the gas mask.

'Of course it was. But why should anyone think it wasn't me, once I'd admitted to meeting you and thereby saved your bacon?'

'And meanwhile you were in Brighton, at my flat, killing O'Connor. Then you went back up to London, got the photographs off Ingram, and came down again to get me out of gaol.'

'Precisely. Did you spot the tattoo, by the way? If you did you kept very quiet about it.'

'Yours or his?'

'Hopefully both.'

'Actually, all three.'

'What?'

It was one of my few bits of solid evidence, but it was safe now. 'That's what I found at his flat yesterday. A copy of your tattoo, so that he could draw it on his own arm – temporarily, of course.'

Tremaine tutted again. 'I knew you'd found something. He was supposed to burn it. He hadn't even scrubbed his arm properly. I made him do that before I killed him.'

Until then I'd not been certain I'd got it right. It seemed unnecessary. 'But why bother with it all?' I asked.

'Why not just get Ingram to deal with O'Connor for you?'

'He wasn't a killer. It's not easy, you know, to kill a man – not face to face. It takes a certain something. That's one of the things they look out for when they're recruiting you.'

'They look out for gamblers too?'

At that moment a train rolled by, on the far side of the cutting, building up speed as it pulled away from the station. I hadn't even noticed it coming, its noise hidden by the mounting pain in my skull. When Tremaine chose his moment, I'd be easy meat for him.

'Yes, they do like gamblers, not so much my kind, though.'

'Losers, you mean?'

'That's not a pleasant word.'

'And how much have you lost?'

He breathed in deeply. 'Thousands.'

'And no family income to support you?'

'In my entire life, every penny I've ever had, I've earned.' He laughed. 'I am truly working-class.'

'Was Metzger the first?'

'Not by a long chalk. But every one of them has to be done differently.'

A sudden pulse of agony ripped through me. I let it pass before speaking again. 'The problem for me was in working out who you could possibly hope to fool. Not Metzger – not his superiors either. You convinced O'Connor that he was really taking those pictures in secret, but that wasn't the main idea. And then I got it: it was your own bosses you had to deceive.'

'Running an agent inside the German Embassy takes a lot a resources. A lot of money. More than they pay *me*. Those pictures convinced them I had Metzger twisted around my finger, just like all the others. It's really very lucrative.'

'Don't they expect information?'

'I do have a few genuine agents who provide enough to

keep them happy. Eventually they'll suspect something, but who cares? There'll be a war soon, and Herr Metzger will be back off to the Fatherland with the rest of them.'

'Did it take you long to find someone who looked enough like Metzger?'

'They're not really that similar. And I wasn't actually looking. But when I saw Vince up at the racecourse, well, a plan formed. You know how these things go.'

'But then O'Connor got in the way.'

'O'Connor got in the way of everything. He was putting the screws on me, and a dozen others too. He got hold of an address for me – from Frank Dudley, one presumes. Sent his filthy little blackmail note there. It was *poste restante*, of course, under the name of Holsworth, so he couldn't link it to me.'

'So why worry?'

Tremaine gave a tight smile. 'He *would* have found me ... eventually. Luckily I found him first, thanks to Mr Mullender's sense of professional ethics. I employed O'Connor, told him I remembered him from the Gilbert case. Told him I had a couple of jobs for him; maybe more if he did well.'

'And the first job – the photos – was for real.'

'Seemed worthwhile to kill two birds with one stone. I needed those pictures taken.'

'And then you asked him to burgle my flat.'

'Yes, that was more my idea than his. I had to have a reason for him to send you up to London. And he was happy to do it ... until he climbed in through the window and discovered that I was already there, waiting for him.'

'And the file you stole from me – Grove Street?'

'I just grabbed something at random, in case I needed it later.'

'To incriminate Ingram.'

'As it turned out. It was easy enough to plant some extra bits and pieces in there.'

'Did you really need to kill him?' I hadn't noticed that

I'd moved, but I was squatting right down now, almost curled into a ball, my hands at the side of my head.

'Are you *sure* you're all right?' No one could have doubted the sincerity of Tremaine's question.

'I ... suffer ... from migraine.' I could hear the involuntary pauses between my words.

'Oh, I say, how awful for you.'

'I asked if you needed to kill him.'

'It was you that killed him. Once you found those other pictures, Metzger was lost as a suspect. And then, when you ran into him at Miss Westby's, I knew he'd have to go sooner or later.'

The mention of Rachael's name cleared my mind momentarily, but only because a wave of fear passed through me as I wondered what he might have done to her. 'She told you?'

'She told me ... everything. A very accommodating girl, it turns out – though I think we'd both guessed as much.'

I felt sick. Sicker than I did already. If Tremaine had dealt with Ingram and was about to push me under a train, he'd have no qualms about doing something similar to Rachael. Perhaps he already had, just after he'd made her call and arrange to meet me at the cinema. I was glad for the other people whose names he didn't know, Lottie and Sylvia for a start. I wondered if he'd make it look like suicide for Rachael, too. Or perhaps he'd make it look like she'd been killed by one of her tricks – it was a likely enough way for a brass to end up. Then I remembered what he'd said about the reason for my suicide, about how she'd broken my heart. Perhaps it would be made to appear that *I'd* done it.

I looked up at him. 'I won't write a suicide note, you know. Not like Ingram did. You won't make me.'

Tremaine laughed lightly. 'I didn't make him write anything.'

'You forged it, then? The coppers'll spot that.'

'Not at all. He wrote it perfectly willingly, but in a quite different context.'

'Wrote it to you?'

'That's right. Said he was quitting my employ and heading back north. Very long and apologetic, but the last couple of lines served my purposes entirely. I don't suppose you'll have written anything quite so useful. To Miss Westby, perhaps?'

I didn't give him a response. My eyes were squeezed shut and I pressed the heels of my hands against my temples as hard as I could, half hoping that my skull would shatter and that the pain would be able to escape. I heard the crunch of his feet on the gravel and saw that he had dropped down to stand beside me.

'If the good people at the Southern Railway are sticking to their timetable, then there'll be another train along before very long. Seems unfair to take advantage of a man in your unfortunate condition. But, on the other hand, it will make things a lot easier. Can you get up?'

'It's too late,' I said.

'I don't think so. A few minutes' delay at Fishersgate, perhaps.'

I couldn't help but smile. His charm hadn't abandoned him, even now. 'Too late for you, I mean. He knows everything, or he will soon.'

'Who does?'

'Sir Vernon Kell – your Director General.'

'K? Knows all about this? You're bluffing.'

'I put it all in the post last night.'

'Well, thank heavens for that. He won't be in till Tuesday, if then. Plenty of time for me to get hold of it.'

'Not to him. You ever hear of Brigadier Graham Woolf?'

'A relative of yours, I take it?'

'Great-uncle.' I could barely form a coherent sentence now, but I had to get my message across. 'Sent it to him. Read it by now. Knows Kell well enough. Same club.'

There was silence, followed by 'Shit!' A sprinkling of

soil and chalk rained down on me. I thought Tremaine had begun climbing away but, when I looked up, he was still there, deep in thought.

'You'd do better to make a run for it,' I said.

He looked down at me, smiling, and shook his head. 'Too convenient. You may be telling the truth, but I'd be a fool to let you live, either way. Come on.' He leaned forwards and offered me his hand. 'Let's get you on your feet.'

There was another cascade of rubble from the cutting above. We both looked up. A dark figure was descending by the same route we had taken, dark because of the uniform he was wearing: a police uniform. Above him at the top of the cliff, I could just make out another figure peering down at us.

'What the devil are you two up to?' With the mess my brain was in, I couldn't recognize who was speaking, but Tremaine evidently did. He raised his hat – and his voice.

'Lovely to see you, Inspector!'

'You didn't think I'd fall for that call from Rachael, did you?' I hissed.

Tremaine looked down at me. Even now his manner was as calm and insouciant as always. 'I think perhaps I'll take your advice.'

He turned and walked briskly alongside the rails, towards the gaping tunnel mouth. I managed to haul myself to my feet and watch him go. After only a few yards he found he was running out of space, and so he skipped nimbly across the electrified rail to walk along the track itself. From the roaring noises that echoed inside my skull emerged a single, identifiable, recognizable sound, quieter than the uproar that raged within me, but cutting through it precisely. It was the sound of a train: the insistent hum of the electric motors and the clicking of the wheels on the joints between the rails. I squinted and saw that it was on the other line, pulling away from Brighton. Slowly it caught up with him and then began to overtake. The driver sounded his horn when he saw Tremaine, but Tremaine's only reaction was to break into a run. Before half the train's length had passed him he had disappeared into the dark, subterranean passageway, perhaps to join the Morlocks.

The next moment, the police constable dropped down beside me, just as Tremaine had done earlier. Another sound accosted me, this time from the rails closer to us, a high-pitched whine, as if they were singing.

'You hear that?' said the constable. 'There's another one coming.'

I looked up as another train emerged into the light at the end of the tunnel, on the same set of tracks that Tremaine had been walking along. It was coming at quite a pace, not yet slowing for the station. The first train still hadn't completely disappeared and the two of them were momentarily side by side at the tunnel mouth. I gazed at them, not fully aware of what was happening, not able to comprehend the speed at which the train approached, nor the danger that it brought for me.

Then it was passing me, a flickering procession of windows and doors, and the occasional gap between the carriages. I didn't notice myself stepping away from the track and into safety. It was only once the train was past that I realized I hadn't, not of my own volition, anyway. I felt the constable's hand hard on my chest, pressing me back against the chalk cliff. I pushed him off me and stepped out, looking upwards to see if Marchant was still there. I couldn't make him out, or indeed anything much, but still I shouted for all I was worth.

'Furze Croft! Flat 202! Get there now!'

CHAPTER 22

I was in no state to climb back up out of the cutting and so we waited. It seemed like an eternity. I tried to measure time by counting the trains passing in each direction. In the end, I think it was less than an hour before they managed to get a rope down to us. By then the migraine was beginning to recede. It hadn't been the worst attack I'd ever known, but I was still weakened by it. I simply let them pull me up, using my arms and legs only to keep myself from scraping against the chalk.

At the top, Sergeant Purvis was waiting for me along with a number of uniformed colleagues. We climbed back over the wall and he bundled me into a car, which set off immediately.

'We've got to get to Furze Croft,' I said. I felt my strength returning with every second.

'That's where we're going.'

'What's happening there?'

'I've no idea. The inspector's already there, and he told me to bring you.'

We sat in silence for a few moments. The journey wouldn't take long. 'I didn't see you,' I said. 'At the cinema.'

'You'd already gone in. You didn't give us much notice. But I saw you both coming out, and followed you. When you climbed down to the railway, I thought I'd better call it in. Took a while for reinforcements to arrive.'

'I wasn't sure Marchant believed me when I telephoned.'

'He wasn't convinced about Ingram, whatever he said to Tremaine.'

'Have you caught him? Tremaine, I mean.'

We were just pulling up outside the block of flats. Purvis stepped out of the car even before we'd stopped moving, then held the door for me. 'One thing at a time, eh?'

There were three other police cars already parked outside the flats. A couple of bluebottles were leaning against one of them, smoking and chatting. Purvis pressed the buzzer and the latch opened without any enquiry as to who he was. We went up to Rachael's flat. I felt weak again, not from the migraine but out fear of what I might discover once we arrived. When we got there the door was ajar. Purvis pushed it open to reveal Marchant standing on the far side of the room, staring out of the window. As he turned his face was grim. He gave Purvis a brief nod, then turned to look across the room at something I couldn't see. Purvis stepped back and finally allowed me to enter. I went in. There was no point in hesitating. I turned straight to look in the direction of Marchant's gaze.

It was Rachael. She was sitting just as I had first seen her, on her chaise longue. She had her spectacles on and in her hand she held a cup of tea. She was fine, though her expression didn't hide the fact that she was annoyed by the intrusion. The natural thing to do would have been to run over and embrace her. But I didn't. The fact that she was alive had implications which made it a senseless thing to do.

'Mind explaining what's going on?' asked Marchant. 'Why you sent me racing across town to interrupt this young lady's morning.'

'Don't you recognize her?' I asked.

'No I don't.'

'Rachael,' I said, prompting her. She turned to face Marchant and took off her glasses, shaking her hair a little, as she did. She beamed at him. The inspector looked at her for a few moments, then began to blush, redness filling his face from the chin up, like beer being poured into a glass. He turned away from her.

'I see,' he said. 'I thought I knew all the tarts in Brighton.'

'I'm from London,' she said. 'Just moved down.'

Marchant ignored her and continued speaking to me. 'I suppose I should congratulate you on finding her. But it doesn't explain why you sent us rushing over here.'

'I thought she was dead. I thought Tremaine had killed her.' I looked directly at Rachael, not attempting to disguise the edge in my voice. 'Seems I was wrong.'

'Tremaine?' Marchant's voice showed that he still didn't understand, whatever his suspicions.

'Like he killed Ingram – and O'Connor. Like he was going to kill me.'

'You've got proof?'

'I sent it to someone, but I'm sure they'll let you in on it eventually.' He grimaced. It was much the same line that Tremaine had spun him, emphasizing how lowly he was in the true scheme of things. I didn't enjoy his discomfort as much as I'd expected.

'Who the hell is Tremaine?' Rachael's voice cut through our conversation.

'Holsworth,' I replied.

'Oh!'

'How long have you known him?' I asked.

'Not long. Only since I moved down here. But he pays well.' Marchant raised an eyebrow. 'Not for that,' she snapped. 'Not for himself, anyway. He just pays people to … help him out.'

'Like you helped him out by telling him I was on to Ingram?' I suggested.

She nodded. 'That's right. Yesterday, after you left. I didn't think it mattered, but he was furious.'

'Yesterday?' Marchant pounced on the word. 'But Ingram *died* yesterday. How could Tremaine have organized it so quickly?'

'He's a man who plans ahead,' I explained. 'He cut the suicide note off the bottom of a letter he'd received from Ingram. That must have been earlier in the week. Even when he killed O'Connor, he knew he might have to pin it on Ingram eventually.' As I spoke, I studied Rachael intently, looking for some reaction but there was none. Either she already knew, or she didn't much care. Marchant was more responsive.

'Tremaine killed O'Connor?'

'Yes, didn't you know?' I put my hand to the side of my head. The pain was almost gone now, but it was worth reminding him – everyone – of the reason I might have forgotten to convey this vital point to him.

'But he was in London ... with you. You saw him.'

'That was Ingram.'

'It couldn't have been. His dabs were on the photographs – his, yours and O'Connor's. No one else's.'

'He only gave you some of what I gave Ingram. Ingram only touched a few of them, the top ones. When Tremaine took them off him, he made sure he handled the rest and then gave them to you. Made sure he'd given you a set of his prints on that coffee cup too.'

Marchant's lip curled a little. He'd thought he'd outsmarted Tremaine on that point. 'And what did he want to kill O'Connor for, anyway?'

I began to tell the whole story from the beginning, though there could have been a dozen places to start. I kicked off with Tremaine's gambling debts and the fake spy rings he used to squeeze money out of his department. Along the way I mentioned where Rachael fitted in, and gave her the chance to confirm or deny what I said. She corrected me on a few details, but broadly I'd got it right. Even then I couldn't be sure. She was being cagey, judging what I'd guessed and offering nothing further. I finished with Tremaine's telephone call to her that morning. She corrected me; he'd come round in person. I considered for a moment whether the truth was that he'd actually woken up here, but she'd already denied that aspect of their relationship. I wondered why I even cared. He'd asked Rachael to call me and pretend she wanted to meet me at the Duke of York's. From there, Marchant knew the rest.

'And you've got evidence for all this?' he asked.

'Most of it's gone to Tremaine's superiors – anything concrete. But you can always ask the people I spoke to. And you should be able to get O'Connor's notebook off Dudley, if he's not destroyed it. A search of Tremaine's place wouldn't go amiss, but I don't think that one's down to you.'

'You know where he lives?'

'*They* will, though God knows how much he's been keeping from them.'

'You think this one can tell us any more?' He nodded towards Rachael. Her eyes flashed with anger at being talked about rather than to.

'I doubt it,' I said. 'Why would Tremaine take the risk? He knows how much her loyalty's worth.'

'I'll still have to take her in.'

She was outraged. 'Why? I've done nothing illegal.' She relented a little. 'Nothing serious anyway. You don't waste your time locking up tramps like me down here, do you?'

'No,' said Marchant, as if with a bitter taste in his mouth. 'Not usually. But when we're done with you, probably best you get on back to London, don't you think?'

'Don't worry, I'm gone.'

I felt suddenly exhausted. I'd been on my feet since we'd got here, but now it took me only a couple of steps to collapse into an armchair. I leaned my head back, gazing at the ceiling, my mouth hanging open.

'You all right, Woolf?' Marchant's concern sounded genuine.

'Migraine,' I muttered.

'My wife gets headaches. Terrible sometimes.' There was always someone – a wife, a relative – someone that meant they understood what it was like. But they didn't.

'I'll be fine. I'd best get home. There's nothing more for me here.' I meant it.

'I'll get one of the boys to give you a lift.'

'I'll take him, Governor,' said Purvis.

I managed to stand, without feeling too shaky, and walked towards the door.

'Send my regards to your mum, Charlie.'

I turned and looked at Rachael. It was hard to know what she really meant by that. Hard to understand anything about her. I let my emotions flood through me for a moment, imagining that I could rescue her from Marchant's interrogation, from her whole filthy lifestyle, and imagining her gratitude for it. Then I pushed such thoughts away. Better to end it here, quickly. Even then, I couldn't be cruel. 'I will,' I said, with an attempt at a smile. I turned to Marchant. 'And let me know when you catch him – Tremaine. *If* you catch him.'

The inspector looked at me, then at Rachael, then at me again.

'They haven't told you?'

*

The following day was Whit Sunday. My night's sleep had been long and deep and I awoke utterly refreshed, as always after suffering an attack. It was as sunny as it had been yesterday and I picked up where I'd left off, collecting my equipment and jumping on to a tram that took me down to the Old Steine. From there it was only a minute's walk to the Palace Pier.

The gruesome news didn't seem to have deterred the tourists. I shouldn't wonder if it didn't actually attract a few of them, at least to the station where it had all happened, and once there they'd be fools not to sample the joys that the rest of the town had to offer. I wondered whether it was an accident or suicide. Tremaine had known the game was up, but he always seemed to plan ahead. I'd have expected him to have a stash of money somewhere, and a forged passport. Enough to start again abroad. Surely he must have seen that train approaching and, even with the carriages going past him on the other track, he could have pressed himself against the tunnel wall and kept himself safe. They'd have little alcoves in there, I imagined, where workmen were supposed to shelter when a train passed by.

But if Tremaine had meant to end things quickly, he'd done a poor job of it. The driver didn't see him, not before the collision, nor after. Tremaine wasn't killed outright. He was caught up in the coupling and dragged along, too low down to be visible from the cab. The driver must have wondered what was happening as he pulled into the platform at Brighton – all those passengers standing there, waiting, their faces one by one turning to expressions of horror as they saw the mess that was hanging off the front of the train.

It stopped short of the buffers. There was nothing unusual in that; they were just for emergencies. A couple of the station porters jumped down to try and help. He was still alive, even then, and conscious, but not really coherent. They pulled him free and laid him on the platform. He died before an ambulance could get there. There were no last words, nothing about the Morlocks and the Eloi. But he'd been right: in the end the Morlocks had got him. *We'd* got him.

'Oh, please, Billy. It's only five bob.'

I looked up. They were studying my sign.

'You could get a photo for less.'

'But this is more, you know, personal.'

'A photograph could never do justice to a face such as yours,' I interrupted. It was a line I used a lot, and it could mean different things to different customers. In this case the compliment was genuine. She was pretty, so there wouldn't be much for me to alter.

'Go on, then,' said Billy, tilting his head towards the chair and assuming an air of generosity. 'Anything for you.'

She sat down with her hands in her lap and an excited

smile on her face. Her eyes twinkled. She looked a bit like Deanna Durbin. I knew I'd have to change the hat, though. The hat was all wrong.

I began to draw.

ACKNOWLEDGEMENTS

While so many people have helped me both directly and indirectly with my writing career, there are a few who require particular recognition for their help with *Late Whitsun*. I'd like to thank my agent, John Jarrold, for his ongoing support and Katie Piatt for her insight and feedback. Chris Horlock is a Brighton local historian who provided countless details both through his books and to me directly. Thanks also to Mark Yexley for help and support with marketing and publicity. Peter Lavery deserves enormous gratitude for editing the whole thing and transforming what I was trying to say into something that makes coherent sense. Finally, I'd like to thank Helen Casey for repeated proof-reading and advice, and simply for being able to live in the same house as me when I'm writing.

COMING SOON ...

If you enjoyed *Late Whitsun*, get ready for the next two Charlie Woolf mysteries.

THE STALACTITE MAN

The body must have been there for six months, strung up amongst the girders that support the West Pier. As the rain dripped from the walkway above it deposited its minerals, caking the dead man's flesh in a stony shell. That's why the newspapers christened him the 'Stalactite Man'.

Charlie Woolf recognized him. His name was Harry Waverly. It can't have been very long before his death that he'd come to Woolf's office with the offer of a job. All he needed was someone to act as a witness when he opened a parcel – just in case it contained something ... illegal. The parcel's contents were as much as surprise to Waverly as they were to Woolf: a pair of cufflinks and a birthday card.

Woolf never saw him again and wouldn't have made a connection with the body under the pier if the papers hadn't printed a description of those distinctive cufflinks. He goes to the police to identify the body, but he could have saved himself the effort – half a dozen others have already come forward. Harry Waverly was surprisingly well known.

Woolf sets out to solve the crime, but before he can get very far his problems are doubled. Within a week another murder takes place, this time in London. On the face of it there's nothing to connect the two deaths, but one thing stands out: in both cases the victim was Harry Waverly.

TO MUDDY DEATH

Charlie Woolf may be a private detective, but he trained as an artist. Neither profession makes him much money, but he takes what work he can get. And you can't turn down a job if it's a favour for your mum. An old friend of hers –

Edith Ward-Grosvenor – has fallen on hard times. She needs to sell a family heirloom; a landscape by the renowned English artist Sir John Everett Millais. But the painting has a sentimental value too. Can Woolf make a copy – not a fake, merely a duplicate – so that something can still hang in pride of place above the mantelpiece?

Woolf makes the copy, but signs it with his own name – he has no desire to be accused of forgery. The sale of the Millais goes ahead, but that's not the end of the story. Just a few days later Edith is found dead, drowned in the brook at the bottom of her garden.

In the dead woman's house, the painting is still hanging. Woolf has no doubt that it is his own work, but the original has vanished. As he examines the copy in detail he sees that there has been one slight alteration. Woolf's signature has been replaced with Millais's own.

Charlie Woolf embarks on a search for the missing painting, confident that when he finds it, he will find Edith's killer too.

ABOUT THE AUTHOR

Jasper Kent was born in Worcestershire, England in 1968. He attended King Edward's School, Birmingham and went on to study Natural Sciences at Trinity Hall, Cambridge, specialising in physics.

Jasper has spent over twenty years working as a software consultant and trainer in the UK and Europe, whilst also working on writing both fiction and music. In that time, he has written the *Danilov Quintet*, comprised of the novels *Twelve*, *Thirteen Years Later*, *The Third Section*, *The People's Will* and *The Last Rite*. In addition, he has produced the short stories *The Sergeant and the General*, *Ben* and *The Tangled Web*, and the plays *Beside the Kitchen Table* and *Comin' Thro the Rye*.

He lives in Brighton (well, Hove, actually) with seven rats called Masha, Olga, Irina, Star, Aura, Bugby and Beau, a dog called Bilbo and a person called Helen.

Find out more at www.jasperkent.com
or email info@jasperkent.com.